Burning Girls

and
Other Stories

BURNING GIRLS

AND

OTHER STORIES

VERONICA SCHANOES

A TOM DOHERTY ASSOCIATES BOOK
NEW YORK

BURNING GIRLS AND OTHER STORIES

Copyright © 2021 by Veronica Schanoes

Foreword copyright © 2021 by Jane Yolen

Edited by Ellen Datlow

A Tordotcom Book
Published by Tom Doherty Associates
120 Broadway
New York, NY 10271

www.tor.com

Tor® is a registered trademark of Macmillan Publishing Group, LLC.

The Library of Congress Cataloging-in-Publication Data is available upon request.

ISBN 978-1-250-78150-5 (hardcover)
ISBN 978-1-250-78151-2 (ebook)

Our books may be purchased in bulk for promotional, educational,
or business use. Please contact your local bookseller or the Macmillan Corporate
and Premium Sales Department at 1-800-221-7945, extension 5442, or by email at
MacmillanSpecialMarkets@macmillan.com.

First Edition: March 2021

Printed in the United States of America

0 9 8 7 6 5 4 3 2 1

For Jenna A. Felice (1976-2001)

CONTENTS

A WITCH FOR OUR TIMES

Veronica Schanoes, an academic who writes fiction like the best of the modern fantasy writers, works in prose both lush and spare. She creates stories that catch both the mind and memory.

Her expertise in folklore and fairy tales is there, but her academic credentials never overwhelm the tellings. Never underwhelms them either. In a very short time, Schanoes has become a master of the short story and novella, known for her stunning prose and her work with revisionary fairy stories. She is already picking up awards: The title novella in this volume, *Burning Girls*, won the Shirley Jackson Award and was also nominated for the World Fantasy and Nebula Awards. "Phosphorus" was nominated for the Shirley Jackson Award.

There is a lyric beauty in all her tellings, and coherent plots, something fairy tales often lose along their ages-old winding path of mouth to ear resuscitation. And many of the stories employ a metanarrator who—we are to believe—is Schanoes herself, though she reminds us throughout that all writers, all tale tellers, are liars. Something, she emphasizes, we must never forget.

The tales in this book are full of Jewish fabulism—and by

that I do not mean only full of dybbuks and maggids, but personal shoahs as well. Plus fairy-tale rejiggerings that go far beyond the grim and begrimed Bruder Grimm recitations. She has circled her lyrical wagons around hidden histories, those small acts of brutal anti-Semitism that have marked the lives of Jews in Slavic and German towns. Few but scholars have read the now-rejected Grimm's stories that have been thrown out of the canon, certainly when printed for young readers. Stories like "The Jew Among the Thorns," which Schanoes has mined brilliantly here for the opening tale.

My ancestors, all of whom fled either the Ukraine or Latvia in the late 1800s, early 1900s, just steps ahead of the Cossacks, the tsar's brutal "Fists" would have recognized their own stories told here in *Burning Girls*, though without any actual magic.

And the Irish will certainly find Schanoes's flawless "Phosphorus"—about the phossy girls who go on strike for better work and wages even as their jaws are breaking into pieces from the bite of the poisonous phosphors they have handled for so long—a bitterly truthful bit of magical realism. Based as it is on Andersen's "Little Matchgirl" tale, Schanoes turns it into a piece of work that is both depressing and uplifting at the same time. And all without sending her dying girl (as Andersen did a century earlier) directly to her mother's arms in Heaven, but instead letting her live to fight bravely to the very end.

Surprisingly, Alice in Wonderland makes a number of appearances as well, always bizarrely. But that makes sense given that she is the newest of the many odd characters that take a turn on this stage, even while not being strictly folkloric.

"The Path of Pins and Needles" also appears as a refrain, not Schanoes's own invention, but lifted and reworked from the French version of *Red Riding Hood*. Here the grandmother adds like a seeress from some storied past: "You will eat roots. Eventually you will eat stones." I shiver with recognition. But the way Schanoes *uses* the path is her very own. I stand in awe. Or rather I sit in awe and keep turning the pages. *That* kind of book.

Many of these stories made me shiver. One—about rats under the skin—literally. But there is more here than just the cold hand on the back of the neck or the light frisson of terror down the spine. There is mordant humor in Schanoes's take on the "Twelve Dancing Princesses" where twelve princes are consigned eternally to a filthy dance hall bar 'til twelve young women come to rescue them. And with the tale comes an ending that is both surprising and earned.

This is a book of short stories, not a novel, with no attempt to link the stories. What holds them together in a loose sort of way are the old tales they spring from.

However, make no mistake—these are *not* those old tales, the ones that wobble about on the superhighway of retellings, often losing both plot and characterization from the long years of tongue polishing. Rather these stories come from an unconfined imagination soaked in the old stories, but told by an author who has studied them with a microscope, and has carved them into her heart. She has also developed along the way a critical understanding that—to make their mark in this century—the characters need real agency, not just chance meetings with old ladies in the woods. Not just a kind fox or rabbit or wolf to show them the way.

As a modern storyteller knows, Schanoes also understands she must crack the stories open like a nut on Christmas morning, she has to bite the head off the haman cookie to reveal the real flesh beneath. Her tales have a pace, a language that is bitter, sharp, even ragged and raw at times. Her characters are often the same—they bleed onto the pages and she does not always stop to wipe up the messes as she flushes the old openings/closings down the nearest commode.

Her sometimes outrageous matching tales to the world's histories are folkish at the core. "Emma Goldman Takes Tea with the Baba Yaga." Really?! A brilliant story that has biography, autobiography, history, plus the greatest female anarchist and the most famous witch in folklore all in one storied place. And Emma holds her own here. How could you ask for more?

So—do I like the stories in this book? "Like" is too soft a word for the way I feel about them. These are stories for our future, not our past. I can't wait to reread them. They read as if they were composed on the guillotine of that fairy-tale opening "Once upon a time" when such storytellers gained either the king's patronage or were swung from his gibbet as an enemy, a spy, a wizard, or a witch.

At the same time, Schanoes has carved a different, difficult path. Maybe pins and needles, maybe charcoal and chalk. Perhaps roots and stones. It is a tough walk, full of the dark. There are not always happy images or endings. Yes, you can find some footprints ahead of hers—Catherynne M. Valente's, Gregory Maguire's, Isak Dinesen's, Angela Carter's. And if I am feeling presumptuous, possibly mine.

But Schanoes has a particular place here, has both daring and a deep core understanding of the old fairy and folktales. I expect she is not nearly done with the old stories yet. They are a cauldron that keeps giving and giving.

She is the one who will be running ahead of the rest of us dawdlers if we are not ready for the race, signaling what is to come. Or as she writes in the Emma Goldman story: "Truth can be told in any number of ways. It's all a matter of emphasis. Of voice. I have not lied about anything yet."

Watch out for that "yet." She is warning us what is still to come. Not a leap off the path of needles and pins. Or perhaps we all need to make that leap together. The Grimms and their cohorts may have seeded many of these stories, but Judaism, Marxism, feminism, and twenty-first-century pop cultural biases have plowed these fields as well. The next generation of fairy-tale scholars will have a field day with her stories.

And if you rise up shouting with joy at this line, where Emma is about to meet the great Russian witch, and is drumming her fingers on the fence: "*da-da-dum, da-da-dum, da-da-dum*, the anapest of boredom" without mistaking it first for a county in Russia, then this book is for you. And if you expect any story in this volume to remain a story and not become today's history, or tomorrow's, then you have mistaken Veronica Schanoes for someone like Spielberg. She is much more lyrical, and much less doctrinaire than he is. Rather she is a seeress, but perhaps one you don't quite believe yet. And much more a witch for our times than you or I really know.

—JANE YOLEN

BURNING GIRLS

AND
OTHER STORIES

AMONG
THE
THORNS

They made my father dance in thorns before they killed him.

I used to think that this was a metaphor, that they beat him with thorny vines, perhaps. But I was wrong about that.

They made him dance.

Just over 150 years ago, in 1515, as the Christians count, on a bright and clear September morning, they chained a Jewish man named Johann Pfefferkorn to a column in our cemetery. They left enough length for him to be able to walk around the column. Then they surrounded him with coals and set them aflame, raking them ever closer to Herr Pfefferkorn, until he was roasted alive.

They said that Herr Pfefferkorn had confessed to stealing, selling, and mutilating their Eucharist, planning to poison all the Christians in Magdeburg and Halberstadt combined and then to set fire to their homes, kidnapping two of their children in order to kill them and use their blood for ritual purposes, poisoning wells, and practicing sorcery.

I readily believe that poor Herr Pfefferkorn confessed to all of that.

A man will confess to anything when he is being tortured.

They say that, at the last, my father confessed to stealing every taler he had ever possessed.

But I don't believe that. Not my father.

They say that in their year 1462, in the village of Pinn, several of us bought the child of a farmer and tortured it to death. They also say that in their 1267, in Pforzheim, an old woman sold her granddaughter to us, and we tortured her to death and threw her body into the River Enz.

Who are these people who trade away their children for gold?

My parents would not have given away me or any of my brothers for all the gold in Hesse. Are gentiles so depraved that at last, they cannot love even their own children?

I was seven when my father disappeared. At first we did not worry. My parents were pawnbrokers in Hoechst; my mother ran the business out of our house and my father traveled the countryside of Hesse, peddling the stock she thus obtained, and trading with customers in nearby towns, during the week. He tried to be with us for Shabbos, but it was not so unusual for the candles to burn down without him.

It was almost always only a matter of days before he came back, looming large in our doorway, and swept me into the air in a hug redolent of the world outside Hoechst. I was the youngest and the only girl, and though fathers and mothers both are said to rejoice more greatly in their sons than in their daughters, I do believe that my father preferred me above all my brothers.

My father was a tall man, and I am like him in that, as in other things. I have his thick black hair and his blue eyes. But my father's eyes laughed at the world, and I have instead my mother's temperament, so I was a solemn child.

When my father lifted me in his arms and kissed me, his beard stroked my cheek. I was proud of my father's beard, and he took such care of it: so neat and trim it was, not like my zeyde's beard had been, all scraggly and going every which way. And white. My mother's father's beard was white, too. My father's was black as ink, and I never saw a white hair in it.

We had a nice house, not too small and not too big, and we lived in a nice area of Hoechst, but not too nice. My parents grew up in the ghetto of Frankfurt am Main, but the ghetto in Frankfurt is but a few streets, and there are so many of us. So we Jews are mobile by necessity.

Even though it is dangerous on the road.

And Hoechst is a nice place, and we had a nice home. But not too nice. My mother had selected it when she was already pregnant with my eldest brother. "Too nice and they are jealous," she told me, "so not too nice. But not nice enough, and they won't come and do business. And," she added, "I wanted clean grounds for my children to play on."

We had some Jewish neighbors, and it was their children I mostly played with. The Christian children were nice enough, but they were scared of us sometimes, or scorned us, and I never knew what to expect. I had a friend named Inge for a while, but when her older sister saw us together, she turned red and smashed my dolly's head against a tree. Then she got to her feet and ran home, and her sister glared at me.

I was less friendly after that, although my father fixed my dolly when he came home that week and put a bandage on my head to match hers when I asked him to.

Some feel there is safety in numbers and in closeness, but my mother thought differently. "Too many of us, too close together," she said, "and they think we're plotting against them. Of course, they don't like it when we move too far into their places, either. I do what I can to strike the right balance, liebchen," she said.

This was my mother, following the teachings of Maimonides, who wrote that we should never draw near any extreme, but keep to the way of the righteous, the golden mean. In this way, she sought to protect her family.

Perhaps she was successful, for the Angel of Death did not overtake us at home.

Death caught up with my father when he was on the road, but we did not worry overmuch at first. My mother had already begun to worry when he was still not home for the second Shabbos, but even that was not the first time, and I did not worry at all. Indeed, I grew happier, for the farther away my father traveled, the more exciting his gifts for me were when he arrived home.

But Mama sat with my uncle Leyb, who lived with us, fretting, their heads together like brother and sister. Even though Uncle Leyb was my father's younger brother, he was fair-haired, like my mother. I loved him very much, though not in the way I loved my parents. Uncle Leyb was my playmate, my friend, my eldest brother, if my brothers had spent time with a baby like me.

But Uncle Leyb was also old enough to be my parents' confidant. Sometimes he went with my father, and sometimes he stayed and helped my mother.

I am grateful that he stayed home for my father's last trip. I do not think he could have done any good. But Leyb does not forgive himself to this day.

"Illness, murder, kidnapping," said my mother calmly, as though she were making up a list of errands, but her knuckles were white, her hands gripping the folds of her dress.

"It will be all right, Esti," said my uncle. "Yakov has been out on the road many times for many days. Perhaps business is good and he doesn't want to cut off his good fortune. And then you'd have had all this worry for naught."

"They kidnapped a boy, a scholar," said Mama. "On the journey between Moravia and Cracow."

"Nobody has kidnapped Yakov," said my uncle. He had a disposition like my father's, always sunny.

"If we sell the house," Mama went on as if she hadn't heard him, "we could pay a substantial ransom."

"There will be no need for that," my uncle said firmly.

My mother's fears did not worry me. Though I was a serious child, my father was big as a tree in my eyes, certainly bigger than Mama or Uncle Leyb or most of the men in Hoechst.

And my parents were well-liked in Hoechst. My father drank and smoked with the younger Christian men, and when he offered his hand, they shook it.

When the third Shabbos without my father passed, Uncle Leyb began to worry as well. His merry games faded to silence, and he and my mother held hushed conversations that broke off the minute I came within earshot.

After the fourth Shabbos had passed, my uncle packed up

a satchel of food and took a sackful of my mother's wares and announced his intention to look for my father.

"Don't go alone," my mother said.

"Whom should I take?" my uncle asked. "The children? And you need to stay and run the business."

"Take a friend. Take Nathaniel from next door. He's young and strong."

"So am I, Esti," my uncle said. He held her hand fondly for a moment before letting it go and taking a step back, away from the safety of our home. "Besides," he said, noticing that I and my next elder brother, Heymann, had stopped our game of jacks to watch and listen. "I daresay that Yakov is recovering from an ague in a nice bed somewhere. Won't I give him a tongue-lashing for not sending word home to his wife and family? Perhaps I'll even give him a knock on the head!"

The thought of slight Uncle Leyb thumping my tall, sturdy father was so comical that I giggled.

My uncle turned his face to me and pretended to be stern. "You mock me, Ittele?" he said. "Oh, if only you could have seen your father and me when we were boys! I thrashed him up and down the street, and never mind that he was the elder!"

I laughed again, and my uncle seemed pleased. But as he waved at us and turned to go, his face changed, and he looked almost frightened.

The fortnight that he was away was the longest I have ever known. Mama was quick-tempered; my brothers ignored me, except for Heymann, who entertained himself by teaching me what he learned in cheder. I tried to pay attention, but I missed my uncle's jokes and games, and I missed my father's hugs and kisses. I took to sucking my thumb for consolation, the way I had when I was a baby. Only when my brothers couldn't see, of course. My mother did catch me a few times, but she pretended not to notice so I wouldn't be embarrassed.

My brothers were out when I saw Uncle Leyb coming home through the window. His face was distorted, and I could not tell if it was an effect of the glass rippling or of some deep distress.

He seemed calm by the time Mama and I met him at the front door, having dropped the forks from our hands and abandoned our meal. My mother brought him into the kitchen and settled him with a measure of kirschwasser. Then she told me to go play outside. I was moving toward the door with my brothers' old hoop and stick as slowly as possible—they were too big for hoop rolling by this time, but I still liked it—when my uncle raised his hand and I stopped.

"No," he said firmly. "She should stay and listen. And her brothers, where are they? They should come and hear this as well."

My mother met his eyes and then nodded. She sent me out to collect my brothers. When all four of us returned, my mother's face was drawn and taut. For many years I thought that my uncle had told my mother the tale of my father's last day privately after all, but when I was older, she said not; she said that when she had seen that Uncle Leyb was alone, she had known already that she would never again lay eyes on my father.

The four of us sat between them, my eldest brother holding our mother's hand. My uncle held his arms out to me and I climbed onto his lap. I was tall, even as a child, and I no longer quite fit, but I think it was his comfort and consolation even more than mine, so I am glad I stayed. At the time, I was still obstinately hoping for good news, that Papa had struck a marvelous bargain that had taken a lot of work, and now we were all wealthy beyond the dreams of avarice, that even now Papa was traveling home as quickly as possible, his pockets loaded with treats.

My uncle wrapped his arms around me and began to speak quietly and deliberately. "Esti, Kinder. Yakov is dead. He will not be coming home. I buried him just a few days ago. With my own hands, I buried him."

My mother sighed, and somehow her face relaxed, as though the blow she had been expecting had finally landed, and it was a relief to have it done.

My brothers' faces looked blank and slightly confused; I suspect mine did as well. I did not quite believe what my uncle said. Perhaps, I thought, he was mistaken. But I could tell that my uncle was genuinely sad, so I reached up and patted his face.

"I fell in with Hoffmann after a few days, and told him of our worries"—Hoffmann was a peddler my father and uncle crossed paths with every so often and saw at shul on the high holy days. He lived several towns away, but he took much longer journeys than did my father. It was strange, though, that he should have been peddling among my father's towns.

"He said that word had spread that my brother's territory was going unattended; otherwise, he never would have presumed to visit it. He offered to join me in my search, so we pressed on together until we came to Dornburg. 'Burg' they call themselves, but they're not even as big as Hoechst. As we approached, the town lived up to its name, thornbushes on every patch of scrub by the road.

"Yakov's body was hanging from a gibbet mounted by the side of the road just outside the town.

"We waited until nightfall, cut him down, and buried him under cover of darkness. I left a few stones at the graveside, Esti, but otherwise, I left it unmarked. I didn't want to risk them digging him up. Let him rest."

My mother's face was stone, and my uncle's voice was calm, but the top of my head was damp with my uncle's tears. I was still confused, so I turned around on my uncle's lap so I could face him.

"So when will Papa come home?" I asked him. I can make no excuses. I understood the nature of death by then. Perhaps I just did not want to believe it.

My uncle put his palms on either side of my face and held my gaze. "He will not come home again. The people of Dornburg killed him. He is dead, like your baby brother two years ago."

"How?" I could not imagine such a thing. My papa was big as a bear and twice as strong in my eyes. He could swing me around and around and never get tired. He could wrestle my two eldest brothers at once. He could even pick up my mama.

"They made him dance, liebchen. They made him dance in thorns, and then they hanged him."

"For what?" The cry burst from my mother. "For what did they hang him?"

"Theft," said my uncle, not taking his eyes from my face. "They said he had stolen all his money; rumor has it that they gave all he had to some vagabond fiddler, and he set himself up nicely. What's little enough for a family of seven is plenty for one vagrant."

"My papa never stole anything," I said. It was then that I realized what had happened. These people could say terrible things about my father only because he was dead.

"Not since we were boys," Uncle Leyb agreed.

I put my hands over his and stared into his eyes intently. If my father could not bring justice to those who slandered him, I would. "I will kill them," I told my uncle. My voice was steady and I was quite sincere. "I will surround that town with death. I will wrap death around their hearts, and I will rip them apart.

"I will kill them all. Every one."

My uncle did not laugh at me, or ruffle my hair, or tell me to run along. Instead, he met my gaze and nodded. Then he took my hands in his and said, "So be it."

He said it almost reverently.

The residents of Dornburg were proud of their story, how they had destroyed the nasty Jewish peddler. How a passing fiddler had tricked the Jew into a thornbush and then played a magic fiddle that made him dance among the thorns, until his skin was ripped and bloody, and how the fiddler would not leave off until the Jew had given over all his money.

How the Jew had caught up with the fiddler at the town and had him arrested for theft; and how the fiddler had played again, forcing everybody to dance (the residents of Dornburg often omitted this part, it was said, in order not to look foolish, but the other gentiles of Hesse gladly filled it in) until the Jew confessed to theft. And how the Jew, bloody and exhausted and knowing he would never see home nor wife nor children again, did confess, and how he was hanged instead of the fiddler, and his body left to hang and rot outside the town gates as a warning.

How one morning, the town of Dornburg awoke to find that the Devil had taken the corpse down to Hell.

Uncle Leyb said that Papa would come home to me nevermore, but I did not quite believe it. I waited every night for years to

hear his footsteps and pat his black beard; I waited every night
for his pockets full of treats and his embrace.

I still do not understand why I waited, full of hope. I knew
what my uncle had said.

My baby brother had died of a fever two years before; my
parents had been heartbroken, and I still missed his delighted
laugh when I tickled his face with my hair. But he had come and
gone so quickly, a matter of months. Papa had always been with
me; I think that I could not conceive that he would not be with
me again.

I knew better than to tell anybody that I was waiting, but I
waited nonetheless.

I think that I am waiting still.

My mother never quite recovered from Uncle Leyb's news, and
when the story of the Jew at Dornburg became commonplace,
her soul suffered further. She had been so careful, so alive to
the delicate balance that would placate the Christians so that
we could live a good life; finding that her best efforts were so
easily overcome, that the mayor and the judge of a town where
my father had traded for years would hang him at the behest of
a vagrant fiddler, and that the townspeople from whom he had
bought, to whom he had sold and loaned, with whom he had
drunk and diced and sung, would gather and cheer, it was too
much for her to bear, I think.

She became a wan, quiet shadow of the mother I remember
from early childhood. She stayed indoors as much as possible,
and avoided contact with nonfamily. She ate little and slept for
long hours. I missed her strictness. She had always been the stern
and reliable pillar of my life. And of course, business suffered as

the families of Hoechst enjoyed visiting less and less often, and my mother declined to seek out their company. Too, she suffered strange aches and illnesses with neither source nor surcease.

We would have starved, I think, if not for Uncle Leyb and our next-door neighbors, whose eldest daughter came over to help my mother through her days. Tante Gittl, I learned to call her. There was some talk for a while, talk that I was supposed to be too young to notice or to understand, that she was angling to catch the eye of Uncle Leyb. If this was anything more than talk, she was doomed to disappointment, for no woman ever caught the eye of my uncle, who much preferred the company of other young men, though he was not to meet his business partner Elias until some years later.

Uncle Leyb took over my father's peddling, joined by my eldest brother, Hirsch, who, at sixteen, had hoped to make his way to Vienna, but willingly turned to peddling to keep food on the table. Tante Gittl helped my mother recover herself, and to slowly revive what remained of our business, and Heymann was able to continue at cheder. At thirteen, Josef was already demonstrating that he had the temperament of a sociable man, one who preferred the company of fellows to the rigors of scholarship. He now keeps a tavern in Mainz, having gone to live with our mother's cousin and learn the trade.

Heymann devoted himself to study, seeking in the teachings and commentaries of rabbis both living and dead the father we had lost. But I knew he would never be found there, for my father was never a bookish man, proud though he had been of Heymann's intelligence and aptitude for study.

I was still young, old enough to help around the house, but not much else. I spent much of my time alone with my dolly, running my fingers over the scar where my father had repaired her, sometimes not even aware that my thumb had found its way into my mouth until Tante Gittl, barely two years older than my eldest brother, would remind me gently that I was too big a girl for such behavior, and set me some petty task as distraction.

Eventually I began reading Josef's cast-off books. Heymann, who had always had the soul of a scholar, stole time from his study breaks to play tutor, practicing on me for his future career.

Time passed, and perhaps that is the worst betrayal of all, for life without my father to have become normal. It felt sometimes as if only I remembered him, though I knew that was not so, as if only I missed him, though surely Uncle Leyb felt keenly the absence of the elder brother who had taken care of him in boyhood and brought him from Frankfurt am Main to Hoechst in manhood, the two of them staying together even as so many of our families are blown apart like dandelion puffs, never to see one another again.

Uncle Leyb must have been as lonely as I.

And Mama never remarried.

So perhaps it was foolish to feel that nobody was as bereft as I, but I am sure that my father and I treasured each other in a way peculiar to only the most fortunate of fathers and daughters.

I wonder, sometimes, if the fiddler, Herr Geiger, as he was called in Dornburg, felt that way about his daughter. He always seemed uncertain around her, as if he wished to love her but did not know how to begin. Once he told me he would love her better when she was older and had a true personality. But she has always seemed to have quite a strong character to me, right from the very beginning, even in her suckling.

I could have told him how to love her. I could have told him that to love a baby is to wake up every time she cries, even if you have not had a full night's sleep in days, to clean and change her cloths even when she has made herself quite disgusting, to sit up fretting and watching her sleep when she has a cold, to dance with her around and around the room without stopping, because her delight is well worth your aching legs and feet, to tell her stories and trust that she understands more than she can say. I could have told him this, but I did not.

He was not a bad father. But he was not a good one. And I did not help him.

My mother died when I was seventeen. She seemed to have just been worn out by the treachery of our gentile neighbors. I do believe that the people of Dornburg killed her as surely as they did my father. She kissed me on her deathbed, and prayed to God to guide me to a safe home. And she died, with God having given her no answer, no peace of mind, the worry still apparent on her lifeless face.

I became Tante Gittl's main help after my mother's death, as Josef had left for Mainz two years earlier and Heymann had no interest in the family business. Too, Heymann was—is—studious and intelligent, but not canny. His is the kind of intelligence that can quote Torah word-perfect at length and analyze the finest points of disputation, but he never could add up a column of figures and get the same answer twice. Not if his life depended on it.

And I hope it never does.

I became Tante Gittl's help, but she did not need me. She and my eldest brother, Hirsch, had married the year before, and it made good sense for her to take over the business. She was very good with people, very charming, and she and Hirsch lived in harmony, companions and business partners. Nor did she need me when she became pregnant, for she had her own sisters, even her own mother next door.

I think it was her wish for me to wed her brother Nathaniel, and he was not unkind. The match would have been well made, but I knew that motherhood would destroy any plan of mine to see my father's grave and take vengeance on the man who had ended his life, because of what we owe to our children. To put myself at great risk—that was my choice, my prerogative. But if I'd had children—it is not right for parents to abandon their children, never. I knew too well what it meant to lose one's greatest protector and caretaker, the one in whose face the sun rises and sets, while still young. And I could never have done that to my child. We owe our children our lives.

With my mother in the ground and the youngest of her children grown, my uncle Leyb grew restless. He had met Elias while visiting Worms, and with Hirsch and Tante Gittl well set and Josef in Mainz, he deeply desired to make his life in Worms as well. Heymann and I were left to choose our paths.

There was never really any question about Heymann's future: he lived and breathed the dream of continuing his studies at the yeshiva in Cracow. I told Hirsch and Gittl, and Heymann as well, that I was going to Worms with Uncle Leyb, and there, perhaps among so many of our people, I would find a husband. They believed me, I think, though Heymann, who of all my brothers knew me best, wrinkled his brow in perplexity. Uncle Leyb accepted my decision without comment, and we made plans to depart.

The last night we all spent together was much as our nights had been for some time, with a pregnant Gittl and Hirsch conferring about the future while Heymann talked to me of his plans for study and Uncle Leyb sat by himself writing a letter, this time to Josef, detailing our plans.

Worms, my uncle said, is perhaps four days' travel from Hoechst, provided the weather was good and nothing hindered our progress. But we would be carrying our lives with us on horse and cart, he noted, and would, of necessity, go more slowly than he did while peddling. The three of us—Uncle Leyb, Heymann, and I—traveled together to the regional shul, where the men prayed for good fortune on our journeys, and then we parted ways, the brother closest to me in both age and affection kissing my cheek, swinging his pack off the cart and onto his shoulder, and turning to the northeast and his scholarly future. His face was flushed with excitement, but the journey was six hundred miles, and he would be alone for the first time. For months after, I would picture him alone on the road, set upon by ruffians, or ill among strangers, without any one of us to hold his hand or bring him water.

My uncle and I walked in silence for a while. After perhaps half an hour had passed, he kept his gaze on the road ahead but spoke carefully.

"Ittele, you know, of course, that Elias and I will always welcome you. But you have always been my favorite, and I flatter myself that I know you as well as anybody could. Surely my brave, bright-eyed niece is brewing plans more complex than husband-catching?"

"Yes," I replied. "I am." But I did not elaborate.

When we stopped for dinner, he broached the topic again. As he finished up the bread and sausage we had packed, he poured himself a measure of kirschwasser. He leaned back against the cart and looked me in the eye.

"So, liebe, what are these plans of yours? Indulge your old uncle by taking him into your confidence."

I smiled at him. "I do mean to see you settled, Uncle. And when you are happily ensconced in Worms and have joined your business to Elias's, and are well occupied, I believe it will be time for me to set out once more."

Uncle Leyb raised his eyebrows and gestured for me to continue.

"To Dornburg, Uncle. I will go to Dornburg, and I will watch the fiddler's last breaths."

My uncle poured himself another measure of kirsch and sipped it slowly. "How do you intend to do this, child?"

My voice seemed to come from far away as I spoke, though I had long thought on this very question. "I do not yet know, Uncle. It depends on how I find him. But I must do this. I have known ever since I was a child. The knowledge has lodged like . . . like . . ." I fumbled for words.

"Like a thorn in your heart, my child?" said my uncle.

I nodded.

My uncle finished his kirsch. "Yes," he said.

"You are bravest of us all, I think," he said, and then he stopped. "I should go—I should have been with him—I will go—"

I put my hand on his arm to stop him. "No. You should go to Elias. I am my father's daughter, and I will go to Dornburg."

My uncle relaxed and let go of the tin cup he had been gripping. Its sides were bowed inward. Color slowly returned to his face. "I believe I understand," he said. "And after I am settled, I will see you to Dornburg. Yakov would never forgive me if something should happen to you on the road." He began packing up our belongings in preparation for continuing on to the next inn.

"So be it," he added, just as he had when I was a child on his lap.

I did wonder how I would take my revenge, but I did not wonder how I would escape afterward. I did not expect to escape Dornburg. I expected to take my revenge, and then to meet the same end as my father had. But I did not say this to my uncle. He would not have been so sanguine, I know, had he heard me say that.

That night, the Matronit visited me in a dream. I did not know who or what she was, only that she was nothing human. She was the moon, she was the forest, she was my childhood dolly. But she was terrible, and I was frightened.

She smiled at me, and through moonlight and the rustle of the trees and my dolly's cracked face, she told me to turn away from Dornburg.

"Never," I said. And the moon clouded over, and the trees cracked open, and my dolly's head shattered.

And then she was gone, only a whisper in the air left to mark her passage.

I had this dream a second time the following evening, and

again the following night. But the third time, it ended differently. Instead of shattering and leaving me, the Matronit's
face grew stern and she coalesced before me into the form of a
woman who was a beautiful monster, my beloved mother with
a brow free from fear, claws like scimitars ready to tear and kill.
Her hair streamed out from her head like the tails of comets and
blood ran down her face. Her feet reached down to death and
her head to the heavens. Her face was both pale and dark and she
beamed at me with pride.

I am coming, my daughter.

Worms was much larger than Hoechst, but my uncle had no
trouble settling in. I suppose a peddler who goes from town to
town must be used to a whirl of people and places. I liked Elias
well enough. He had an elegant brown mustache and was very
fond of my uncle. I determined to set out for Dornburg on my
own, so as not to interrupt their idyll, but my uncle would not
hear of it, and neither would Elias.

"Terrible things can happen to a maiden alone on the road,"
said Elias. "Leyb and I have both seen this. But with him escort-
ing you, you will be safe. As safe as anyone can be."

I nodded my head in assent, secretly pleased to have my uncle's company and moral support along the way.

"But Itte," Leyb said, "what of when you are in Dornburg?
You . . . look so much like your father. I see Yakov every time I
look at you, and your father . . . your father carried Israel in his
face."

I remembered the woman in my dream, the woman with
claws like scimitars, with her feet in death and her head burning

in the sky like the sun. And blood, blood running down her face. "I do not yet know, Uncle. But I trust a solution will come."

She came to me that night, while I was sleeping. I opened my eyes, sat up in bed, and words began pouring from my mouth, words in languages I had never heard, let alone studied. I wrested back control of my tongue long enough to stutter, "Dear God, what is happening to me?"

I am here, my daughter, echoed in my head. My mind flooded with pictures of moonlight, forests, and war.

"Who are you? Where are you?"

I am here, the presence said again.

"I am possessed? Inhabited by a dybbuk?"

I felt the presence bridle. *I am no dybbuk,* it said. *I am your dearest friend and ally. I am the mother who protects and avenges her children. I am she who is called Matronit, and I speak now through your mouth. I am she who dries up the sea, who pierces Rahab, I am the chastising mother, I am the one who redeems the mystery of Yakov.*

"Mother?" I gasped.

I am the goddess-mother of all children of Israel. And I am your maggid.

"My mother is dead," I told the empty air. "And I am pious—I have none but Adonai as God."

I have always been goddess of Israel, even now as my children turn away from my worship. And I was goddess in times of old, when I was loved and feared. For was not a statue of me set in the temple of Jerusalem? And did I not oversee the households of the Holy Land? Was incense not burned to me, libations not poured to me, cakes not made in my image in Pathros, when the children of Israel defied Jeremiah? And have I not intervened with Hashem on behalf of the children of Israel,

*not once or twice, but many times? And am I not your maggid, who
will bring you victory if you but embrace me as of old?*

"These were great sins," I breathed. "To depart from the ways
of the Lord—"

He is a jealous god, she continued. *But he is not alone. Was not
your own mother named for me?*

"My mother was named for her grandmother, who was—"

*Esther. Named for me, the goddess of Israel, and I have gone by
many names, including Astarte, including Ishtar. You worshipped me
every time you spoke her name.*

Do you not understand? I will bring your vengeance to pass.

"What mother are you," I said bitterly, "who did not protect a
child of Israel ten years ago, when he was tortured and killed in
Dornburg? And he is only one among many."

There was a silence in my head, and I thought the presence—
the Matronit—had departed, but then she spoke to my soul
again. *I have been greatly . . . diminished. Hashem is a jealous god,
and his prophets have destroyed my worship, and so my power has
dwindled. But still I can be your maggid, and guide you to righteous
victory. And in turn, you will observe the rites of my worship, and
help to restore some of my former strength, just as your brother will
in Cracow, when he learns of me, the Matronit, the Shekhina, in his
studies.*

"My brother will learn only the most pious teachings."

*And he will learn of me, when he advances to the teachings of Kab-
balah. And I will bring you vengeance as your maggid.*

"My maggid?"

*Your guide, your teacher. And something more. I will possess your
body, reside in your soul, yet I will not wrest control from you. I will
strengthen you for what lies ahead, yet I will leave you human. And
when this work is done, I will depart.*

"And you will bring me success? You will enable me to bring vengeance to Dornburg?"

Yes, my child. Through you, Dornburg shall become a wasteland.

In but a minute, I made my choice. I abandoned what I had been taught, not out of impiety, but out of sheer rage, for I realized then that despite all my piety, all my father's piety, all my brother's devotions, Adonai had allowed my father to suffer, to be ripped by thorns and then hanged while townspeople had jeered. What, then, should He be to me? And if this Matronit would bring devastation to Dornburg— "Then possess me, Mother," I said. "I consent to this ibbur. I welcome you, and I will observe your rites."

The Matronit paused before answering. *Then you must know that I must first make your soul ready to receive me. And you must know that this cannot be painless. Your uncle and his partner will see you writhe in fever for seven days and nights. And you will be changed. You will be scorched with the knowledge I bring you.*

I was not foolhardy, for I knew what I was accepting. My soul had been scorched before, when I was seven years old.

My uncle and Elias tended me faithfully as I convulsed with fever. I vomited, they told me, continuously, until my body could bring up nothing more, and then I shook and refused to choke down even water. They told me later that they did not believe I would ever regain consciousness, and Elias whispered privately that my uncle had sat weeping by my bedside more than once. Perhaps it is a blessing that I could not feel that pain, for I do not remember any of it.

What I remember are the visions, for while my uncle sat by my bedside, I was not with him. I was not there at all. I was among those to come, among my people when they were expelled from Vienna five years hence, when they were driven from Poland in the century to come. I saw our emancipation throughout that century, and I saw its collapse—and then I was among riots, watching parents throughout Bavaria clutch their children as their homes burned, as learned professors and their students tore their possessions apart and worse, an old man impaled with a pitchfork, unable to scream as blood bubbled from his throat. Again and again, I saw the pendulum swing, as my people's emancipation drew near and then was wrenched away, slicing through the hands that reached out for it.

And I saw worse. The world around me teemed with flickering images, nightmarish visions of stone roads carrying metal beasts, of burning homes, of people pressed like livestock into mechanical carts, children crying, separated from their parents, toddlers' heads dashed against walls, of starvation, and of our neighbors turning on us, only too glad to agree to our degradation and murder. The visions persisted no matter where I turned my head, and there was no reprieve, nor any justice, no justice anywhere.

"What is this?" I asked the Matronit. "What is happening to me?"

None of this has happened, as yet, she told me. *You see as I see, across not only space, but time. This has not happened, but it will happen. It will all happen.*

"And Adonai? What of Him? Why has—why *will* He abandon my people?" I wailed silently. "Does our devotion mean nothing, nothing at all? What of our covenant? Did Abraham smash his father's idols for nothing? For nothing at all?"

The Matronit chose her words carefully. *Hashem—Hashem . . . is . . . hungry for power. He always has been. He rides the waves of power and he does not care who is crushed beneath them. He never has.*

"So He will desert us?"

My daughter, he deserted Israel long ago.

If I could have, I would have spat. "Then I will desert Him," I told her. "Why should I remain devout, why should I—why should any of us—maintain our rituals or keep our covenant?"

My daughter, if you did not, who would you be?

I awoke with no voice, coughing blood. When I saw Uncle Leyb asleep in the chair by my bedside, tears ran from my eyes for his ignorance, and for his hope, and I cried for Hirsch's baby, and all the children to come. My uncle awoke and wiped my tears as well as my nose. I was able to take his hand and to whisper that I was well again, but this effort exhausted me, and I fell back asleep. I dreamt not at all.

I was not well. I thought I would never be well again.

As I slowly recovered my strength, I kept faith with the Matronit. I poured out wine and lit incense for her; I baked small cakes in her form and in her honor. I did not tell Elias or Uncle Leyb the reasons for my actions. I myself was still unsure whether the Matronit was a demon or the goddess—and how strange it felt to think that word—and if she was the former, I had no wish to lead them astray, for they were good men. But I became convinced she was what she said she was—the diminished goddess of the Jews, she who had intervened on our behalf with Adonai. For how could she speak holy prayers otherwise? Even if Adonai was no longer with my people, the holiness of our prayers could not be denied. So I prayed for her strength to return, every night and day.

After such a long illness, it was many months before my uncle would allow me to travel. But recover I did, and soon even he could not deny that I was strong, stronger even than I had ever been before. And so we two set off for Dornburg, leaving Elias in Worms to manage the business.

When we had traveled for two days, my uncle turned to me and told me that he was not a fool. He had heard me talking to the Matronit, he said, and he told me he would not allow me to continue unless I could explain what seemed to him like madness. He would not, he said, abandon a woman touched in the head to a strange town.

I weighed my options.

"I have a maggid, Uncle," I said at last. "My soul is hosting a righteous spirit who is leading my steps. Please trust in it as I do."

My uncle looked strangely relieved. "I am glad to know it, Itte," he said. "I will feel better knowing that you are not on your own. Tell me the name of this spirit, so that I may honor her as well."

I paused for a moment, wondering if I should invoke the name of some learned rabbi, but I could think of none. "The Matronit," I said. "It is the Matronit-Shekhina."

My uncle said nothing. I hoped that he would remember her in his prayers, and that his prayers would add to her strength.

He left me five miles from Dornburg. I know my uncle did not like to turn back to Worms alone; I know he worried. He tried to disguise it, but I was less easily fooled than I had been ten years previous. And despite my maggid, after I had walked for two hours and found myself standing alone outside the walls of Dornburg, staring at the gibbet where my father's body had rotted a decade ago, I found myself gripped by terror. I looked for the rocks my uncle told me he had placed atop my father's grave, but without much hope. It would have been strange indeed if they had not been moved in ten years. Finally, I placed the stone I had brought from our garden in Hoechst at the foot of a birch tree.

Then I paid my toll to the guard at the gate and entered the town.

It was morning when I entered Dornburg. My uncle was right; it was not even as large as Hoechst, and after having been in Worms, it seemed even smaller than I would have thought it before. A cluster of women was gathered around a well, and a group of children were tearing around after each other, screaming with laughter. As I walked slowly, they caromed into me. One went sprawling and the others ground to a halt, looking embarrassed.

I tried to smile kindly, and I began to speak, but my throat was suddenly dry. In the pause, the boy who had fallen spoke.

"I'm sorry, Fräulein. I didn't see you—we were playing,

and I wasn't looking where I was going, and then you were there—"

I lifted him up and helped him brush the dirt off his clothing and hands. "It's no matter, liebchen. I too knocked into my share of grown folk when I was little. They move so slowly, you know?"

We shared a conspiratorial grin.

"Were you playing a game I know, kinde? Tag? Or—" I said, noticing some crude musical instruments in the children's hands, "war? Are you piping brave songs to hearten the soldiers?"

"Neither," laughed the child. "Dance-the-Jew! I'm the Jew, and when the others catch me, they must make me dance 'til I drop!"

I recoiled involuntarily. "I—I don't know that game, child. Is it . . . new?"

"Dunno," said the boy. "We all play it."

I took a deep breath and exhaled, trying not to shake. "Well. Run along, then. Run along and enjoy yourselves."

The children took off again, shrieking in delight.

"They will know," I whispered to the Matronit. "They will know and they will hang me as they did my father, and then children will laugh for years afterward!"

They will not know, she said. *They will not know, because they do not see your true form. I have glamoured you, my daughter. They do not see your true face, and they do not hear your accent. Be calm in your heart.*

Slowly I made my way to the well at the center of town, past a tavern called the Dancing Jew. There, I found three or four women talking amongst themselves, but instead of happy, boisterous gossiping, they were speaking in low tones of worry and sorrow.

"Well, it's not the first time one so small has been lost, and it won't be the last, either," said an older matron briskly, but with tears in her eyes.

"But for such a great man," said a younger woman, "the loss is doubly sorrowful."

"Guten morgen, Frauen," I began. "I wonder if there is work in this town for one who is willing."

"You have chosen a sorrowful day to come to Dornburg," said the youngest woman. "For one of our finest bürgers has lost his wife in childbed just two days ago, and will soon lose his baby girl as well. And he is a fine man, who helps anybody in our town in need."

"Is the babe sick?" I inquired.

"She will take neither cows' milk nor goats' milk, but she screams and turns away from any who try to nurse her. She will not last much longer."

I felt the Matronit move in my body, and a sudden heaviness in my breasts, almost painful.

"I think I can help," I said.

He has three gifts, the Matronit told me as I was being taken to Herr Geiger's house. *He has the fiddle that compels all to dance when it plays. He has a blowpipe that hits whatever it is aimed at. These two objects are on display, so that he may have the pleasure of telling of his triumph over the wicked Jew. The third is not tangible, but it is the most valuable of the three. No mortal can resist his requests.*

"No—but then, if he asks me of my background—"

I will strengthen you. That and your appearance I can do right now. And you will meet his will with your own.

My fear subsided and I thought clearly again. "So he could

have requested that he be set free, and gone on his way without consigning my father to the gallows, then?"

Yes.

"But he preferred to torture my father and take all he had and see him hanged?"

Yes.

Herr Geiger made only the most cursory inquiries into my background. I was a widow, I told him, and had lost my man last month in an accident in Hoechst. After my husband's death, I said, his family had refused to take in me and my baby due to bad blood between them and my late parents. I had set out for Worms looking for work, but had lost the baby to a fever only days ago on the road, and could not go on. It was a very sad tale.

Herr Geiger took my hand in his and wept with me over the loss of my child. He asked me its name.

"Jakob," I said.

I did not worry that he would connect this lost baby's name with the Jewish peddler he had murdered a decade ago. I do not believe Herr Geiger ever knew my father's name. I am not entirely certain that he ever realized that my father had a name.

When I first saw Eva, she had hair like the sun, yellower than my mother's. My mother was fair, her hair pale blond, but Eva's was true gold. Her eyes, though, were dark and brooding, the kind of stormy blue that, in a baby, will soon change to brown. She lay in her cradle, too weak to do more than mew sadly as she turned her head this way and that, searching for her mother's breast.

When I lifted her to mine, she gripped my braids with more strength than I thought she had left in her entire body and seized my nipple in her mouth. I closed my eyes and for a terrible moment thought nothing would come, but surely I knew that if the Matronit was any kind of goddess at all, she would be well-versed in the powers of the female body, and soon Eva shut her eyes in long-awaited bliss, and her suck changed from frantic to strong and steady, an infant settling in for a long time.

I shut my eyes as well, exhausted by my journey and my anxieties. When I opened them, Eva was asleep in my arms, and we were alone in the room.

Herr Geiger thanked me the next morning. He had tears in his eyes and his breath smelled of schnapps.

I nursed Eva carefully. As carefully, I lit incense and poured out libations to the Matronit. And as Eva got stronger, so did my maggid.

Eva stared up at me with her storm-night eyes as she nursed. When she was sated, she would push her head away and sigh contentedly. Sometimes, I thought I saw my reflection in her eyes, the reflection of my true face, but I knew I must have been fooling myself.

Her hair began to curl, like my mother's.

I spent my days caring for her. I sang to her when she wept.

Her first laugh came when I set her down on the floor and stepped out of the room to retrieve a blanket. As soon as I got out of her sight, I popped my head back in the room and said, "Boo, baby girl!" She laughed and laughed. We did it ten times in a row before her giggles calmed.

She was a jolly baby with an open heart.

Her first word was "Jutta," the name I had chosen for myself when I translated my own name to its Christian equivalent. When I kissed her, she beamed up at me and tried to kiss me back, but was not quite clear on how. She opened her mouth and bit my nose instead. I laughed so hard she did it over and over again, and we rolled around together laughing and kissing each other.

I had not been so happy since I had flown through the air, swung around and around by my papa.

One night, after Eva was asleep, Herr Geiger called for me, and I found him in his study, stroking a violin.

"Are you fond of music, liebchen?" He was well in his cups.

"As fond as anybody, I believe."

He lifted his bow.

"But not, I think, now, Herr Geiger."

He lowered the bow. "I take it you have heard of my conquest of the Jewish rascal whose ill-gotten gains gave me my start in life?"

I lowered my eyes modestly.

"Indeed, how could you not? Dornburg has made its fortune on that tale. I have always been a generous man—am I not so to you?"

"But of course, Herr Geiger. I am very grateful to you after so many difficulties."

Herr Geiger waved off my thanks and offered me a glass of schnapps. I accepted warily.

"After my first job, for a man so miserly he might as well have been a Jew, I set out to seek my fortune. I had not walked ten miles before I saw a poor old woman begging by the side of the road, and I gave her three talers, all the money I had in the world. What do you know but she was a fairy in disguise, and in recompense for my kind heart, she gave me one wish for each taler. I asked her for a blowpipe that would hit anything I aimed at and a fiddle that would compel all who heard its music to dance, and one more wish that is my secret, my dear!" He paused and waited for me to attempt to wheedle the secret of the third wish out of him.

I remained silent.

"Well," he said awkwardly. "I kept on with my journey, and not two days later, what did I find but a nasty Jewish swindler by the side of the road, muttering some sort of hex. I didn't quite understand all he was saying, but to be sure, he was up to no good, with his eyes fixed on a brightly colored bird in a tree. Quick as anything, I used my blowpipe to bring down the bird. Then, all politeness, I asked the wicked old fiend to fetch me my kill. I waited until he was just crawling through a thornbush and then—out with my fiddle and on with the dance!"

Herr Geiger laughed at the memory and poured us both more schnapps.

"Such fine dancing you've never seen, my dear! With the blood running and his clothing in tatters, still he had to keep on dancing! He begged me to stop, and I did, on one condition—that he hand over all his sacks of money! And he did—there was less there than I had hoped, but plenty still, so on I went with my journey, having made a good beginning.

"But oh, that vengeful, petty Jew—of course he couldn't let me have my triumph, of course not—they are a vindictive race, my dear, grasping and vindictive. He followed me straight to Dornburg and had me arrested with some trumped-up story about how I attacked him on the road! I would've hanged, my dear, if you can believe it, had I not pulled out my fiddle again, and this time I didn't leave off playing until the Jew had confessed to all his crimes. He hanged before the day was out, and I was rewarded with all he had—for of course, you know Jews, he'd kept back some money from me at our first bargain. And that's how I got the capital I needed to set myself up well, here, and they honor me as one of their first citizens! You can see how well I've done for myself."

"I can, indeed, Herr Geiger." I kept my face turned to the ground, not out of modesty, but so as not to show my feelings. I say again, my father never stole, and was never petty. He ever had open hands and an open heart, and never turned away a request for help. I remember him, I do.

"All I lacked was a companion to share my happiness with. I thought I'd found my heart's desire in dear Konstanze; we were so happy together. I never thought in my youth that I'd wish to give up bachelorhood, but as a man ages, my dear, his thoughts turn to the comforts of hearth and home. Poor Konstanze. She was always delicate, and childbirth was too much for her."

Herr Geiger lapsed into silence while I considered the lot of the late Konstanze.

"But Jutta, a man cannot live forever alone. It's not right. It's not healthy. It's not Christian. And Jutta, I know what a good mother you will be. Are you not already a mother to my child?"

Now I did look up, startled. "Herr Geiger—you know not what you are saying—you know so little about me—you are still headspun with grief—"

He leaned forward and took my hands in his. I tried not to lean back. "Jutta, my darling, let me hope. Give me a kiss."

I felt the force of his request coursing through my body, the pressure to bend toward him and part my lips. This was different than just a request for information, to which, after all, I at least had pretended to accede. I felt the Matronit's strength behind my own, and I redoubled my resolve. Never. Never. Not even to lull him into complacency.

I think that if I had not been able to resist, I would have strangled him right then and there.

But I did resist. The Matronit lent me strength and I directed it, meeting Herr Geiger's magic with my own, stopping his will in its tracks.

I stood up. "Alas, Herr Geiger. I regret that I cannot give you cause to hope. But my loyalty to one who is now gone prevents it. I will care for Eva faithfully, but to you I must never be any more than your daughter's nurse."

He gazed at me in wonder. I spared a thought for the late Konstanze and wondered if she had been tricked into marriage by such a request, if she had mistaken his desires and magical compulsions for her own inclinations.

"Good night, Herr Geiger." I walked out of the room and left him staring after me, eyes wide.

The following morning I took time during Eva's morning nap to bake cakes for the Matronit. I stayed in the kitchen as much as possible, trying to avoid Herr Geiger's eyes. I suppose it had been many years since anybody had been able to refuse him a direct request. I did not care to encounter his scrutiny.

But I could not avoid it forever. I became aware of . . . how shall I put this . . . his eyes upon me. And he took to accosting me without warning and asking me to do things. I acceded, but when he would ask for a kiss, I would not, and then his curiosity would redouble.

"When?" I pled with the Matronit. "When? I cannot stay near this man much longer, Mother. When will you be strong enough?"

Soon, she replied. *But every time you must refuse a request of his, my power is depleted. Are you so sure you will not—*

"I am sure," I told her. "I will not endure the touch of his lips. Not now. Not ever."

One morning, a month later, she said, *Tonight.*

I devoted myself to Eva that day as if I would never see her again, for I did not believe I would. I could not take a Christian baby, not after all the lies told about us. This is not a thing we do, stealing children.

But did Eva not belong to me? By love if not by right? Her face lit up when I picked her up from her cradle in the morning, and when she was fretful, only I could calm her. She laughed at my games and clung to me with both her fists whenever someone else tried to hold her. Even her father.

I did not like to think of what would become of her with the rest of Dornburg dead. For I could not kill an infant, not an infant. I am not a monster.

But how could I take her?

Eva became drowsy at dusk, and I cuddled her and sang her to sleep as gently as I could. After she fell asleep in my arms, I curled myself around her and napped, drifting in and out of sleep. I felt at peace; I felt that all the world had fallen away, and only Eva and I remained, coiled together in love.

The clock at the center of town tolled midnight. I shifted, but did not rouse myself. I did not want to leave Eva. I wanted only to have her in my arms forever.

Rise! The Matronit's voice was mighty, implacable, and I was instantly fully awake. *The time is now.*

I sat up and reluctantly pulled away from Eva's small body. She stretched out an arm, looking for me in her sleep, but was otherwise undisturbed.

I had been ready, I think, for a decade.

First I went to Herr Geiger's study and collected his fiddle and his blowpipe. Then I silently left the house. The judge who had ordered my father's death had been an old man then, I had learned over the months. He had died not long after. But the mayor and the hangman, they were still in the prime of life. The hangman had several children and a lovely house, some distance from the other homes, it's true, for nobody loves a scharfrichter, but nonetheless, he had a good life, and was respected if not celebrated. I walked to his home by moonlight, my cloak wrapped tightly around me. Standing outside his house, the Matronit told me to shut my eyes, and when I did, she granted me a vision.

The scharfrichter, Franz Schmidt, and his wife, Adelheide, were sleeping in their shared bed. All was peaceful.

What is your desire? asked the Matronit.

"Give him a dream," I told her. "Can you do that?"

But of course.

"Give him a dream. He is in chains, being led to the scaffold. He is innocent of any crime, but nonetheless, the faces of the crowd are filled with hatred. He thinks of his wife, his children, and how they will long for him, grow old without him. The noose is fitted around his neck and he finds his tongue, pleads for mercy, but the judge and the crowd only laugh. The platform drops out from under him, but the rope is not weighted correctly, and instead of his neck breaking instantly, he is slowly strangling, dancing in air. Oh, how he dances!"

The vision the Matronit granted me changed—Schmidt is twisting and turning in bed, unable to wake, unable to breathe. His face is pained and panicked.

I waited, wondering if I would feel pity, or remorse, or forgiveness. I felt none.

"Stop his heart," I said.

Schmidt convulses once, and then is still. His wife has never moved.

I then went to the house of the bürgermeister.

Strangely calm, I returned home; I returned to the house of Herr Geiger.

Herr Geiger awoke to find me seated on a chair at the foot of his bed. "Jutta?" He yawned, all confusion. "What are you doing here?"

I did not answer. Instead, I brought the blowpipe out of my pocket and snapped it in two.

"Jutta! What are you doing?"

I then smashed the fiddle against his bedpost. It was nothing, then, but shattered splinters and catgut. I threw it to the ground.

"Jutta!" Herr Geiger was on his feet, looming in front of me, grabbing my shoulders. "Do you know what you have done?"

Still I did not answer. My braids undid themselves and my hair, my true black hair, stretched out toward the fiddler, becoming thorn-covered vines. He shrieked and tried to back away, but my vines caught his arms and legs, lifted him into the air, and there was nobody to hear his shrieks except Eva, who awoke and began crying in the other room. The maid and the cook came in daily but lived with their own families.

I stood.

My vines twined ever tighter around his arms and legs, and blood ran down his body freely as the thorns dug through his skin. He twisted in pain, trying to wrench himself free, but succeeded only in digging the thorns in more deeply. My vines suspended him in the air in front of me, and I watched his struggles dispassionately. They did not bring me pleasure, but neither did they move me to pity or compassion.

"Why, Jutta?" he gasped.

"My name is Itte," I told him. Then I spoke to the Matronit. "Let him see my true face." I watched his eyes as my disguise melted away and my own features showed forth.

"You killed my father," I told him. "Ten years ago, you killed him. For ten years I have missed his embrace and smile. And never will I see them again."

"Jewess!" he spat.

"Yes," I agreed.

The vines grew further, wrapping themselves along his trunk, and they began burrowing into his flesh. He screamed.

"Did my father scream like that?" I asked him. "Did he scream when you made him dance in thorns?"

Eva continued to cry.

"Please, Jutta, spare me!"

Again, I could feel the force of his request marching through my body. The Matronit was channeling all her strength into the vines of my hair. I had only my own resolve with which to meet his power, but that power had been weakened by my breaking the blowpipe and the fiddle, for all things are more powerful in threes. I met his will with my own.

"For Eva's sake, spare me!"

I stared into his eyes. "You know nothing of Eva! Do you know which solid foods she can stomach, and which she cannot? Do you know on which day she began to crawl? Does she even babble your name?"

I thought of my father, swinging me through the air, patching my dolly, cuddling me to sleep, and I thought of him exhausted, breathless, limbs burning like fire, skin torn, confessing to crimes he had never committed, knowing he would never see me nor my brothers nor my mother again, and my resolve strengthened.

"I will not spare you, Herr Geiger," I said. A new vine formed from another lock of my hair, and even as he gibbered in terror, it wrapped itself around his throat.

"Eva—" he began.

"Eva is mine," I told him. "You destroyed my family. I will take her and make a new one."

At my nod, the vine gave one jerk and snapped his neck.

The vines let him fall, and they began shrinking and turning back into my plain black hair, which replaited itself. I took one final look down at what had been Herr Geiger. Then I nodded again and turned and ran to Eva.

As soon as she caught sight of my face, she stopped crying, and she beamed at me through her tears and held out her arms. I picked her up and began to soothe her. I changed her cloth, for she had wet herself, and nursed her back to sleep.

"I am taking her with me," I told the Matronit as I threw my belongings into my sack. "I do not care what is said about us. I will not leave her here to be raised by strangers, to be taught to hate Jews."

It would be a terrible thing to do to a Jewish infant, said the Matronit.

I paused. "She is not Jewish."

She is the child of a Jewish mother.

"Konstanze was Jewish?" I asked.

No. Konstanze is not her only mother.

"She is not my daughter."

She is. Your milk gave her life. She knows she is your daughter.

"Why did she not cry when I picked her up?" I asked. "She has not seen my true face before, only my disguise."

She has never seen any face but your true one, the Matronit said. *She knows you. She knows your face. She knows you are her mother.*

I had finished packing. I picked up Eva and she opened her eyes to peer drowsily at me. She smiled, nestled her head against my chest, and fell back asleep. I tied her to me, picked up my sack, and left Herr Geiger's home with my daughter.

Outside the town walls, I stood and watched as bushes and vines of thorns grew. They blocked the gate and rose to enclose Dornburg.

"What will happen to the townspeople?" I asked the Matronit.

They will wake tomorrow to find the sun blotted out, the sky replaced by a ceiling of thorns, and no way out of the eternal night their town has become. The sun will not shine. The crops will fail. No traders will be able to penetrate the thorns. They will starve.

I watched for a while longer and found myself troubled. I could not shake from my mind the memory of the grin the little boy had given me on my first day in Dornburg. Apparently I had some pity, some compassion after all.

"Is this just?" I asked. "To destroy the lives of children for what their elders have done before they were born?"

The vines paused in their growth.

Do you question me?

"I do," I said. "Children are powerless. Is this divine retribution, to murder the helpless? I do not wish it. Matronit, you should not do this."

The Matronit was silent. And then—*Very well. I will spare the children. You may take them away to safety.*

I remembered an old story, of a man in a many-colored suit leading away the children of Hamelin. But is this what I wanted? To take charge of a town's worth of children who by the age of six were already playing at killing my people?

"No," I said. "What you suggest is impossible. How should I do such a thing? And is it mercy to take children from the only love they have ever known, to make them wander the earth without family? Without home? Is this kindness?"

What do you suggest? The Matronit did not seem pleased with me.

I thought again, looking at the thorn-vines. "I know another story," I said. "Of a princess asleep in a tower, and a forest of thorns sprung up around her."

And this is your vengeance? asked the Matronit. *Sleep for a hundred years? They will sleep and wake and your people will still be suffering.*

"No," I agreed. "A hundred years will not suffice. But . . . let them sleep . . . let them sleep . . ." I thought of what the Matronit had shown me of the future. "Let them sleep until their loathing for my people, Matronit, for your children, is only a curiosity, an absurdity, a poor joke. Let them sleep until they are only antiquities, laughingstocks. Let them sleep until Hesse—and all the lands that surround it—are safe for the Jews."

The Matronit was silent once more.

"Will that suffice?" I prodded her.

That will be a long time, my daughter.

"Yes," I agreed.

That . . . will suffice. They will sleep until realms of this land—all this land, all Europe—are safe for the Jews. And you are satisfied? This is different enough from death?

I struggled to explain. "If they do not wake . . . if they cannot wake . . . it will be only their fellows in hatred who are to blame. Not I."

I stroked Eva's head, noticing the darkness growing in at the roots of her hair. "Will you guide us, Matronit? Will you guide my footsteps?"

I will guide you. I will guide you to Worms, where you will see and speak with your uncle Leyb and Elias, and then you shall take them with you to London.

"London?" I asked, surprised.

London is open to my children once again. And there will be no pogroms there, not in your lifetime. Nor your daughter's. Nor your daughter's children's, and their children's after them. I will guide you to London, and then I must depart. But you will keep my rites, daughter. Keep my rites.

"Yes," I agreed. "I will keep your rites."

I stood outside those walls with Eva bound to my chest, my old dolly tucked in next to her, and I carried my pack, which contained only those things I brought with me—I no more steal than my father did—and some of Eva's necessary items. She was sleeping peacefully, and I could feel the damp warmth of her breath against my neck. No feeling has ever given me greater pleasure.

The vines of thorns had almost reached the top of the town walls when I turned and did what my father had not been allowed to do. I walked away from Dornburg.

HOW TO
BRING
SOMEONE
BACK
FROM THE
DEAD

1. PAIN

It hurts to come back from the dead. And it hurts to bring someone back from the dead.

2. THE JOURNEY

There is always a journey and it is often long. You will have to take the path of pins and the path of needles. You will walk on the pins and your feet will bleed. You will walk on the needles and your feet will bleed, red like your jacket (You must always wear bright colors when you go to the underworld). This is your body mourning. It hurts to bring someone back from the dead.

You will need to be brave and to go into the woods. It is dark and cold, close and damp. You will be there for a long time. You will be on foot. By the time you come out, flashing lights and bright colors will confuse you. You will not be able to respond to them. Your open eyes will not focus, and you will not remember how to turn your head. You will long for the woods and you will not understand how to leave, how to be in the world outside of the woods. The woods will be the only real place. That is why you must bring bright colors with you—dressing all in black is a mistake. You will carry a torch in each hand as you search. Your feet will bleed. If the dead drink the blood, they will be able to speak to you, but they will not come back with you. Be careful. Do not let the person you want to bring back drink your blood.

You will travel for a long time, holding your two torches. You must not stray from the path and you must not pick the flowers. You may ask for help. You will ask the sun for direction and you will ask the moon. Neither will help you; the moon is not able and the sun is not willing. Triple Hecate will have heard screaming and she will tell you where. You may ask an old woman who sits by the path mumbling to herself. If you walk by without a word she will reveal herself to be a witch and eat you in two bites, but if you ask her for help and offer to share an apple with her, she will give you guidance. Do not throw stones at ravens. You may ask wolves for help, but you should not believe what they tell you. They do not think carefully. They do not think as we do.

You will travel a long ways in the dark. Perhaps you will have to make your way through thorns and brambles. The thorns will rip your skin and lay the delicate, palpating network of your veins exposed to the cold wind. You may be caught and the thorns will reach over to block out the sky. All you will be able to see will be the walls of thorns and you will forget that you even knew anything else. The world will become patterns of thorns, patterns whose repetitions you'd counted and memorized years ago and never thought you'd have to see again. You will not want to leave; nothing outside of the thorns will seem real. Perhaps the thorns will take out your eyes and you will not see anything at all.

You will eat roots. Eventually you will eat stones.

3. JOURNEY'S END

You will finally find your beloved. She will be chained in outer darkness wailing for you in her sleep. She will be covered with dust and cobwebs. She will be surrounded by others sleeping like she sleeps. Or perhaps she will be in a clearing, behind glass like a dead duck in the window of a Chinese restaurant. She will shine like a roasted duck as well. She will be surrounded by little men muttering little words. You will not hear them.

Perhaps the men will be wearing white coats. The shine comes from the sweat on her skin as her fever climbs. She is having no dreams.

Will you recognize her? Her face will be porridge, too hot and too pale, slumped like snow on a fallen scaffolding. Her hair will be pulled back. There will be pallid fluorescent lights and no color on the beige walls. The floors will be in washed-out squares like the floor of your high school. Her high school, too. You will sit down next to her and take her hand. She is not there. You can see her. You can touch her. You can smell her. But she is not there. Her chin is hanging in a very peculiar way.

Her eyes are too big and so are her teeth. She is bleeding. She is dying, Egypt, dying. She is dead. She is in chains, long whisper-thin chains. They are as slender as the skein of wool you have unwound as you walked.

Did I not mention the skein of wool?

Do not forget the wool. It is your memories, your time.

The chains are not silver. They are not metal. They do not make a clinkety-clankety clattering noise.

They are pale and fuzzy. They are colorless. They look like dust bunnies stretched out, like gray hairs knit together by dead skin. There are so many of them, they cover your beloved completely and hide her face. She cannot breathe. The dust is in her throat and she cannot breathe.

4. YOUR BELOVED

She is one of many and you cannot find her. You cannot recognize her. Also, you are exhausted. You have come such a long way already.

You will always know her. She is young and she has long blond hair. She is young and she has cherry-red lips and hair black as the raven's wing. She is old, so old that she is dead, with short white hair almost all fallen out.

She has hair like yours, short and coarse, dark and curly. She wears cat's-eye glasses. She is shorter than you are. She has a mole in the center of her neck and a scar on her right temple from a cat's scratch.

Cats are never up to any good.

Her fingers are swollen. Her tongue is swollen and chapped, and it has been bleeding.

She has a short tongue.

She is young enough to be your daughter.

She is your daughter.

She is only bones.

Her fingers are swollen. Her rings don't fit anymore.

He looks like you, a warrior-king. Lean. Muscles. Scars.

She looks just like you, only she is dead.

5. WHAT YOU WILL DO

You will kiss her. Everybody knows that.

6. WHAT ELSE

You will kiss her.

You will jar her or perform the Heimlich maneuver. She might be choking on an apple or some pomegranate seeds or maybe a plastic tube. Help her.

Play music. Play her favorite song on your wonder horn. Play a wild tearing song. Play a love song. Play sixty-nine.

Draw the needle out of her arm with your lips. Stop the blood with your mouth. The tube and the needle are not helping anymore. And she hates them.

It will hurt. Paint your face now, so that you look like a warrior. There will be snakes crawling beneath your skin. You will vomit from the pain, and because it is disgusting to be filled with snakes.

Lower the guardrail at the side of her bed. Check her hair for poisoned combs. Unsnap the shoulder of her gown.

Lie down next to her very carefully. Wrap your arms around her. She will not hug you back. Rest your head on her shoulder. You will have to go to where she is. Close your eyes. It might hurt. It will hurt.

You can cry. It won't help.

7. AFTERWARD

She will turn her head and look at you. Call her name. She will recognize you and smile. She is so tired. And she hurts. She hurts so much. She is confused. She doesn't know where she is. She won't thank you. She will blink and sit up.

Take her by the hand. Hold her tightly.

Give her one of your torches.

Don't worry if she doesn't talk at first. Voices take a long time to come back. And anyway, her throat hurts from the tube. Or the apple. The pomegranate. Whatever.

Lead her out. Don't look back.

8. HOW TO BRING SOMEONE BACK FROM THE DEAD

There is no way to bring someone back from the dead. But you will make the journey anyway.

ALICE:
A FANTASIA

1. INA FIRST

For it's very easy to forget Elsie, eldest of the treacle sisters, as she sits at the bottom of the well and waits to come up, but it was she who met Uncle D. first, after all, and she who first took tea with him back when her sisters were all too young—babies, really—for such a treat, and it should be easy to see how she should have been first in his love, and through him first in all our hearts.

But look at the photographs and think, who could be captivated by such a one as her? A face only a mother could love, and that's the truth. With her oversized brow and her sulky expression, it is not a lory she reminds one of so much as an egg. No, she could never be the heroine of the tale, but perhaps she could have been Humpty-Dumpty, teetering on the edge of a precipice and hurling glory and scorn down on her sister in contemptuous tones, glory and veiled threats of murder.

For alas for poor Ina! Even if Uncle D. had been taken with Ina first, first Ina with her high brow and set sausage curls, the curls that hung down bedraggled and unloved around her surly face, his heart was soon lost forever and always, to her younger sister, whose name he set among the stars. Alas, alas, for the little lass, alias Miss Alice, had a dark and disturbing gaze, bewitchingly delicate eyebrows, and a darling little pointed chin. The dark glow in her eyes set her apart, the glow of the abyss.

And yet, what was so special about Miss Alice? Nothing, thinks Ina, but what Uncle D. made of her, for isn't the muse the invention of the artist, the beloved the creation of the lover? Wasn't Alice a stolid, clever, regular little girl, nothing so remarkable after all? For didn't she grow into an icy, unpleasant, unremarkable woman? Or perhaps she *had* been an ebullient, otherworldly delight of a girl and that spirit had been beaten out of her by the rigid switch of the nineteenth century. But who could accuse the Golden Age of flower fairies and children's fantasy of destroying such a sprite as Uncle D. had imagined existed in his favorite? No, no. After all, aged Ina thinks, Alice must have always been the straight and narrow, the iron child, the respectable dullness that she later became, all the rest must have come from the heart of the lover, the eye of the beholder.

But could it truly only ever have been Uncle D.'s vision and not the creature he beheld? wonders Ina. For if it *was* thus, why should he not have fastened on me (a knotty problem)? Was it always, is it always, will it always be a matter of prettiness? That little Miss Alice was a dainty elfin creature next to which Ina looked large, pale, slow-moving, and ill-tempered? Could Uncle D.'s vision not pass through that exterior to light upon the spirit beneath?

Or perhaps, and here was a frightening thought, perhaps she had no spirit after all. Perhaps she was as dull and respectable and tame as her sister. Or perhaps she did have a spirit and it was a nasty, vicious thing, not at all congenial to flights of fancy or journeys of adventure. Perhaps the exterior did reflect the interior, in which case Alice must have been a sparkling, ethereal, unsettling spirit after all, because not even Ina could deny that her sister was beautiful, so beautiful as to merit a white stone.

At least, she had been when she was a child. An exceptional child, then, but a stunningly unremarkable adult. Something had been lost in the transition from girl to woman, but then, something always is.

And now, see what has happened! Even I, with the best of intentions, have wandered from Ina to Alice, and instead of elaborating on the plight of the elder sister, I find myself speculating on the spirit of the younger. How easy it is to pass over sulky Ina for ethereal Alice. Is it any wonder that Uncle D. did the same?

So perhaps the prudent thing is to refrain from further discussion and to return to the chapter title. Ina was first, first into the world, first into Uncle D.'s arms, and first to be photographed. She cannot be blamed for being the girl she was and not her sister. So for just a moment, consider Ina first, Ina first, Ina first.

2. ALICE HAS MIRROR-SIGN DELUSION

Alice has a secret, but not the one you think.

All her life, Alice has looked in the mirror and seen somebody else instead of herself. She is the only one to be so replaced—the images of her sisters, her mother, her father, all appear in the looking-glass where they ought to be, as clear as day. Alice recognizes them, knows them as she would know her own face, if ever it appeared in the glass, which it does not.

Instead of seeing her own brown bob, unsettling eyes, and pointed chin when she gazes into the pier glass, Alice is confronted with another little girl, quite different from herself. The other little girl she sees has long, stringy blond hair and no bangs at all. Her hair, all one length, straggles down her back like straw. Her face is round and dull, without any of the questioning gaze that Alice is told can be found in her own eyes. The other little girl never smiles. No matter what delight Alice takes in Uncle D.'s riddles and stories or how often she wins at croquet, Alice's other-girl-reflection never seems at all pleased or excited, let alone transported with joy. The other-girl-reflection adopts expressions ranging from mildly irritated to viciously angry, no matter how Alice herself is feeling.

And Alice is feeling afraid. She is starting to suspect that this other little girl is plotting to take over her life. After all, the other-girl-reflection follows her around, absorbing every aspect of her existence, and nobody else seems to be able to tell the difference between them. Her mother and governess and nurse fix her hair and dress her in her finest clothing and then tell her to admire herself in the looking-glass. When she looks into the mirror, only she can see the other girl, plotting away and thinking nasty thoughts. All others around her insist that it really is her in the glass and eventually Alice stops arguing. But she is worried that one day the other little girl will step out of the mirror and, quick and brutal as a nightmare, push her through to the other side of the glass, where she will be trapped, helpless to intervene as the other little girl plays with her sisters, kisses her mother, and goes to tea with Uncle D. Every morning when she wakes up, Alice opens a book to make sure that she hasn't been taken to looking-glass land while she slept.

One afternoon, while she and her sisters are on a boating expedition with Uncle D. and his friend the Duck, she sneaks a peek over the edge of the boat to check her reflection in the water. Sure enough, the ill-tempered stolid blond girl is looking back at her, daring her to disrupt the summer idyll by making a fuss about something that only she can see. In anger, Alice is about to bring her fist down on the reflection's face when she glances up and catches Uncle D.'s eye. He looks away quickly, down at the reflection, and then his eyes flick back up to her face, startled. She realizes that he can see the other girl, too. He knows. Alice sighs with the relief of the perfectly understood, the perfect harmony, and lets her hand fall gently into the water.

For this curious child was very fond of pretending to be two people, thought Uncle D., as he was telling a story to Alice and her sisters. He considered the two girls sharing the name of Alice, the quick-witted, pretty-faced child with a dark bob and profound eyes on the one hand, and her reflection, the sulky plump blond girl with long hair, reaching through to grab the first girl's soul, on the other. He has read fairy tales of wicked magicians who stole shadows and mirror-reflections as a way of stealing souls, but never in all these tales has he read of a foreign reflection being sent to take the place of a stolen one.

He shades his eyes against the afternoon sun and watches the three girls making daisy chains.

Or should he say, the four girls?

The rest of the afternoon passes in a dream for Alice. Uncle D. saw the other girl. She knows that he will not betray her, for they have secrets together, she and he, mainly that she is going to marry him when she grows up. Together, she is sure, they can thwart the wicked plans of the looking-glass girl.

Later that week, Uncle D. invites Alice for a photography session. This is not at all uncommon and it is one of the reasons Alice loves him so; Uncle D.'s photographs are the only way she has of knowing what she actually looks like. She poses as a beggar girl, in her best dress, and in Chinese costume. And then it happens. Something wonderful.

"Alice," says Uncle D., "would you like to help me in the darkroom? I shall show you guild secrets."

Would she? To assist in the dark alchemy of mixtures that sometimes stain Uncle D.'s hands quite black! To be allowed into the sanctum sanctorum, the room of no light, there to assist in the mysteries of artistic creation! To move from mere muse to able assistant!

Of course she would.

So, carrying the photographic glass plates in both hands, Alice is ushered into the darkest of rooms. She brings over bottles of foul-smelling chemicals at Uncle D.'s direction and watches as he bathes the glass plates in shallow tubs. After she watches him treat two plates, he sets up another tub of mysterious substances and asks Alice to take charge of the third by herself.

Thrilled and solemn, Alice carefully, gently rocks the glass plate back and forth, back and forth. And for the first time, she sees, O wonder of wonders, she watches as first a trace and finally a speaking likeness of her own face appears on the glass.

For her part, the looking-glass girl lurks in the mirror, in the water, and waits. Her time will come, she knows. She needs only to bide her time. Long after dark-haired Alice and her sisters have faded into old age, long after Uncle D. is dead and buried, she will still be reigning in triumph and majesty. She can afford to wait.

3. ALICE AT THE CLANG ASSOCIATION

The Red Queen, the dread clean lead mien calls the Clang Association to order, to water, O my daughter. O daughter Alice, alas, a lass, the dafter daughter with laughter ought to jump down, drown in her wonderland, under hand, the sundered band, a hundred grand wild creatures, mild teachers, O child's features, peering staring quizzically physically from a glass plate, a raucous fate stilled in pages, filled in stages as malice goes underground with wonder found.

O Malice! O Mouse! Let me douse the fire of your pyre, the mire of your gyre, you ferocious liar! And the moral, O adorable malice, is to take care of sense and the sounds will take care of themselves, but what selves! What delves into the dense sense of tragic magic and emerges in surges of blue? Only a few of the merry cherry toothsome dairy, running true and fast at last, in all kinds of mauled minds with lightning tightening like ice, callous Alice, cruel and caustic, a ghoul, a girl, a true dew pearl afloat in milk and honey.

Thundering hands, wondering lands, wandering sands, brushed with silk and money, hushed and lush with giant mushrooms and sticky sickly treacly bloodred falls and squalls. The tea party departing in a ruffled huff paused with its claws dragging and snagging, dripping and clipping, clapping and snapping, catching and snatching at the hair that needs cutting, ruddy in the fading light, the light kite that shudders through the heir.

O airy fairy free! To be own invention, the known convention of flight, lily-white child, wild in her eyes, shifting size and losing temper. For the egg and the sheep and crystalline sleep join hands at the feast. O beast of burden at the final curtain, weep for the shining sea.

Down that hole in the all she calls for the gold, but who holds the pen? The tears on the beach, calling to each duck, dodo, eaglet, and wren? The race and the bill taking in their fill, O fill with the day's kill the eager mouth—see how it stands to bite the hands hid amid the lilies' press-gangs. Lilies and rushes in armfuls and bunches melt into air at the touch—for the glory, the crush, the uncertain hush, the story's own lurking rush.

The serpent that wriggles at the tops of the trees, giggling, snickering while the eggs take their ease, the pig in the rig figures on the trigger as she gets bigger than any set of keys. The looming head, the booming dead, cries off with the moth in the boat. While the beautiful soup and contraband tarts soften damned hearts on the grounds, the winter abounds with uncertain hounds tracking the stops of the story's great pet, the reflected, perfected, inflected girl. Girl! Churl! With nary a curl of the lips as she slips through the gray mist into the gardener's train—for a queen *again*! O heartless, vain, and needless meme. The fawn is soon gone with fear drawing near and alarm at the child's bright charm. And the boys in the fright of the night's black-winged kite, the sheep in the shop and the wool by the wall before the big fall, and down will come baby, cradle and all.

The trying lion in the might fight ate plum cake from the red right hand of the monster. It's my own invention, he said, that two-tone convention, the dry bone and the golden crown. All around town, another queen, the mother dream, at the midnight feast with the right lease and an explosion of hankering hunger.

So she grabs the unfed dread red and shakes and shakes and shakes her—

and it was a kitten, it was all written, only a kitten after all that fall, only a kitten after all.

And life, all life, rife with strife and agleam with dreams, moves phantomwise in deep disguise, in saddened but still brilliant eyes.

PHOSPHORUS

A man can strike a Lucifer on anything—the wall, the bottom of a shoe, a barstool. Sometimes the white head of the match will flare up from the friction of being packed at the factory, and an entire box bursts into flames, releasing the rough poison of white phosphorus into the air, and the box goes on burning until the girl who was packing them stamps it out, and then the Bryant and May Match Company fines her.

London in the nineteenth century is marked, inside and out, by the black, burnt trails left whenever a Lucifer is struck. A series of black marks, scoring the city's face, like scars.

The Lucifer allows an easy way to kindle fires, to provide light and heat and smoke without the unreliable and frustrating business of flint or the danger of Congreves, matches prone to exploding into burning pieces upon being struck, and so banned in France and Germany. And Lucifers are cheap, much cheaper than matches made from red phosphorus, which can be struck only on the side of the box, anyway. Lucifers are so cheap that, in the words of William Morris, "the public buy twice as much as they want, and waste half."

Herbert Spencer calls the Lucifer "the greatest boon and blessing to come to mankind in the nineteenth century."

The pathways the Bryant and May matchwomen take home from the factory every night are marked by piles of phosphorescent vomit.

It begins with a toothache. And those are not uncommon, not where you live, not when you live. Not uncommon at all. But you know what it means, and you know what comes next, no matter how hard you try to put it out of your mind. For now, the important thing is to keep it from the foreman. And for a while, you can. You can swallow the clawing pain in your mouth just as you swallow the blood from your tender gums, along with your bread during the lunch break. If you have bread, that day. A mist of droplets floats through the room, making the air hazy, hard to see through. They settle on your bread.

Your teeth hurt, but you can keep that from the foreman. You can eat your bit of bread and keep that secret.

But then your face begins to swell.

Property is theft, wrote Karl Marx, and for almost thirty-five years, Karl Marx lived in London. Private property, he said, is the theft from the people of resources hitherto held in common. And then that property can be turned to capital, which can be used to extort labor from workingmen and women for far less than its value. Another theft. Theft of communal resources, theft of labor, and for these women and girls, the matchmakers of the Bryant and May match factory at Bow, it could also become theft of bone, theft of flesh, and, finally, theft of life.

Not that they don't put up a good fight. Fighting is something they're good at. Fighting, dancing, and drinking, those wild Irish girls of London's East End. That's what reformers and journalists say, anyway.

Your old Nan came over with her husband back in 1848, during the famine—forty years ago, long before you were born, but you and your siblings and cousins, you still have the map of Eire stamped into your souls.

Your Nan has the sight, or so she says. When you were naught but a small girl, not working yet, but only a nuisance underfoot, hungry all the time, she would distract you by telling you all the lovely things she could see in your future—a husband handsome and brave, fine strapping sons and lively daughters, and a home back in Ireland, with cows lowing on the hills, and ceilis with the neighbors every weekend, and all the cheese and bread you could eat.

You couldn't quite picture the countryside she described—the closest you could come was a blurred memory of Hampstead Heath, where your family had once gone on a bank-holiday outing, and being a London girl, you weren't quite sure that you wanted to live there, but you liked the sound of the cheese and the ceilis and the husband that your Nan promised you. And you believed her implicitly, because your Nan had the sight, didn't everyone on the street know that?

But perhaps she'd been mistaken because now your teeth hurt like hellfire and your face has started to swell. You can think of only one way for this to end, and it doesn't involve any ceilis.

When you were little, the youngest of your family, the first thing you remember is your mum telling you to be quiet while she counted out the matchboxes she made at home. Your mum would put you into the arms of your sister, Janey, four years older, and shoo the two of you and your brother and any cousins who happened to be around outside to play, and there you'd be until late at night, when the matchboxes were dry and could be stacked in a corner out of the way, and you kids could unroll mats and blankets and sleep fitfully on the floor.

When you were old enough to be a bit more useful, soon after your mum died birthing one baby too many, you would sit with your Nan, cutting the rotten bits out of the potatoes so that she could cook them more easily, back in the days before she lost her vision, the vision of this world, anyway. Once you'd lost your temper and complained about how many rotten spots there were, and your Nan shook her head and told you that the half or third of good flesh you got out of one of these potatoes was a bounty compared to the famine years. "All rot and nothing else," she said, "and you could hear the keening throughout the countryside, until you couldn't, and that was all the worse, the despair and silence of those left behind." She looked at the potato in your hand, took it from you, and dropped it in the pot. "And every crop melting into slime, and the English shipping out fat cows and calves and anything else they could get their hands on."

Sometimes your Nan would lapse into Irish, the language she and your granddad had spoken before emigrating. You don't speak it; your mum spoke a bit, and so did your dad. Janey and some of your older cousins speak some, but after that, there were just too many kiddies to make sure of what they were saying. When your Nan uses Irish, you don't know what her words mean, but it's easy to make out the general tone.

In Irish, the potato famine of 1845–1852 is called an Gorta Mór, the Great Hunger, or an Drochshaol, the Bad Times. During those seven years, around one million Irish died, most likely more, and at least another one million emigrated, reducing the country's population by one-quarter. England exported crops and livestock, off-limits to the impoverished Irish, to its own shores throughout the disaster. The food was exported under armed guard from ports in the areas of Ireland most affected by the potato blight.

The sultan of the Ottoman Empire attempted to send ten thousand pounds in aid to the people of Ireland; Queen Victoria requested that he reduce his charity to the sum of one thousand, as she herself had sent only two thousand. The sultan agreed, but nonetheless sent three ships of food to Ireland as well. The English courts attempted, unsuccessfully, to block the ships.

In America, the Choctaws had endured the death march known as the Trail of Tears sixteen years prior and apparently saw something familiar in a people being starved to death and forced off their land. They sent $170 for the relief of the Irish.

Sir Charles Trevelyan, the government official responsible for England's relief efforts, considered that "the judgement of God sent this calamity [the potato blight] to teach the Irish a lesson."

Your Nan lost her first two babbies, a little girl of two years who starved to death before she and your granddad left his farm, and another one that had yet to be born on the way over to England. Now she looks forward to holding both her babes once more when she meets them in paradise, which she describes as sounding much like County Cork in happier times.

When she used to tell you of your future life in Ireland, an Ireland under home rule, perhaps, an Ireland of Parnell's making, and blessed O'Connell's memory, she put herself there, too, back in County Cork in her old age, sitting by your fire.

When you were a little girl, you promised that you would bring her back to Ireland with you, and that when she died, you'd see her buried in the graveyard of the church where she'd been baptized and married.

Where will she see you buried? you now wonder.

There are no outside agitators in the factory at the end of June, and the only socialists are the same socialists who are there every day, dipping and cutting and packing for five shillings a week.

The only new thing is a bit of newspaper being passed around furtively, read out in whispers by the girls who can read to those who cannot: an article from *The Link* entitled "White Slavery in London," telling the middle-class folk of London about work at the Bryant and May factories.

You read with interest the details of your own life, and you make haste to hide the paper when the foremen come in.

A letter at your workstation states that the article is a lie, and that you are happy, well paid, and well treated in your work.

You rub the place at the bottom of your swollen cheek where the sores first opened up.

Instead of signing the preprinted letter to *The Times*, which has become the mouthpiece for middle-class outrage at Bryant and May, you spit on it.

Not one of the women in the entire factory signs the letter.

In the entire factory, the only letter with a mark at the bottom is the one with your spittle on it, shining faintly in the dark.

Fourteen-year-old Lizzie collects the unsigned letters and hands them to the foreman, staring him straight in the eye, and in that moment you know that it was Lizzie who'd gone to *The Link* with the story. And so does the foreman, perhaps, because he smacks her across the face with the sheaf of papers. Lizzie spits between the foreman's feet.

Lizzie is sacked the following Monday. When she's told to leave, she considers for a moment, then breaks the foreman's jaw with a single punch. As she turns to leave, all of you, you and your friends and rivals, put on your hats and follow her out.

The strike flares up like a Lucifer. When you look back at the long line of women behind you, you have to blink to be sure that there aren't white trails of phosphorus smoke floating off all of you, disappearing into the sky.

They said it was Annie Besant's doing, that Mrs. Besant had been the ringleader, an outside Fabian socialist agitator. And perhaps there is some truth to it, as she did write and publish "White Slavery in London," the article that so shamed Mr. Bryant that he tried to get his workers to repudiate it.

But Mrs. Besant called for a respectable middle-class boycott, not for working-class girls and women to take matters into their own hands. The strikers did not contact her until some days after the initial walkout.

The East End of London did not need middle-class Fabians to explain socialism.

In the seven years leading up to 1888, the women of Bryant and May had struck three times. They were unsuccessful, to be sure, but practice makes perfect.

You're getting ready to go out marching, collecting for the strike fund, when you hear your Nan calling for you. You hold off on wrapping up your suppurating face and turn to find her, bent almost double with her dowager's hump, staring up at you with her milky, sightless eyes.

"Yeh've got the phoss, acushla," she says. "Had it for a while, I reckon. When were yeh plannin' to tell me?"

You shrug, saying nothing, then remember that your Nan can't see you. You open your mouth to talk when she turns and shuffles back to the chair she had been sitting in.

You find your tongue. "You can smell it, eh, Nan?"

She swats at the air. "Can't smell a damn thing. Haven't been able to since before you were born. Makes all the mush I eat taste the same. Not that I figure what I eat tastes of anything worth eating anyways." She shakes her head. "Nah. I just know. Known for a while."

You wait to see what, if anything, she'll say next. Her eyelids droop, and before you know what you're doing, you burst out angrily, "And what about my children and husband and cows and ceilis every weekend? When will I get them, Nan?"

Her eyelids snap up again. She makes a sort of feeble fluttering gesture with her hands, which still look surprisingly youthful. "Never, acushla, my darling. Never for you."

Your eyelids widen in shock, and for the first time you realize that part of you had been hoping that your wise, witchy Nan would pull an ould Irish trick from up her sleeve, send the phoss packing, and send you away to Ireland, away from Bryant and May.

"I lied to you, my love," she says. "All those times, for all those years, I lied. I never saw nothing for you. Just a greenish glow where your long life should have been."

"Why?" you ask, glacial with the loss of hope.

"Ah, darling. Don't you know yeh've always been my favorite?"

You turn abruptly and resume tucking your scarf around your decaying jaw.

After a few seconds, your Nan speaks again, softly. "Darling, don't be so wretched. The phoss in your jaw is a horror, it's true, but it'll soon be over, it won't be long now."

You picture yourself coughing up blood, your jaw twisted, black, and falling to pieces, and you take little comfort in the image.

"Worse off by far," says your Nan, "are those who get the phoss in their souls. They'll never see paradise at all."

We'll hang Old Bryant on the sour apple tree,
We'll hang Old Bryant on the sour apple tree,
We'll hang Old Bryant on the sour apple tree,
As we go marching on.
Glory, glory, hallelujah . . .

—matchgirl strikers' marching song, 1888, sung to the tune of "John Brown's Body," a song popular among Union soldiers and abolitionists during the U.S. Civil War

A few days after the walkout, you and Annie Ryan from next door make your way to the Mile End Waste. You don't say much on the walk. Moving your jaw has become too painful, every slight flex of your facial muscles redoubling the bone-grinding ache, the soreness stretching poisoned tentacles out from your slowly decaying jaw to grip your skull and bore into your brain.

You've taken to eating the same soft, gray pap your Nan lives on. It saves you chewing and leaves more hard bread for your brothers and sisters and their kiddies. And since you're constantly queasy if not worse, you don't even miss it.

Some days you don't want the gray mush either, but your Nan won't eat unless you do. And some days you've half a mind to let the ould bitch starve, serve her right for lying to you all these years.

But after all, she is your Nan.

You leave your scarf on inside, even at home, so as not to scare the kiddies, but they avoid you anyway. It's the smell.

When you were a wee lass yourself, you and the others used to play on the corpses of horses, worked to death and left to putrefy in the street. Nothing still walking around should smell like that.

So you walk in silence toward the rally, even as the men and girls around you break into song. And in a crowd of thousands, your patch of silence isn't likely to be noticed.

Annie draws your arm through hers. "You've a marvelous singing voice, Lucy," she says, pulling you near, near enough that you can see her nostrils flare as she works to give no sign that she's noticed the smell. "Don't you remember when we were only small, and you made up that skipping rhyme about Mrs. Rattigan's warts? You sounded like an angel, counting off her warts as you skipped."

You nod, and even that hurts.

"They've got to hear us, Lucy. All the way to Mayfair and Parliament. Maybe all the way back to Ireland. That'd make old Parnell proud, wouldn't it?"

Annie leans in even closer. "You know nobody'd ever put you out, Lucy, don't you? And even if they did, well, you'd just trot down the block and come stop with me and mine. Take care of you right to the end, we would."

You nod slightly and she squeezes your hand. "Make the end come a bit sooner, too, if need be."

She draws away again, and after a moment you find your voice.

You can barely hear your own singing above the noise of your headache, but you see that Annie and the other girls can, and that, you suppose, is what counts.

When you return home, you finally relax and remove your hat and scarf. Something small, like a pebble, falls to the floor.

It's a piece of your jaw.

In 1889, Annie Besant exchanged socialism for theosophy. Despite its esoteric reputation, theosophy reflected conventional Victorian values in at least one way.

According to the teachings of Madame Blavatsky, theosophy's

founding mother, each and every person has exactly what he or she deserves in this life. Theosophists believed that sickness, suffering, deformity, and poverty were punishments for sins committed in a past life. This belief can be dressed as God's will, or as social Darwinism, but it comes to the same thing.

It is a reassuring thought to those whose lives are not thoroughly saturated with such suffering. Sometimes it can be a comfort even as one is led to the guillotine or faces the firing squad.

When Besant traded in socialism for theosophy, she bought spiritual certainty at the price of her compassion.

Though Annie Besant was by no means a strike leader—indeed, she had written on more than one occasion about the futility of trying to organize unskilled laborers—she'd had enough sympathy with the strikers and care for her good journalistic name to counter management's claims of innocence by publicizing the working conditions, wages, and abuse that Bryant and May expected the striking matchwomen to accept.

And she had a word with her good friend Charles Bradlaugh, MP.

As you and the other girls make your way to Parliament, heads turn at the sight of so many tattered dresses, the sound of so many rough accents outside the East End, and not in any uniform, either.

"What're you lookin' at?" Lizzie shouts at a group of young

ladies who, having forgotten the manners drilled into them by their governesses, stare and gape as you walk past.

The young ladies drop their eyes and turn away quickly. After a few seconds, you hear a shriek of laughter.

By the time you reach Westminster, traffic in the streets has slowed to a crawl as cabs and buses come to a full stop so their drivers and passengers can take a good, long look at the poor women walking en masse toward Parliament, just as if they have a right to.

Perhaps if you weren't in so much pain, you tell yourself, you could be as brave as Jenny, old Jenny Rotlegh, forty if she's a day, and bald as an egg from years of carrying wooden pallets on her head. Jenny sweeps off her bonnet right then and there, in front of the three MPs who had received your delegation.

"Look," she says. "Look what they done to me! Ain't that worth more 'n' four shillings a week, less fines?"

You listen to the gasps from the fine gentlemen and wonder if you should undo your scarf and expose what remains of your blackened jaw, and the line of sores reaching now up to your temples. You come as near as raising your hand to the scarf around your throat and taking one of the ends in your fingers. You untuck it and pause, thinking of the gentlemen staring at your melting face.

Jenny is an object of pity, an exemplar of abused and mistreated femininity.

But you have become a monster.

There is a difference between shocked pity and horrified disgust. It is human nature to turn away from the latter.

You tighten the scarf and retie the knot, more tightly than before.

Annie Besant wasn't the only established activist late to the party. There was also the London Trades Council, the last leading bastion of craft unionism, which had previously turned up its nose at unskilled laborers. The council met with a delegation of matchwomen. Perhaps out of the desire to retain its preeminent place as the voice of the urban worker, perhaps out of a paternalistic sense of noblesse oblige, perhaps even out of a genuine sense of fellow feeling and solidarity, the LTC offered to send a delegation of workmen to negotiate a settlement agreeable to both parties.

The firm received the overture genteelly, which must have made it all the more humiliating when that deputation returned empty-handed. The men reported only that Bryant and May were willing to allow most of the strikers to resume their old places, if they returned immediately, while reserving the right to refuse reemployment to the women they termed "the ringleaders."

The strikers didn't bother to send a reply.

The evening after the meeting with the MPs, your Nan asks you to lay your head on her lap. When you do, she rests her hand on your hair.

"You're angry with me, acushla," she says.

You say nothing. You watch your words more carefully than your sisters watch their farthings now that you slough off flesh with every motion of your mouth.

"Well, you've a right," she continues. When you remain silent, she sighs and is quiet herself for a while. After some minutes drift by, she draws breath to begin again.

"The strike will end," she says conversationally. "I seen it." This time she doesn't bother to pause for responses you will not give. "But you won't see it. You'll die first. I seen that, too."

Sooner's better than later, you think dully, and wonder if she'll tell you how long the strike will last, and if any of you will have jobs by the time it is over. You'd like to know that Annie won't starve, at least. If your Nan really does have any sight at all, if she hasn't been lying about everything, all this time. If she isn't just some crazy ould biddy.

"You won't see the end of this strike," she repeats. "Not unless I help you out. And I figure, I figure, I owe you at least that much."

You gently take her hand from your head and sit up, moving slowly, the way you have been for a while now. You hold her rough hand between two of yours, and you know for sure now, her mind is broken and gone, and she'll never see Ireland again.

She pulls her hand away from you irritably, as though she can hear your thoughts, and swats at you.

"Not a crazy ould one," she says. "Not like my own gran, there was madness for you, if that's what you're thinking. A life, it's like a flame, y'see, a candle flame. An' if I put that flame into a real flame, a real candle, well, you'll keep right on living as long as that candle keeps burning.

"And a candle held in the left hand of a hanged man, that candle, it can't go out. You can't put that out with wind nor water nor snuff it with yer fingers. Only good white milk can put out a Hand o' Glory.

"I can do that fer you," she says. "I can do it, if yeh can bring me what I need. It won't exactly be living, more sort of not dyin'.

But I don't know that what yeh're doing now is living, so much, either."

You say nothing once more, but this time more out of shock than deliberately.

"I'll give you a list," she says.

"Hand of a dead man?" you manage to slur.

"Hanged," she corrects you. "Left hand of a hanged man. Or woman'll do as well, o' course. Dunno how we'll get that one. We're neither of us well enough for grave robbing. But we'll manage."

After a doubtful pause, she repeats, "We'll manage.

"And those pieces of your jawbone that keep fallin' off. Start saving 'em."

Here are some of the reasons given by Bryant and May for fines taken from their workers' pay packets:

—dirty feet (3d.)
—ground under bench left untidy (3d.)
—putting burnt-out matches on the bench (1s.)
—talking (amount not specified)
—lateness, for which the worker was then shut out for half the day (5d.)

Here are deductions regularly taken from the matchwomen's pay packets:

—6d. for brushes to clean the machines (every six months)
—3d. to pay for children to fetch packing paper (weekly)

—2d. to pay the packer who books the number of packages (weekly)

—6d. to pay for stamps, to stamp the packages (weekly)

—1d. to pay for children to fetch and carry for the box-fillers (weekly)

Bryant and May employed no children to fetch and carry for the box-fillers. The box-fillers fetched and carried for themselves.

Nan says that you don't have the time to make a tallow dip. You wonder how much time you do have, as you collect what she told you to, and if it's worth living as you do now until the strike is over and broken. Perhaps it would be better to go now, while the girls are still going strong, fueled by high hopes.

But love is a hard habit to break, so you do as she tells you, scavenging strips of paper, a wide-mouth jar, and a length of wire from the trash heaps, and stopping at the butcher's for what lumps of pork fat he'll give you for your pennies. You've found that shopkeepers give you better prices these days. Perhaps they feel sorry for you.

Perhaps they just want you out of the shop as quickly as possible, so you don't scare off custom.

Either way is fine by you, as long as you can walk away with all the pork fat you need, which isn't much. You bring your parcels home to your Nan and lay them at her feet, like offerings.

What you do next isn't hard; you've made paper wicks before, rendered pork fat before, and it stinks, but it doesn't stink as badly as you do. While you do these things, your Nan takes the pieces of your jawbone that you've saved and grinds them into a fine powder, using a mortar and pestle. They crumble so easily.

Dust to dust.

While you stir the melted fat, your Nan leans over from her chair by the fire and tips the dust of your bones into the small pot. Then she slices across the veins of your forearm with an old knife. Straining against her arthritic knuckles, she squeezes and massages your arm to get as much of your blood into the mix as she can.

After you give the pot a few more stirs, the tallow looks no different from any other bit of tallow you've ever seen, grubby and nasty, and smells no different either, rank and putrid. You pour it into the glass jar, watching it pool and pile up around the paper wick held stiff by the scavenged wire.

While you scrub out the pot, your Nan mutters some Irish over the makeshift candle and sets it aside to harden.

"It's a good thing we neither of us eat much," she says to you. "With neither of us bringing anything in."

You nod. After a minute, you ask her the same thing you did the previous evening.

"Hand of a hanged man?" you force out.

She seems troubled, but she pats your hand. "Leave that to me," she says, and then again, more slowly, "leave that to me."

Before you sleep that night, she whispers in your ear, "I'm goin' out tonight. You be in the cemetery. The unconsecrated ground, an hour before dawn. Bring the small axe and the candle. And a few matches, o' course."

Your sleep has been unquiet for a long time now, with the effect that you find it harder and harder to rouse yourself. This is probably because you are dying.

Whatever the reason, by the time you force yourself fully awake, it's long past when you should have left for Bow Cemetery. On your way, you wonder anxiously if you'll be there in time. However it is that your Nan plans to find you a hanged man, you want the cover of darkness.

You don't know the way as well as you do to the churchyard at Saints Michael and Mary on Commercial Road, the Catholic church not yet built when your Nan came over. You've been there plenty, standing by the gravesides of the very young, the very old, and all between.

But your Nan wouldn't dig up a good Catholic.

Surely she didn't have the strength to dig up anybody else, either, come to that. And she didn't tell you to bring a shovel.

It's summer, and small pink flowers dot the ground of the graveyard. They remind you of the morning that an anonymous benefactor sent a cartload of pink roses down to all the girls on the picket, to wear as badges. That morning, the fragrance of roses had blotted out even the stench you did your best to trap in the folds of your scarf. For that one morning, the scent of roses surrounded you, and you let yourself pretend that you weren't rotting away, like the corpses interred in the ground beneath your feet.

The unconsecrated ground is a newer part of the graveyard, and it holds unbaptized babies, suicides, and those of strange and foreign faiths, or perhaps even no faith at all.

But they all rot in the same way, you figure, 'cause the worms probably don't know the difference.

Or maybe they do. Maybe they feel a tingle of the divine wind round them as they cross from unconsecrated to holy soil, and the whisper of loss and chilly despair as they pass back the other way.

You spot your Nan's figure swaying by an oak tree. That's to be expected, of course, the swaying, but she seems somehow to be taller than you think of her being, and she's not holding her stick.

When you draw nearer, you see your Nan's stick lying on the ground where she dropped it, next to the lidded milk pail and near the kicked-over step stool, all of which she must have dragged out to the cemetery last night. Nan herself sways and twists gently, her feet a foot and a half off the ground, one end of a stout rope around her neck, the other tied to a branch over your head, a branch high enough to keep her feet from the ground, but low enough that she could reach it from the step stool.

She rocks back and forth, and you watch her, waiting for the tears to come. They don't, though, perhaps because there's nothing left inside you at all.

"Oh, Nan," you whisper, and you don't even feel the pain as what remains of your jaw and tongue move clumsily.

You sit just near her swaying feet and begin to feel a certain leaden weight in your limbs, beginning at your hands and feet and creeping upward. It is death come for you, you know. As you decide to sit calmly and wait for the leaden feeling to spread, a gust of wind sets your Nan's corpse to swinging violently. You look up at her contorted face.

It is less repellent than you imagine your own to be.

You get to your feet, straighten the stool, and pick up the axe, so your Nan, who had loved you enough to lie to you, enough to relinquish her place in paradise and her chance to see her lost babbies again, shouldn't have done so for nothing at all.

For isn't suicide a mortal sin?

Using the axe, you cut her down and lay the body on the

ground, her left arm stretched to the side. And as the sun rises, you bring the axe down on her left wrist.

You move mechanically, so as not to waste a moment, and in any case, the cool, rough skin of your Nan's hand is less horrifying than the dead flesh of your face and neck. You close her fingers around the candle, and they grip it tightly, as if your Nan is still there, holding on to what remains of your life for all she is worth.

You take a match from your pocket and strike it against the handle of the axe. It flares up, and for a moment the familiar smell of white phosphorus hovers in the air.

You hide the axe in the bushes on the grounds of the cemetery and walk home carrying the corpse, the burning candle protected by her good left hand hidden in the lidded milk pail dangling from your arm.

The old lady is heavy, so much heavier than she had seemed when she was alive. She'd become small and frail, but the body that lies in your arms is heavy as sin.

Even in the East End, people do not usually stroll out just after dawn carrying a corpse. Heads turn as you go, and your neighbors recognize you, recognize your Nan. Nobody speaks.

You lay your Nan's body down in the room you shared with her and your sister, her husband, and their kiddies, and then you rouse the rest of the family.

You say little when they ask what happened. But then, you say very little these days anyway. They assume that your Nan's hand was missing when you found her.

At least, you think they do. You do catch Janey looking at you intently, her brow wrinkled, her head tilted to one side, a bit suspicious-like, and for a minute she looks so much like your late mother, with her constant expression of worry, that it takes your breath away.

Or it would.

You realize that you are no longer breathing. You bring your fingers to your throat, pushing through the layers of your scarf, and feel for a pulse. You find none.

Later, in private, you peer into the milk pail, and the candle your Nan made and holds is still burning.

Early in the afternoon, you go back for the axe.

Bryant and May gave in, just over two weeks after the walkout. They gave in so quickly and so completely that with the benefit of historical hindsight, one wonders if the matchwomen should have demanded more. On July 18, 1888, Bryant and May acceded to every one of the strikers' terms.

—The firm agreed to recognize the newly formed Union of Women Matchmakers, the largest union of women and girls in England.
—The firm agreed to abolish all fines.
—The firm agreed to abolish all deductions.
—Matchworkers could take any and all problems directly to the managing director of the firm rather than having to go through the foremen.
—The firm agreed to provide a room for eating lunch separate and apart from the working rooms.

This last item was so that the matchwomen could eat without

white phosphorous settling onto their food and from there mak-ing its way into their teeth.

It starts with a toothache, after all.

On August 14, 1889, just over a year after the matchwomen's vic-tory, a group of London dockworkers walked off the job. These workers were mainly Irishmen: the husbands, sons, brothers, and sweethearts of the matchwomen of the East End. Within two days, twenty-five hundred men had turned out, demanding a wage of a sixpence an hour, a penny more than they had been earning. Solidarity with the dockworkers spread across London. Black workers, usually brought in as cheap replacement labor, refused to scab. Jewish tailors went out. Hyde Park played host to a rally of one hundred thousand people, serenaded by bands playing "The Marseillaise."

By the end of August, more than 130,000 workers were out on strike, and the families that were making do without their men's wages were withholding rent.

The strike lasted a month, and the dockworkers won nearly all they asked for. Years later, historians refer to the Great Dock Strike of 1889 as the beginning of the militant New Unionism: the organization of unskilled and industrial labor that swept Britain and replaced the old craft union model. By the end of 1890, almost two million of Britain's workers held a union card.

John Burns, one of the dockworkers' great leaders, spoke out at rallies, urging solidarity in the face of the starvation that threatened strikers and their families.

"Stand shoulder to shoulder," he thundered. "Stand shoulder

to shoulder and remember the matchgirls, who won their fight and formed a union!"

On July 18, 1880, the new terms are settled and accepted by the newly born union and by Bryant and May, still in shock (but also pleased that they'd not had to cede more). That afternoon and evening, there is jubilation in the East End.

Streets and homes fill with happy, loud women in the bright, loud clothing the matchgirls are known to favor. Women talk, laugh, dance, and drink. There might even be a few fights, to tell the truth, but if so, they are all in good fun.

Even journalists are right, some of the time.

You switch out your regular scarf for one in bright blue and your everyday hat for your best one, allover red roses and feathers. You wear your best clothing and spend the evening with Annie at the Eagle in the City Road, even dancing on the crystal platform, just as you did before, when your heart beat and your jaw was whole.

When your Nan was alive.

Your Nan, your poor Nan, not laid in the rich soil of County Cork, not now in a better place clutching once more her babbies to her breast, but lost to heaven completely, for had she not been a witch, and a suicide to boot? Sure, she was laid to rest in the consecrated ground of the Catholic churchyard, but only because when Father Keene had interviewed your sisters and brothers, they had all sworn that she had been out of her head with grief for some time, ever since her favorite granddaughter had started showing the signs of phossy jaw. Sure to God, she'd never have done a thing like this while in her right mind, never.

And Father Keene had looked over at you, you sitting in the

corner with your face hidden in shadows, and had felt in his heart that what they said was the truth, and he had thought, Wouldn't it be a shame to bring scandal and more suffering to this family?

But your Nan hadn't been out of her head at all. All you had to do to see that was to look into the covered pail where her candle still burned, or to search in vain for the heartbeat that used to pulse under your left breast. Your Nan hadn't hanged herself because she was out of her mind with grief.

Your Nan had hanged herself for this: so that this night you could dance a breakdown on the Eagle's crystal platform, so that you could put your arm through Annie's and watch the sun come up, knowing that she and the others were going to be all right, maybe. That when she'd told her man, Mick O'Dell, lived over a few streets and worked on the docks, that she was expecting, he'd told her to set the date just as soon she could.

But you aren't going to hang around for the wedding. Nothing less lucky than a corpse at a wedding, even one that can dance.

You and Annie watch the sun rise from the churchyard at Saints Michael and Mary. You have one arm through hers, and in the other, you hold the pail with the candle inside, still burning, and a small bottle of milk.

Just a bit, you figure, to douse the candle, and then the rest for Annie to drink, for the coming babby, and you'll do it yourself. No need to make a murderer out of Annie, no matter her offer, and then you'll follow your Nan to perdition, so she won't be without family to help her in her trials.

You and Annie turn and walk slowly and a bit unsteadily (the worse for drink, both of you) through the churchyard, toward the freshly filled-in grave of your Nan. There's a small headstone, just her name, Bridget O'Hea, and the years, 1827–1888.

You'd been there yesterday to lay flowers. Other than the pink and yellow wildflowers you'd picked on Hampstead Heath, already wilting and going brown by the time you placed them on the grave, there had been nothing.

But now the flowers you laid yesterday are not wilted at all. They've taken root and are blooming. You give them a gentle tug to make sure they're real, not a trick.

You and Annie clutch at each other's waists as you watch an honest-to-God oak tree sprout from the grave, from sapling to full grown in an instant, with a rich canopy of leaves, wreathed in mistletoe. You step forward and run your hand across the rough bark. A large snake coils around the trunk of the oak, several times, and the thing must be yards long.

You stare for a moment before turning to look at Annie, to see if she's seeing what you are, or if what is left of your brain is playing tricks on you. She steps forward and plucks a leaf from the oak and holds it to her lips in wonder.

The snake turns its head to look at you, and you find yourself looking into your Nan's eyes.

You blink and the snake, the oak, and the mistletoe are gone, but the flowers you brought are still growing from the grave soil. After a moment's pause, you meet Annie's eyes and step carefully onto your Nan's grave. You settle yourself against the headstone, and Annie sits next to you. You take the candle, still held in your Nan's left hand and set it on the ground and pass the bottle of milk to Annie. She begins to pry the cork loose, but you still her hand.

Instead, you slide the fingers of your Nan's hand back, and they uncurl as smoothly and gracefully as barley bending in the wind. The candle slips free.

It begins to burn in earnest then, guttering and smoking like the cheap tallow that it is, but burning more quickly than any candle should have a right to, as if making up for lost time. You have ten, maybe fifteen minutes, at the rate it is going.

Annie takes your hand, and together you watch the candle burn down.

Near the end, her grip on your hand tightens, and you close your eyes.

We have remaining to us two photographs, and only two photographs, of the striking Bryant and May matchworkers. The second photograph is more formal. It is of the official strike committee, and the women in it have done their hair and put on their Sunday best. They are arrayed across a stage, carefully posed in chairs. They seem confident, proud, intent.

But the first photograph is the more interesting one. It is of seven women standing in front of the Bryant and May factory. Their faces are gaunt, taut, and serious. More than one look a bit dazed, as if unsure of what they have done and what future it will bring them.

This photograph is famous now. More than that, it has become a symbol of working-class courage and resolve, displayed in the windows of London union offices.

Two of the seven women have almost certainly been identified by recent scholarship.

At the leftmost edge of the photo stands a woman half cut out of the picture. We see her left arm, the left half of her body, and most of her head, which she must have turned toward the camera. She is wearing a velvet hat, like some of the other women, and has a fringe of straight hair reaching almost down to where her eyes should be. Her face is nearly impossible to make out. It is a blur. Perhaps she moved as the photograph was being taken, though nothing else is blurred, not her hat, not her hand, not the scarf knotted around her neck, not a hair of her fringe.

The original print, now lost, belonged to John Burns, the leader of the dockworkers' strike, who urged his men to remember the matchgirls, who had won their fight and formed a union.

But her face is gone.

BALLROOM
BLITZ

I remember when the very air pulsed with music, raucous shouts and double-time beats mixing with the eerie wailing of tortured guitars. We were all of us young and wild; my brothers and I wore tight black jeans and ripped T-shirts and stood around looking tough and combing our hair 'til it was slicked back just right to show off our sideburns. The girls wore short skirts and strong boots, ripped fishnet stockings ending inches below their hemlines. We all wore boots, come to that, engineering boots or motorcycle boots or combat boots or Doc Martens, as though we had to be ready for a forced march. And we may have been under a curse, but I remember us always laughing. The air was gray with smoke and our heads spun—not a full glass but we emptied it, not a pill but we popped it, not a leaf but we smoked it, and we laughed even when we were on our knees. The air was drenched with beer and whiskey, and we danced those boots so thin we could feel the floor through our socks.

We were young, I said, but of course my brothers and I couldn't age, could we? We were bound, and that kept the twelve of us from growing any older no matter how much time passed. We couldn't set foot outside the club, but inside we couldn't grow old, couldn't die. Bands appeared and disappeared, DJs spun in and out, and we were always there, game for anything, hopped up on speed and lack of sleep, dancing our boots thin and shouting our voices hoarse. We'd been there for years before we found the girls, or before the girls found us.

I remember the rest of it, too, waking up wanting to die, the hacking coughs, the bleak despair driving me—driving us—to drown ourselves in the neon darkness, the impossible wish to see sunshine just once more, the imprisonment. But when I look back, everything glows with false freedom, and I remember us always laughing.

The music never stopped, even when your head was screaming, when the beats that had blasted you off your feet drilled behind your eyes, and it felt like your head would break open from the pain. The air never cleared, and the smoke that had sustained us and cushioned us like amniotic fluid turned harsh, bitter, and sticky like tar with sharp teeth, extending tendrils to wrap around our limbs and keep us moving but stop us escaping. And the dancing that had transported us became a cage of knives, spitting electrodes forcing us to move, even when our very bones were splintering in agony.

Each morning I woke up shaking, my vision blurred and doubled. I was begging Cynthia for a drink before my eyes were even fully open, but she just stood behind the bar with her arms folded, black hair tightly braided back, and shook her head.

Even picking my head up off the bar made my guts flip over. I'd forgotten what it felt like to sleep in a bed, to wake up without pain and nausea. Staggering a little, I would wake up my brothers.

We all woke up like that: black eyes, broken jaws, teeth missing, nausea, spitting blood. I woke up shattered and begging like the rest, but I was oldest, the one in charge, the one who looks after his brothers, cleans them up, gets them out of trouble, gets them in trouble. And it was my fault. So I would get to my feet somehow and go to wake up my brothers. My hands shook, my whole body trembled, and I could feel blood trickling out my ears, my ribs cracking and shattering every time I tried to draw a breath.

We felt like that every morning, and we'd heal by nightfall.

So I'd go to wake up my brothers, and for me that was the worst of it. My third brother, who's always been an asshole, woke up spitting with rage, calling me names and blaming me for our troubles, which was fair enough, I suppose, and my twelfth brother, my youngest brother, just wept silently at every waking, tears running down his face like rain against a window. At least one of us would wake up choking on vomit. Sometimes it was me.

We had to wash the place down, and the bar was like us: no matter how well we'd scrubbed the toilets, the bar, the floor, the basement, by the next morning they'd be covered in puke and grime and shit again. And with joints cracking, doubled over and hunched up like old men, we had to shine it up again. We had to take care of that hellhole like it was our baby, and afterward, if we'd done it well enough, Cynthia would order us some food from the diner down the street. Never enough, though. I remember always being hungry. Also dirty. There was a small sink in the men's room where I rinsed out my shirt every so often and tried to splash myself clean, but there wasn't much in the way of soap, and I lived in a cocoon of sweat and bile and dried blood.

My youngest brother, I had to make sure he didn't get ahold of my pocketknife. He'd cut himself if he did—maybe he still does, I don't know anymore—and the cuts wouldn't heal by evening.

He's got scars up and down his arms and legs. One of the cuts got infected once and he ran a fever like I'd never seen before. I pleaded with Cynthia to bring in a doctor, promised her I'd do anything, but as she pointed out, I had nothing to bargain with. Eventually she tossed me some antibiotics, but the fever singed his brain, and he hasn't been the same since, and none of this is his fault. He just fell in with the wrong crowd. Me.

Even when he didn't have my knife, I'd have to keep an eye on him. Sometimes he swiped the knife Cynthia used to cut up lemons and limes.

My sixth brother killed himself once.

I found him hanging from the light fixture in the men's room by his belt, and he was stone dead. I remember how heavy his body was when I brought it down, how mottled his face was, his tongue lolling obscenely out of his mouth. And I remember him waking up the next morning, whimpering like a puppy, with purple bruises around his throat. He's held his neck funny ever since.

My third brother, that asshole, he just pummels the wall when it gets to be too much for him. It fucks up his knuckles, leaves blood smears on the walls that we have to scrub off again, but I don't think he's thinking about that when he does it. I think he likes the pain it brings.

And me? I drink. We had plenty of money when we first got here, and I drank it away. Not by myself, of course. We ran out a long time ago, so I do my drinking at night. At night we don't pay, I don't know why, except I think Cynthia's giving us the chance to do the night over, to do something right. I see myself in the mirror and I can tell the alcohol is wrecking me, but that's better than the alternative. I feel the liquor corroding my body from the inside out, breaking me down into dust and poison. Or maybe just releasing the poison that had been there all along.

My hands still shake, if I don't concentrate on keeping them still.

Those were the days of living death. But the nights were something else entirely. In the years before the girls showed up, at night we felt okay again, and okay was so much better than we'd felt during the day that we went wild. But by the time the girls got there, there was damn little of that left. By the time the girls got there, we were spending the nights slumped at the bar, bleak hopelessness etched into our faces.

The girls were obviously slumming, but then, so were we, or we had been at first, pretty boys down from the big house to mix it up with the squatters. Now we had the broken noses and rotten teeth of real diehards, but we hadn't started out like that. I carried a switchblade, but I never pulled it. Anyway, the girls were clearly coming from Daddy's mansion to rock out with the real punks. Twelve of them with ratted hair and liquid black eyeliner making cat's-eyes an inch long, black leather bustiers and Doc Martens. They might have been meant for us, and I swear, I could see our salvation in their eyes. We all could, I think.

But we played it cool, leaning up against the bar and downing beer and eyeing the girls when they weren't looking, while they were still blinking in the dark, trying to get their bearings among the pounding beats and flaring matches.

The oldest made her way to the bar, right where I was waiting for her. Maybe she'd seen me eyeing her after all. I sauntered over a few steps and met her.

"Buy you a drink?" I asked.

No, that's not right. The music was shaking the floor, glasses were rattling behind the bar, and I leaned over to her and half shouted, half mouthed, "Buy you a drink?" close enough to her ear that she could feel my breath on her face, my breath, which smelled of smoke and beer and late nights and rotten hope and self-destruction.

She cut her eyes at me, and her eyelids glittered with caked-on silver eye shadow. I wanted to bend her over backward in a movie kiss right then and there, but I kept my hands to myself, took a drag off my cigarette instead while sonic fireworks exploded around us. I could see my brothers gravitating toward the other girls.

Then she smiled, shouted "Why not?" at me, and mouthed, "cider."

I put my arm around her waist and she let me. I got her a cider—we never had to pay, not at night, because we were paying every day—and gave her a cigarette, and lit it for her. She coughed and pretended it wasn't her first. I remembered my first, how I hadn't coughed at all, but had sucked the coarse, harsh smoke straight down into my heart, where it wrapped around that beating machine like a protective cocoon. The smoke's still there, but it's been getting thinner, no matter how much I force down my throat.

She stood with her hip pressed up against my leg. "What do you want?" she shouted in my ear.

"I want to dance with you," I shouted back. "Because . . ." I didn't know how to finish that sentence, so I just let it hang in the air like an afterimage.

She drained her glass and slammed it down on the bar, but the music was so loud that I couldn't hear it hit. Her face lit up, flushed with drink and heat. "Let's go, then!" She grabbed my hand and together we pushed and shoved our way to the middle of the seething mass of people, my brothers, her sisters, and we became the center of the storm and the lightning struck and we danced. We danced the band dry and the DJ sore, and still we moved like machine gun fire, like the St. Valentine's Day Massacre, and I knew that this was it, that she and her sisters were the ones.

We danced the sun up, not that we could see the sun through the tattered walls. No, we were lit by neon and dim incandescence and the flares of cardboard matches, but the space emptied out and the music faded until finally we could hear each other speak, and there were holes worn through the soles of our boots.

"Where d'you live?" she asked me as we leaned against the bar sharing a bottle of whiskey.

I gestured around the room a little unsteadily. My socks were damp with sweat and with something nasty on the floor. "Here," I said. "We live here."

"You got nowhere you could take me?"

"Honey," I said, "I can't leave."

She took a pull off the bottle. "Why not?"

I ground out my cigarette and told her.

My brothers and me, back when we were really young, not trapped in youth, but genuinely new, we heard the beats from our black disks and they pulled each of us by the balls. We knew we had to come here, that here was where our life should be, in the dark and in the noise. So we got the gear first—went down to Trash and Vaudeville with ready cash and remade ourselves.

We swaggered in here like young Turks, chains clinking against our legs, our hair combed just right, and we tore up the dance floor, and we knocked back shots of tequila, and we hassled the girls. We were real assholes, spoiling for a fight.

It was me who got one.

Not even a fight. You couldn't call it a fight. He was just a kid, barely older than my tenth brother, barely shaving. He was just a fucked-up kid. But I was always angry, and when this junkie kid barreled into me on his way to the men's room and puked on my boots—part of it was wanting to impress Cynthia with how hard-core I was. I didn't know about her then, didn't know what kind of power she had, just that she was the bartender, and she was cute—long black hair pulled back in a French braid and bright red lipstick. Knotwork tattoos. But then a lot of it was pure rage. I was always seething, always about to boil over. I don't know why. Testosterone, maybe. Or maybe just being cramped inside my skin, of needing to get out, of needing release.

It doesn't matter why, I guess, but I beat the shit out of that kid. He didn't . . . look okay afterward.

Cynthia came out from behind the bar with the Louisville Slugger she keeps back there, but I didn't even feel it hit me, I was so hopped up on adrenaline, so it wasn't until my brothers pulled me off the kid that I stopped and saw what I had done to him. Sometimes I wonder if he survived the night.

Sometimes I wonder if I did.

Cynthia gave twenty bucks to the kid's friends and told them to get him to the nearest hospital, NYU, I guess. Then she turned and looked at me.

"You," she said. "Out. Don't come back."

But the fire was still burning through my blood and the shame was starting to seep in through the cracks in my rage, so I stonewalled. "Fuck, no," I said. "That kid owes me new boots."

"That *kid*," she said, "owes you *nothing*. Get out. You're eighty-sixed."

I sized her up. Cynthia's not a tall woman. I looked around and didn't see a bouncer. "No. I'm not done drinking."

"This is my bar," she said, "and you're done."

"I'm not leaving."

"You're not?"

"No," I spat. "And neither are my brothers. We'll fucking sit and drink and dance until we're *ready* to go home. If you don't like it, call the fucking cops."

"No cops in my bar, boys," Cynthia said, kind of husky, and back then I thought it was capitulation, but now I think it was a warning. She looked around at my brothers. "He speak for all of you? Any of you leaving?"

My brothers stood tight next to me. I . . . I'm still a little proud of that, still a little grateful. They must've heard the menace in her voice, but not one of them budged. Not even my third brother.

Cynthia's gaze lingered on my youngest brother. He's only fourteen, and he looks it. "You sure?" she said, and she spoke kindly, for her. "You sure you want to stay with him?"

My youngest brother looked at the door, looked at me, and didn't say anything, but he didn't move, either.

Cynthia nodded. She went back behind the bar and turned the music back on and I thought I'd won. And she acted like nothing was wrong, like I hadn't beat a kid maybe to death in front of her, like I hadn't flung her authority back in her face. She set us up rounds and even smiled so sweetly at me that I thought I had a shot with her.

When I woke up that first morning and saw her behind the bar setting up for the night, I just thought I'd passed out and she'd left me there. I felt beat to shit, but I'd woken up feeling that way before, and not remembering why. Then I tried to leave.

As soon as I tried to set foot outside the door I curled up in agony. The air felt like knife blades skinning me alive, the rising sun seemed to pour molten metal down on my skin, and the ground, ah, the ground seemed to swarm up around me like a mountain of stinging beetles. Every inch of my body blistered and burned.

I crawled back into the bar on my hands and knees, gulping the stinking air. I couldn't feel anything but pain and rage.

I woke up my brothers, and when my third brother realized what had happened to us, he actually went for Cynthia and she broke his collarbone with the Louisville Slugger. He fell down and she stood over him—she seemed to tower over us.

"What did you do to us? What *are* you?" I asked her hoarsely.

"I'm the *bartender*," she said. "And don't you *ever* fuck with me. Not in my bar."

Cynthia's always here, and I don't think she sleeps.

So every morning, I told her, we wake up in the same beaten shape I put that kid in, and every day we do everything Cynthia tells us and we can't set foot outside the bar. But it could end, I told her, if there are girls, if there's dancing, 101 nights straight, we could leave. Maybe even go home again. If we still have a home. Maybe we could find a home.

All the time I told this girl our story, she drank whiskey and nodded in the right places.

"Home's overrated," she said.

I thought about asking, but didn't. "Look," I said. "I'm not like that anymore. I don't do that. I just . . . I don't. I mean, if somebody gives you trouble, I'll lay him out. But I don't . . . I don't let the rage take over anymore."

She nodded. "How long has it been?"

I shrugged. "Dunno. Years. Things don't change here. People

come and go. We don't age, but the circles under my eyes, they get darker."

"Yeah," she said. "First thing I noticed about you. Under your eyes, the skin looks like charcoal."

She put her hand on my thigh, leaned over, and kissed me. I put my arms around her, and she broke it off and pulled away. While I caught my breath, she put the whiskey bottle in my hand and slid off the barstool, her purple miniskirt riding up to the very bottom of her ass. She tugged it back into place.

"I'll see you," she said.

"You coming back tomorrow night?" I asked as her sisters began filing out. I tried to keep the desperation from my voice.

She grinned. Her dark lipstick was smeared from our kiss and her black eyeliner cat's-eyes were long gone, sweated off while we danced. The rips in her stockings had gotten bigger. "Yeah. We'll be back."

"And the night after that?"

"Could be," she said. "You never know."

"Wait," I said. "You know about me now. I'm Jake. What's your name?"

"Isabel," she said.

"What's your story?"

"I don't have one yet," she said.

"Come on," I persisted. "What brings you here?"

She grinned again, but this time it looked a lot more brittle. "Nothing." She shrugged. "Hey—anything you want? From outside?"

I thought about pushing her harder for a minute, about trying to find out what it was she wanted to get away from, and decided against it. I couldn't risk pissing her off, not when I still barely knew her.

"A clean T-shirt," I said. "Maybe a peach? I kind of miss peaches. They used to be my favorite."

"Wrong season," she said. "Peaches won't be any good for months."

"An apple, then?"

"Okay." She smiled at me, and then she walked out. The door slammed and bolted, locking my brothers and me in for the day.

Our first few weeks in there, we'd torn the place apart every night, wrenched the stools apart and used them to smash up the bottles and the mirror behind the bar. But the club just rebuilt itself around us. It didn't heal completely—the mirror was still shattered like a mosaic and walls were charred in places. But the place didn't look much different from the run-down punk dive it was when we'd first walked in. The cuts on our fists took a lot longer to heal.

After the girls and the other patrons—the ones who came and went as they pleased—had left, my brothers and I settled in for the day, after that first night, contorting ourselves on benches and against walls.

"It's gonna happen," I said happily.

"I don't like them," my youngest brother said.

"What do you mean, you don't like them?" I asked. "They're our girls, the ones who are going to set us free. You can't not like them."

"The one I was dancing with was boring," he said.

"And mine didn't like it here, I could tell," said my fifth brother.

"We want to get out of here, don't we?" I said reasonably.

"You're just cheery because you and your girl were making out on the dance floor," snarled my third brother. He's always been the worst of us.

"Look, guys," I said. "There're twelve of them. Twelve of us. They're the ones. Just go to sleep."

My third brother was right about one thing. I was deliriously happy. I haven't felt that way since.

They came back the next night and the night after that, and I danced with her all night, 'til our boots were worn through and our heads were caved in with the beats. And we drank so much that when we fell down we bounced, and when we got hurt we roared with laughter instead of pain. We were wrecks, me trying to shuck what was left of the bullying asshole I had been, and her running from . . . whatever she was running from, two drunken, dancing banshees. Twenty-four, really.

She told me about the weather, which I liked. The bar was cold in the winter and hot in the summer, but I'd almost forgotten about the beating sun and gray pinpricks of rain. She told me about her calculus class, which made me feel stupid, but I didn't really care. She smelled like parks and asphalt and street fairs and the outside that I missed. Every few nights she'd come in morose and rageful. She wouldn't talk and wouldn't smile. All she would do was knock back shots of bourbon and dance. By the end of the night I was holding her hair out of her face while she vomited into the toilet. I didn't mind. I guess I was falling in love. I think she was just falling. She'd do that for a few nights in a row, and then come in back to normal, chirping about her cousin's new baby and showing me pictures. I couldn't remember the last time I'd seen a baby.

We both had our hands full taking care of the others. I'd laid down the law to my brothers: no bitching about the girls to me. I didn't want to hear it. But they didn't get along with them any better, and it was just as clear that the girls didn't like my brothers. The oldest was the only one who bothered to dress up;

the others slouched around in jeans and T-shirts, which was fair enough, because that's what we were wearing. My third brother pissed off one sister so much that she threw her drink at him. I shoved him up against the cracked wall of the bar.

"What the fuck did you do?" I shouted at him.

"Go fuck yourself," he spat at me.

I banged his head against the wall again. "I swear to God, Max, if you screw this up for us—"

"*What?*" he shouted. "I'll get the shit kicked out of me? That's how I wake up every goddamn morning, thanks to you!"

We stared at each other for a couple of minutes. Finally I turned away. "Just don't, Max," I said.

Isabel had been talking her sister down. "Please don't go," I heard her saying. "C'mon, don't go. Tomorrow'll be better. I promise. I promise."

The next night Isabel brought in a bag of weed and some rolling papers. "I think this might help," she told me, and it did. It helped Max, anyway, who stopped pummeling the walls if we saved enough for him to smoke up during the days. Every night after that she brought in something. I didn't know where she got the drugs or the money for them, but she was able to hold them over us and enforce good behavior.

Sometimes I think the only things that united her sisters and my brothers were the desire for the drugs and their resentment of the two of us. But we took care of them, and we kept them in line.

There was nobody to keep us in line.

A couple of weeks after I first met her, she pulled me into the bar's back room, pressed me into one of the darker corners, and kissed me. My arms went around her and I found the gap between her T-shirt and her purple skirt.

"Better not stop dancing," I whispered to her, and she nodded. But she tasted like cider and cigarettes and sweat, so I kissed her again and ran my hand down the side of her breast.

"I know another dance," she whispered back, and slid her hands into the back pockets of my jeans.

We had ended up in a heap at the foot of the wall, and I held her half-on, half-off my lap. I didn't care if we had to start the 101 nights over, honestly, it had been that good, and I leaned over and kissed her hair.

"I love you," I told her.

"You need me," she corrected me, pretty bleakly.

"No," I said. "I love you."

"You barely know me," she replied.

So we danced and screwed our way through one hundred nights. My brothers and I never knew where the girls went during the days, we never found out where they lived. At night they lived with us, amid the smoky, alcoholic squalor of the bar. My T-shirt and her fishnets were in shreds and tatters but my and my brothers' boots miraculously healed each day while we slept, curled up in the dark corners. Sometimes I would have sworn that I could still smell her hair in my sleep.

The hundredth night, Isabel was in one of her poison moods. She wouldn't look at me, wouldn't talk to me no matter what I did or said. By the end of the night my nerves were spitting wires. I never knew what to do with her when she was like this. Nothing worked, nothing felt right, and I was tense, straining for that 101st night like a dog at the end of a leash. It was all I could see. I tried to talk to her, but her averted eyes and mono-syllabic answers reduced me to silence as well. At the end of the night I stared moodily into space while she knocked back shots of Irish whiskey. My tension and mounting excitement curdled into frustration and I began to seethe. Why was she being like this when we were so close? When she paid for her fifth shot, I finally spoke.

"You can't handle that much whiskey and you know it," I said.

She shrugged half-heartedly. "Fuck you, Jake," she said, but without any real malice behind it. No feeling at all, really, not love or anger.

"Seriously, Isabel. Stop drinking. You'll just wind up puking it back up."

"So? Who are you, my mother?"

"Not your mother," I said. "I'm the person who cleans you up afterward, remember." My voice turned ugly and I knew it would be a mistake to keep talking. But I was so aching with tension for the next night and her mood had turned that tension sour. I guess I thought a fight might be the next best thing to fucking, which she certainly wasn't in the mood for. "Me, not your sisters." I kept going, trying to goad her into paying attention to me. "Your sisters, they don't give a shit. They leave you here as soon as the dancing's done."

It worked. Her head snapped around. "Don't you say *one word* about my sisters. You're sick of cleaning *me* up? What have I been doing since I got here but cleaning up after your mess? You think it's easy getting my sisters here every night? They practically *hate* your brothers. You think I want to be here when I feel like this?"

I'd actually . . . never thought about what Isabel's black moods would be like from the inside. I guess I'd just thought about them as part of her mystique—Where did she come from? How did she feel? She was here for me, and that had been enough. For me, anyway.

"Then why do you bother to come?" I snarled at her, to cover up the shame beginning to slink through my guts.

She stared at me for a minute and turned back to her drink. "You're an asshole." She drank down the fifth shot of whiskey and blinked a little in the low light. For the first time I noticed the dark circles under *her* eyes. "I come here," she began, and then stopped. "I come here," she said again, with some difficulty. "Because it's the only time I really feel alive. It's the only time I feel like I *want* to be alive. I can't stop sleeping, Jake. I sleep twelve or fifteen hours a day. Most days showering is too hard and my arms and legs feel like they're filled with lead. I—I feel like I'm not really there most of the time, just looking through the cut-out eyes of a portrait, like in a bad movie. Everything hurts, all the time, even when there's nothing wrong with me. I cry every day. I can't keep my mind together, my thoughts bounce and clatter like a bag of marbles emptied out onto the floor. And everything looks gray to me, like there's a screen of smoke in front of my eyes. And I hate myself for being like this, so weak. Weak and useless.

"And when I come *here*, Jake, I'm not useless. I come *here* because sometimes when I'm here, the music and the smoke and the drink drives that away, and I feel okay. Just okay, and that's a fucking miracle. And sometimes I feel better than that. Sometimes I feel bubbles like champagne in my blood and I can see neon light trails in the air and everything just—just *sparks*, like burning metal and fireworks. But *most* of the time, *most* of the time, Jake, I feel like crap."

I didn't know what to say to her. I drank her sixth shot of

whiskey. "I didn't know," I said. "I never knew. You always seemed so . . . alive."

She looked at me bitterly until I heard exactly how stupid I sounded. "Yeah. I'm good at *that*. And I'm good at calculus, so nothing really bad could be happening, could it? You never noticed, you never took it seriously because you needed me to be the girl who would save you. You *don't* love me and you *don't* know me. You *need* me. And you never once thought about what I needed, or even noticed me counting ceiling tiles while you were fucking me."

"That's mean," I breathed. "That's mean, and it's not true. I did think about what you needed, why you were here, I asked—"

"Oh, shut up, Jake," she said, and slid off the barstool. "I'm going to go throw up, and I'll hold my own fucking hair back, and then I am *leaving*."

After she left, I put my head down on the bar. It was aching already. I could tell Cynthia was standing over me, tapping her foot. After a long silence, I heard her say, "You get one chance, Jake. You know that, right? Just one."

"I figured," I said, pressing my fingers against my eyelids.

"You haven't learned anything, have you?" she said. "You're an idiot."

"I know," I said. I sat there and waited to fall asleep, waited to wake up in misery.

The next night, the 101st night, we were waiting from the moment the sun went down, but the girls didn't come. And the time ticked by.

"Where are they?" asked my youngest brother.

I shrugged.

"They're not coming, are they?" he whimpered.

"They're coming," I said.

And we waited, not even tapping our feet to the music. I could hear the sound of each second falling to the floor.

"They're not coming," said my youngest brother again a few minutes before midnight.

"And it's your fault," snarled my third brother. "All your bullshit threats to me, and you go and fuck everything up at the end. What's wrong with you, anyway? Too many fucking blow jobs scramble your brains?"

"Shut up, Max," I said quietly. "I swear to God if you don't shut up, I'll break your fucking jaw."

My other brothers slowly cleared away while Max stepped up close. I could hear him breathing. "You couldn't take me when were kids, Jake, and you can't take me now."

"Not in my bar, boys." Cynthia's warning voice seemed to come from miles away.

The door slammed open and the girls staggered in. She wasn't wearing much makeup and she wasn't dressed up. She was wearing a pair of hot-pink jeans and a black cotton tank top.

Her eyes were swollen, like she'd been crying.

She grabbed my hand.

That night my feet felt like lead and the music sounded like so much static. Each beat felt like a hammer blow to the head and every step was like pulling teeth. But we ground it out, nothing if not determined, and by the end of the night there were holes in the soles of my boots as big as nickels.

There was a silent pause for a minute while my brothers and I stared at each other. Then my youngest brother walked tentatively toward the door, licked his lips, and stepped outside. More silence, and then we could hear his scream of joy, sharp as an arrow in my heart. Nine of my brothers stampeded for the door.

Max waited uncertainly and then came over and put his hand

on my shoulder. "Come on, Jake." His voice sounded almost affectionate.

I shook him off me and he shrugged, cast one last look at me, and left. He closed the door gently behind him.

"You're free," Isabel said.

I didn't feel it.

"So go on," she said. "Get out of here."

"I didn't think you were coming back," I said.

She shrugged. "We were so close." Her voice sounded dull, and I didn't know if she meant that she and I were close or that we had been so close to the end of the 101 nights when we fought.

"I'm sorry," I said. "I shouldn't have said that, about your sisters. And you know I don't care how much you drink, not really."

"I know," she said. "But it's not about that, is it? All this time, and you never really noticed anything wrong with me, did you?"

"There's nothing wrong with you," I said.

"I can't feel anything when we have sex," she said. "I don't feel anything but bad anymore."

I didn't know what to say to that.

"I used to feel things, here, with you. I used to feel good. And then . . . it kind of fell away, and I was just coming to help you. Maybe I used myself up."

"I'll help you," I said. "I can do that, for you. Like you've done for me."

"I don't think you can. You only ever thought about yourself and your brothers, really, like you're the only ones under a curse. You only ever thought about what I could do for you—bring you cigarettes, get you off, set you free. Even tonight—you just worried about yourself, didn't you? Did it ever cross your mind that I wasn't here because . . . I had . . . because something had happened to me? You wouldn't know how to help me."

I tasted salt and realized that tears were running down my face. "Don't leave me. I'll learn."

She shook her head. "I don't think I get to have that." She was crying, too. "I've got to go."

"Give me your phone number," I said.

She shook her head. "It's better, because you won't get bored trying to help me, when you can't."

"Did you get bored trying to help me?"

"You aren't *like* me," she said impatiently. "There's nothing wrong with you. You're kind of a jerk sometimes, but so's everybody. I'm broken."

"I don't believe that," I said.

But she left anyway.

I stared out into space for a few minutes after she left. There didn't seem to be anywhere worth going.

After a little while Cynthia came over and stood in front of me with her arms folded. "Time to go, Jake," she said quietly.

I shrugged.

"You can't stay here any longer," she told me. Then she poured me a glass of brandy. "On the house," she told me. "To celebrate. Drink it and get out of here."

I sipped the brandy. "Can I come back, some evenings?"

"Sure," she said. "Any time, if you've got the money. And you behave yourself."

My brothers made good. They have good jobs, nice places to live. I stayed with them sometimes, one after another. I made myself enough money to drink.

"Plenty more pussy out there," my third brother said to me, right before I decked him.

It wasn't true anyway, not for me. It was like when she went away, something broke inside me. I saw other girls, girls who weren't her walking by, and I felt nothing. I only got hard if I was remembering her, and I felt that slipping away as well.

My fourth brother got me a job at his wife's father's office. The soles of my Docs had never healed after that last night, so I bought new shoes and threw the boots into the back of my closet. I cleaned myself up and damned if I didn't look respectable. And older. I looked older.

My hands still shook, so I bought an electric razor.

My youngest brother approved. "Put it behind you," he said. "Start over."

But I remember. I remember nights when we danced on tongues of flame and angels, when the world opened up and was ours for the taking, when sparks shot through the air, when drumbeats were gasoline and I had a book of matches.

One night, Max was waiting for me at my sixth brother's apartment when I came home from work, and the two of them were glowering at each other.

"Zach doesn't think I should tell you," said Max. "But fuck him. I found your girl."

I went into the kitchen, took a beer out of the fridge, came back, and sat down in between my brothers. "I don't believe you, Max."

He looked vaguely hurt. "It's true."

"How could you find her when I couldn't?"

"Because you looked like a fucking nightmare when you were searching for her, pal. Seriously. Unshaven, you reeked of alcohol, you think any girl would tell you where her friend was? Now me"—he gestured to himself—"I wear a suit. I'm well-spoken. Who wouldn't talk to me?"

I glared at him.

"My girlfriend's a senior at Barnard," he said. "Her younger sister was at school with an Isabel, Isabel Goldman. Oldest of twelve, counting stepsisters and half sisters. The rumor around school was that she tried to kill herself and her parents sent her to a mental hospital in Connecticut to get her away from her friends here—to get her away from you, I bet, even if they don't know who you are. They have a country house up there. So I looked into it for you. 'Cause I'm a stand-up guy, no matter what you think of me. And it's true. She's there, no visitors, no correspondence except her parents. Pills and electroshock therapy."

I didn't feel anything I had expected to feel. I didn't feel anything. "Tried to kill herself?" I repeated mechanically.

"Tried," said Max, drinking my beer. I guessed Zach hadn't offered him one. "One of her sisters called an ambulance, they pumped her stomach."

"Look," he continued. "You ask me, I think you should stay away from her and vice versa. I don't think you're good for each other. But do what you want. One piece of advice—if you come for her, get yourself together. Clean yourself the fuck up. Get your own place. Be a goddamn man already. She didn't get you out so you could spend the rest of your life crashing on somebody's couch."

He tossed me a brochure, the kind of thing aimed at parents of troubled teens, soft focus and fake understanding, no edge to it. Not what someone like Isabel needed. Not what someone like me needed.

He finished my beer. "So don't say I never did anything for you, Jake." And then he left.

I thought about what someone like Isabel needed, what someone like me needed, and then I quit my job. I'd never liked it and

I don't think I was any good at it; I was never entirely sure what it was. Max had said to get my own place. There was only one place I thought of as my own.

Cynthia didn't look very surprised to see me. "What took you so long?" she asked.

I sat down and asked her for a shot of bourbon. When she brought it to me I sipped it. "I'm going to find her," I said.

"She's not here," said Cynthia. "So you're not off to a good start."

"Yeah, well, I'm not good at starts."

"This is not my problem," she said.

"Come on," I coaxed her. "Don't you ever want to get out of here? Look at the sunlight? Go to the beach?"

"Are you asking me out?" she said. "Long walks on the beach?"

"I'm asking you for a job."

She was silent for a full minute, and then she went down the bar to take care of other customers. When she came back, she drummed her fingers on the bar. "I miss going to the ballet."

"Are you serious?"

She glared at me. She drummed her fingers on the bar again and then went away to wash some glasses. She came back and poured two more shots of bourbon. "You've got a decent ear. You can book the bands and take over a few nights."

I gaped at her.

"What you want to say, Jake, is 'thank you.'"

"Thank you."

She rummaged behind the bar for a few minutes and came up with a set of keys. "You can start tomorrow night. I don't need to train you, do I?"

"I think you've already done that."

"Yes." She slid the keys across the bar to me. "There's an apartment above the bar. I don't live there."

For a minute I wondered where she lived—what that even meant to someone like her. Then I said "thank you" again, just to make sure.

She nodded. "I'll see you tomorrow."

I got up to go. "Oh," she said. "Jake? Don't drink all my fucking profits."

I took Max's car out to Connecticut.

"Don't blow out my speakers. And don't stain my seats when you fuck your girlfriend," he said before he tossed me the keys.

"She probably won't want to come back with me anyway," I said.

He grinned at me. "What're you talking about? She's never been able to keep her hands off you, man."

I saw Isabel in the center's common room and realized it was the first time I'd seen her without any trace of makeup. She didn't look older or younger, just different. Maybe more tired than before.

When I took her hand it felt like the future had finally started, like everything in my life had been stalled, just waiting for her.

"They've fucked up my memory," she said, and laughed a little, but not in a good way.

"Memory's overrated," I told her. "I've come to get you out."

She looked at me like I was an idiot. "I can get myself out. I'm over eighteen now. I can sign myself out any time I want."

"Then why haven't you?"

"Nowhere for me to go, really. Nowhere I want to go," she said, and then paused. "Until now?"

I nodded. "I have a job," I said. "I have a place. The apartment above the club."

"That fucking club." She laughed a little giddily, like she might cry. "You never really left, did you?"

I shook my head.

"Me neither."

"I've got Max's car parked outside," I told her. "We could drive back to my place. We can stop partway and mess up Max's seat cushions. If you want to, I mean."

She grinned at me. "Then we should go, while I still remember who you are."

"Who am I?" I asked her. I tried not to hold my breath waiting for her to tell me who I was, what I was to her.

"You're an asshole, Jake," she said, and stroked my face. "But I've missed you anyway."

"I'm an asshole," I agreed. "But I'm yours if you want me."

"I want you," she said. "I want you, but it'll come back, you know that, right? You've got to understand that. It'll take me again. I'll never be *cured*. It'll never be *over*. I'm not like you. You can go anywhere now. But it will always take me again."

I wrapped my arms around her. "I'll keep you safe."

"You *can't*," she said. "Aren't you listening? You can't keep me safe."

"Then let it take you," I said. "And I'll bring you back. As many times as you need, I'll come and bring you back. I won't let it keep you."

"You won't get bored?" she asked anxiously.

I shrugged. "Maybe I'll get bored. Maybe I'll get bored and cranky and obnoxious and drink too much and throw up in the bathroom. But I'll still come for you. As many times as you need."

She took my hand and interlaced our fingers.

I could see the afternoon sun through the glass door, and I still wasn't used to being out in daylight, even to seeing daylight. I still tensed up every time I walked out a front door, hunching over in anticipation of unbearable pain. But I looked over at Isabel and saw that the hand I wasn't holding was clenched in a fist, that she was flinching away from the sunlight and her face was twisted in something like fear. So I loosened my shoulders and put my arm around her waist.

"It's okay," I told her. "We're going home. I've got the new Glos album in the car and you can turn the volume up as loud as you want."

"Thank God." She smiled up at me. "The music in this place is shit."

And together we walked right the fuck out that door.

SERPENTS

"Will you take the path of pins or the path of needles?"

It doesn't sound like much of a choice to Charlotte. Dark woods, sharp metal. It sounds like some kind of test. Perhaps if she gives the wrong answer, toads and snakes will fall from her tongue whenever she tries to speak. Charlotte wouldn't mind that. She likes snakes: she likes the way they move, twining themselves along the ground. She thinks she might be a kind of serpent herself, sliding along in a smooth sine wave, wise and cunning. Serpents don't sew.

"The path of pins."

The scenery changes, wavers like a snake curving from side to side, and then slides away. While it is swerving and sliding, Charlotte wonders if the world is a snake as well. That would make her happy, to be a smaller snake inside the belly of a larger snake undulating through time and space. The past would be the tail and the future the head, and the massive sinuous body would coil and curve over and under and through itself in a Moebius pattern, and the past would be the head and the future would be the tail and the world-serpent would hold its tail in its mouth, a tale in its mouth, its tale in its mouth.

Snakes never blink.

* * *

Charlotte finds herself on the path of pins. As far as she can see, the dirt path is strewn with pins, safety pins, straight pins, hairpins, hat pins, diaper pins, glittering like scales along the back of a winding serpent. A careless little girl could cut her feet to shreds walking on this path. Charlotte is wearing her purple fourteen-hole Doc Martens and she can't even feel the pins grinding into the dirt floor of the forest under her feet. She walks along, imagining the silver serpent that has shed this skin. It would be huge, she thinks, to shed this many scales, and the pins would almost be more like stiff little feathers than like smoothly overlapping scales. As she thinks this and begins to imagine the cold sapphire eyes of the pin snake and the sharp metal teeth lining its mouth, she realizes where the pins are coming from. The trees lining this path have pins where the leaves should be. These trees would be impossible to climb—one wrong move and you'd have a face full of blood and scratches. You'd probably need a tetanus shot.

While Charlotte contemplates the trees, something is moving very quickly toward the path, making as little noise as possible. It skids right in front of her like a schoolgirl crossing Park Avenue against the light to get to homeroom before the bell rings. Charlotte is thrown off balance; she tries to stop in mid-stride, and almost instinctively, like a snake sensing motion, she whips around to follow the movement. The result is that she tries to balance on one leg, her arms pinwheeling as her left foot waves in the air behind her. She's almost regained her balance when she skids on some pins and falls heavily to the side, bloodying her hands, her knees, and her face.

The sun is setting. Oh my fur and whiskers, I shall be too late.

But Charlotte is not too late; she turns her head aside just in time to avoid an eye full of pins. As she lies where she's fallen, breathing heavily, nonsense phrases slide through her head: *it's all fun and games until someone loses an eye, cross my heart and hope to die, stick a needle in my eye.* Not needles. Pins. Charlotte takes a deep breath and stands up. She dusts pins off her blue skirt and white apron, leaving red streaks from her bleeding hands, streaks the same color as her wine-dark motorcycle jacket, with all the zippers and pockets holding her subway pass, silver eyeshadow, red lipstick, liquid black eyeliner, a fake ID that gives her age as twenty-two, a neon pink cigarette lighter, a pack of cigarettes (she doesn't smoke), some speed, some bobby pins, a thimble, and a box of comfits. She opens her basket and pulls out gauze and tape. After bandaging her knees she puts on a pair of swimming goggles. No pins in her eyes, thank you very much. No needles either. She sets off to find whatever it was that made her lose her balance. She steps off of the path.

Aha, you may be thinking. *We all know what happens to little girls who stray from the path.* Do we, now?

As Charlotte walks carefully and firmly through the pin-grass growing in this part of the woods, she thinks about goggles. Do snakes wear goggles? It depends, she thinks, on whether or not they go in the water. Water moccasins go in the water. So do other snakes. She likes to watch them skimming, sliding along the surface of the water, arching their bodies back and forth. She wonders if sea serpents swim the same way, gliding in S shapes along the surface of the ocean. Probably not, she decides. Sea serpents swim *through* the water, not on it. She imagines a sea serpent weightless in the wine-dark sea, coiling its body in ever more intricate patterns of knotwork, flicking its tongue in and out of the salty liquid surrounding it. She imagines the same serpent pulling a fishing boat down to the ocean floor, twining the rope of its body around the boat as strapping young sailors shriek and hurl themselves overboard. The thoughts make her smile. Sea serpents, she thinks, might wear goggles.

She is tracking the quickly moving creature as she muses. Her Docs make surprisingly little noise as she goes; perhaps she's done this before. She draws closer and sees a white rabbit, breathing heavily and shaking. Blood and mud are smeared across its paws and its fur. Its small pink eyes roll around in an even madder manner than usual.

Charlotte wonders whether or not snakes eat rabbits. Surely swallowing a rabbit wouldn't be much of a difficulty for a boa constrictor, she thinks, remembering pictures she's seen of other smaller snakes with rat-shaped lumps in their bodies. As if sensing the predatory turn her thoughts have taken, the rabbit freezes, its ears triangulating, frantically trying to catch the sound of her breathing, and all at once it leaps down a rabbit hole that had been concealed under a mound of intricately stacked pins piled precariously like sharp metal pick-up sticks. Charlotte throws herself after it and is falling, falling down a hole whose walls flicker with images of pins with duck heads holding diapers onto babies' bottoms, safety pins punched through clothing, straight pins piercing butterflies as they flap their wings vainly, pushpins holding Charlotte's second-grade essay on poisonous snakes to a corkboard, bobby pins twisting her hair too tightly, safety pins through her earlobes (they had already been pierced, so it took only a steady hand and some patience). The hole is quite long and it twists and Charlotte feels as though she is being swallowed by a snake. It is not a bad feeling. She then lands with a rush on a leaf pile of pins.

Her goggles, Docs, and motorcycle jacket serve her well—no pins make it through. But her exposed legs and face are now scratched, cut, and bloody. Charlotte pushes herself up, scraping her hands as she goes. She opens her basket and takes out a bottle of iodine and methodically applies some to every inch of broken skin. She is a wound and its cure, a germ-free adolescent.

Which way is Grandma's now? She forgets about the goggles for a moment and goes to rub her eyes, leaving bloody smears across each lens. From now on, she will see the world through the haze of her own blood.

Something about the tiling of these corridors looks familiar to her, but not until she reaches the glass booth does she realize that she's in the Astor Place subway station. She brings the subway pass out of her pocket and waves it at the token clerk, who is not there anyway, and jumps the turnstile. She sees the rabbit on the platform and begins to run toward it, but the dirty feral creature spots her and is so distressed that it leaps off the platform, launching its battered once-white body straight out over the tracks. As it falls and Charlotte watches, it changes from a rabbit into a small mouse and scurries away into the netherworld of subway vermin.

Charlotte is disappointed. A snake certainly could have swallowed that morsel.

She is not disappointed for long, though. She is thinking about having a cigarette and whether or not her grandma would smell the smoke in the folds of her jacket or the cuts in her skin, and if she did, whether she would believe Charlotte if she told her that the smell was from the show she went to last night, when the train comes hurtling into the station at breakneck pace. Snakes have no necks to break, thinks Charlotte. Or maybe they're all neck until their tails.

Charlotte has always loved the subway system, the dark, dank, smelly stations, the more labyrinthine, the more exits and interchanges, the better. She likes the seemingly random assignments of letters and numbers; she likes the confusion and mourned when the difference between the AA and A was dissolved. She likes it when an uptown local becomes an express on an entirely different track and when the F with no warning starts running on the A line. She likes the small signs that presage the coming of the train—the soft clank of the track shifting, the mice moving quietly to the sides of the track, the faintest pinprick of light down the tunnel, all the things that tell the girl who is paying attention that it won't be long now. Not long. She loves the look of the stations, the steel beams and bolts and cracked concrete— the bones and organs of the city. And when the train comes, she likes that best of all, the free-fall rush of air it pushes before it, the long loud clatter and screech. Subways, Charlotte thinks, are like snakes when snakes ruled the earth.

When Charlotte was little, she used to make her mom ride in the first car so that she could stand at the door at the head of the car with all the warning stickers (RIDING BETWEEN CARS IS STRICTLY FORBIDDEN; NO SE APOYE CONTRA LA PUERTA) and press her face against the glass. As the train hurtled through the darkness, Charlotte would watch wide-eyed as incandescent lights stretched out in bright streaks flashing by like the *Millennium Falcon* making the jump into hyperspace, only better. What Charlotte liked best was the occasional ghost station— 18th Street on the 6. Abandoned, covered with phantasmagoric graffiti, but still kept lit up in perpetual futile wait for passengers and trains that would stop. Charlotte used to dream about getting off in the old stations to explore and then being left behind as the train pulled away, left to fade into the stretched and flamboyant graffiti. They were nightmares, sort of.

Charlotte gets on the train, arranges her skirt, and closes her eyes. She tries to doze but she is just too hungry. Instead she opens her basket and peels a hard-boiled egg, leaving bloody fingerprints, a murder mystery detective's dream, on the shell and on the surface of the white, which gives beneath the pressure of her fingers and then returns to its perfect shape. She is on her second egg when she becomes aware that the shrieks and squawks of the other passengers have been drowned, engulfed by a silence, the silence of people pressing away, the silence of fear and loathing.

As Charlotte chews the second bloody bite of her second egg she realizes that the other passengers are birds, not pigeons or other city-vermin birds, but dodos, lories, eaglets, and hawks. She thinks she even catches sight of a bird with plumage all of pins, which would be painful for a snake to swallow, but perhaps she is mistaken. Slowly and deliberately she finishes her egg as a finch in the little love seat in the corner tucks into a Tupperware of living centipedes. Charlotte shifts position, which is painful because of the way the cuts in her legs are sticking to the seat.

As muttering and chirping starts to replace hostile avian glares, the train judders and shudders, stopping suddenly. The lights go off and then back on. Charlotte and the birds stare straight ahead as seconds and then minutes drift by silently. Then the PA system emits a loud crackle of static. Charlotte doesn't know it, but if she could play that static backward and at twice the speed it would be the sound of her mother as a little girl telling her to be careful on the path of pins. But she can't, so she will never know. To her, it just sounds like a hoarse snake, hissing and spitting and coughing all at once. A snake with strep throat.

But you and I know, and that will have to be enough.

There is a pause in the static, and then the PA starts to play music, particularly insipid sentimental pop that seems to distress the birds as much as it does Charlotte, who has no intention whatsoever of sitting in a stalled-out subway car listening to Celine Dion.

She stands up, walks over to the door leading to the area between the cars, where you're not supposed to ride, and opens it. She steps out onto the ledge and lowers herself onto the track, followed by the birds, who are grateful for her deft opposable thumbs even if she does eat eggs. They are clearly more comfortable following a bleeding egg-eater than they are staying behind in the subway car, which is beginning to fill with hot salt water.

Charlotte walks deliberately and firmly. She is convinced that every so often she can spot a pin glinting up at her from the tracks. She may be right, or perhaps between the lights and the goggles, she is just seeing sparks, little bursts of fire as her neurons flare off and die in a brave show of fatigued defiance. The birds follow silently. Occasionally Charlotte glances over at the third rail lying coolly under its sheltering guard. The lure is strong, like the fear that you might throw yourself off the top of the Empire State Building or try to grab a policeman's gun just because you can imagine yourself doing so. Charlotte pictures herself laying her hand against the third rail and filling from hair to boots with burning electric energy, her consciousness flickering and then running straight into the electric blood of the city, crackling through trains and streetlights, merging purely and quickly with the pulsing islands surrounding her.

She doesn't know if the birds are thinking along similar lines or not.

The way along the tracks is long, much longer than the path through the woods, and the birds are starting to become restless, rustling their feathers and crowding forward, even pecking Charlotte's back, although she certainly can't feel it through her jacket. One of the wrens decides that he can lead the way better and takes off straight into the third rail. His skin turns black and splits, spilling his bones and lungs, still quivering, onto the ground. The smell of burning feathers makes Charlotte vomit and she stops walking in order to rinse her mouth out with cinnamon mouthwash from her basket.

The remaining birds are looking a bit green as well, so Charlotte passes out the comfits for them to suck on.

After they have been walking for what seems like hours, Charlotte finds that they are at the abandoned 18th Street subway station. The funhouse graffiti is layered on over older graffiti; infinite strata of urban fireworks marking successive waves of fucked-up youth. Charlotte walks through the station looking like one of the garish, ghostly images wired to live. Her goggles, her blood-and-iodine-stained face and legs, her bandaged hands, her red motorcycle jacket, and her comet tail of birds all add to her affinity with the phantasmagoria around her. She climbs the stairs only to find her way blocked by an iron gate. She rattles the bars, but the grille is locked. She picks up one of the birds and pushes it through the bars. It flies away and the others get the idea. Soon the only company Charlotte has left is the dodo, who is too large to fit through the gate and can't fly anyway. Together they walk back down the stairs.

Charlotte finds a section of the wall which has less art and is mostly painted with slogans instead. She leans back against RIP HER TO SHREDS and HATE AND WAR, removes her goggles, and takes a nap, right under GOD SAVE THE QUEEN and HEAVY MANNERS. The dodo sinks down next to her, rests its head on her shoulder, and falls asleep as well.

When they wake up, Charlotte is unsure how long she has been sleeping. She lights a cigarette, stubs it out, and passes it to the dodo, who eats it. Charlotte thinks this is all to the good, because she doesn't like to litter. The city has enough trouble. So does she.

She sighs and puts her goggles back on. The red smears of blood are still damp. The dodo looks a bit anxious—perhaps it is reconsidering the wisdom of nestling into a serpentine egg-eater—so as a gesture of friendship Charlotte gives the bird a second pair of goggles from her basket for protection. She tightens the strap around the bird's head and it squawks in appreciation. Then she takes a small bottle of seltzer and a piece of cake out of her basket. She and the dodo share breakfast? lunch? dinner? Neither one of them knows, and neither do we.

After eating, Charlotte examines the bottom of her left shoe and pulls out several straight pins that had stuck in the rubber. While she is doing this, she is oblivious to the dodo's embarrassment at having nothing to give her in return for the goggles and food. Luckily, the awkward bird spots something glinting in the corner of the abandoned station. It is Charlotte's own thimble, which has rolled out of her pocket while she was sleeping. The dodo, ignorant creature, has no way of knowing the shiny thing's provenance. It picks up the thimble in its beak and solemnly presents it to Charlotte. Charlotte accepts it graciously even though she recognizes it and has no intention of using it. Snakes, remember, don't sew. She slips it in her pocket.

Charlotte stands up. As she pulls away from the wall she feels her jacket sticking, but she cannot see why. The graffiti that she was leaning against, old and chipped as it was, has imprinted itself on her jacket like wet paint in a silent movie or a *Sesame Street* sketch. The mirror ghost prints of half a dozen punk slogans crisscross her back.

Together Charlotte and the dodo climb the stairs, and armed with the pins from her boot she begins to pick the padlock keeping the gate closed. It's a fruitless exercise—Charlotte wouldn't know how to pick a lock even if she had a cat burglar's do-it-yourself kit, and these straight pins are causing nothing but pricked fingertips and a steady subway rumble of foul language from Charlotte.

Finally she gives it up and throws the pins away. Sitting back down on the ground, she opens her basket and takes out a large solid key with four different ridged edges that match the + at the bottom of the padlock. She unlocks the padlock, puts the key back into her basket, slides the lock off of the gate, and locks it around a belt loop on her jacket. Then she pushes the gate open. She and the dodo step through together.

They climb up another set of steps. When they come up from underground they are at the very edge of a forest. Looking back Charlotte can see the glint of the sun reflecting off two paths winding through the trees, both of which trail off a few feet away from the entrance to the subway station. Looking the other way she can see her grandmother's cottage two, maybe three blocks away. She checks to make sure she still has everything she needs: goggles, jacket, basket. The dodo watches her uncertainly. It shuffles its feet and clears its throat. Charlotte picks the bird up and hurls it as hard as she can up in the air. The dodo spreads its stubby prickly wings and flaps ferociously, twisting its barrel-like body back and forth as it rises. It hangs suspended for a few seconds, contemplating Charlotte. From this height she looks like a red blur, a bloodstained egg, and compared to the dodo, she is barely more than an egg. The dodo wishes her luck, blows her a kiss, and then continues its ascent.

Charlotte has already turned away and is walking to her grandmother's cottage. There is nothing left in her way, just smooth sidewalks unrolling under her feet. When she gets to the cottage, she knocks gently on the door, and when there is no response she uses her school ID to jimmy open the lock. She walks in.

Grandmother is not bedridden, and her eyes, ears, and teeth are just the right size. She is wearing a green dress and kneeling in front of the crackling, sparking fire in the fireplace. She is crying softly and inconsolably. She does not even turn her head to look when Charlotte comes into the room.

Charlotte kneels down next to her grandmother and takes her hand. "It's okay," she says.

Her grandmother continues to weep over the long tube of patterned snakeskin. "It's dead," she whispers. "It's dead."

"No, Grandma," says Charlotte. "It's not dead."

But her grandmother continues to weep gently, bent gracefully over the shed skin like a delicately branching willow. Charlotte sets her basket down and takes from it a loaf of fresh bread, a quart of homemade chicken soup, and a bottle of red wine. "These are for you," she tells her grandmother, who makes no response. Charlotte takes a red apple from her basket and places it in her grandmother's hand, closing the older woman's fingers around it, but still her grandmother does not turn her head.

Charlotte stands behind her grandmother and begins to undress. She takes off her motorcycle jacket, folds it lovingly, and lays it on the floor. She unties her bloodstained apron, takes it off, and lays it on top of the jacket. Her sky blue dress follows, as do her black cotton underpants and bra as well as her hair ribbon, leaving her standing in only her purple Doc Martens and her goggles.

"It's okay, Grandma," she repeats. "It's not dead. Look."

And as her grandmother turns to look, Charlotte—slowly, slowly—begins to shed her skin.

EMMA GOLDMAN TAKES TEA WITH THE BABA YAGA

1. HISTORY IS A FAIRY TALE

Once upon a time, there was a girl, the third and youngest daughter of a merchant, whose charms lay not in her looks but in her brains and voice. But those brains lay fallow, as her father was one of those who did not believe that knowledge was of any use to a girl. So she set out on a journey and she traveled far from home, over land and over sea, until she came to a strange land.

Or perhaps you would prefer this?

Emma Goldman came to Rochester, New York, from St. Petersburg in 1885. She was sixteen, and she was very, very smart. Despite her intelligence, her misogynist father denied her an education, and had even thrown her study books into the fire.

Truth can be told in any number of ways. It's all a matter of emphasis. Of voice. I have not lied about anything yet.

And in this strange land, she met a young man, a young man who beguiled her with his ability in dancing, and won her heart with his love of reading. But his promises of love and ecstasy were empty, and the girl continued her travels. So she set her sights on a larger city in this strange land, a city booming with glory and misery, and set off once again. She left behind the young man, bitter at the failure of his overtures, and her eldest sister, who felt for her a mother's love.

Here are the same events, told a different way:

After a little over a year in Rochester, she was divorced from an impotent husband and barred from her family's home (her parents had followed her to Rochester soon after her arrival) for "loose behavior." Only her older sister Helena, who had long stood in place of a mother to Emma, supported her. So she packed a bag and headed to New York City. Well, where else?

The fairy tale sounds better, I think, or at least different. It makes Emma's life romantic and mysterious, her emigration a grand adventure rather than an escape from the very real menace of rising antisemitism. As soon as I ground this girl as Emma Goldman, she is no longer on a quest; she's only waiting to become the fire-breathing anarchist.

But the matter-of-fact history is much more succinct. A bit juicier in some ways, too. Good for Goldman, refusing to settle for a lifetime of sexual frustration. What a waste that would've been. Good for Helena, too, the older sister who had supplanted Goldman's harsh, unhappy mother, the sister who loved her and consoled her and brought her up, and stood by her steadfastly even as Goldman became a lightning rod for scandal and political persecution.

Emma Goldman had long been interested in leftist politics, and in New York City, she found anarchism. She had a vision of a humanity unfettered by the coercive violence of the state, cooperative societies without hierarchy. In some ways, collectivist anarchism is what Karl Marx envisioned as communism's ultimate goal, but anarchists know that the state will never wither away of its own accord. It must be abolished at once. In her youth, she believed in what was called "propaganda of the deed" fervently enough to, with her lover Alexander (Sasha) Berkman, plan and execute—well, fumble—an attempt on the life of Henry Clay Frick. Frick was an anti-union Carnegie steel factory manager responsible for the murders of nine striking workers. Berkman was to kill Frick and then himself, and Goldman to explain his deeds and their motives afterward. Their hope was that Frick's murder would inspire a working-class revolution that would overthrow capitalism.

Needless to say, that is not what happened. Berkman got two shots from a pistol off at Frick, missed, and was then tackled by a security guard. He nonetheless managed to stab Frick three times with a dagger before being clubbed on the head by a nearby carpenter. He attempted suicide but was restrained and taken into custody. Berkman ended up serving thirteen years in prison and one in a workhouse. He insisted he had acted alone, and Goldman avoided prison in that instance.

But with her fervent belief, her brilliant orations, and her personal bravery and defiance, she rocketed to radical celebrity in the United States and Europe, speaking on anarchism, sexuality, and art. She read, she wrote, she spoke, she published, she agitated. She ran afoul of the law more than once. She was no longer a girl. She grew stout. She grew white hairs. She still believed in free love and longed to practice it, but found few lovers. She continued traveling, speaking, and loving as best she could. Even after the United States did its worst and deported her to Russia in the midst of its civil war, she continued.

Emma Goldman found anarchism, and the rest, as they say, is history.

It's all history now. Goldman has been dead and buried for almost eighty years, and Red Emma, the most dangerous woman in America, is safe for leftist Jewish feminists such as myself to lionize. She can't open her mouth to reject her elevation to saint-hood. The greatest orator in America no longer speaks. She has become more icon than iconoclast. She is history.

Emma Goldman and Berkman were imprisoned for using her writing and speech to "induce persons not to register" for the draft, illegal under the Espionage Act of 1917. They were re-leased in 1919, and the United States government was out to get them. J. Edgar Hoover at the tender age of twenty-four was already head of the Bureau of Investigation's General In-telligence Division, which was charged with disrupting leftist American activities. He decided to use the Anarchist Exclusion Act of 1903, a piece of legislation designed to keep anarchist immigrants, along with "epileptics, beggars, and importers of prostitutes," out of the country.

Goldman stood upon her citizenship. She was not an alien, but a United States citizen, entitled to freedoms of speech and the press, and she therefore would not answer any questions about her anarchism.

The Department of Labor stripped her of her citizenship.

Remember the impotent husband?

Apparently he had been convicted of some crime or other in 1908 and had his citizenship revoked. Hoover pressured the courts to find that this meant that Goldman, too, was no longer a citizen.

Never mind that they had been divorced for more than twenty years by 1908, and that this was unmitigated patriarchal bullshit of the highest order.

It was easier with Berkman—he had never applied for cit-izenship to begin with. Ultimately, Goldman withdrew her appeal so that they would not be separated. For they loved each other, even if they had not been lovers for many decades, and whither thou goest, I will follow. And Goldman, now a woman and not a young one at that, prepared herself for a homecoming to Mother Russia.

Homecoming is such an important moment in fairy tales, is it not? You can set forth to seek your fortune, to find a bride, to carry a basket of food to Grandmother's house, and at the end of the tale, you must come home again and show your mother what you have achieved, whom you love, the empty basket.

And while you are on your journey, you trust that home will still stand and Mother will be much the same as she always was, because if mothers start running around changing and having adventures, what is there to define yourself against? How can you know you are the foreground if Mother refuses to continue being the background?

But we do change, nonetheless.

Goldman and Berkman and 247 others were put aboard the USAT *Buford* on December 21, 1919, and the ship docked in Finland on January 16, 1920. The following day, the prisoners were put in unheated boxcars and taken as close as possible to the border Finland shares with Russia.

They were then marched through a snowstorm and handed over to the Bolsheviks. Goldman and Berkman saw the other 247 prisoners safely across before crossing over the frozen Systerbak River themselves, where they all received heroes' welcomes and were put on a train to Petrograd.

Goldman had not seen Petrograd in more than thirty years.

She was a celebrity. And she had hopes for the Russian Revolution, for the freedoms and reliefs it might bring the people of Russia. Anarchists had fought alongside Bolsheviks, taking on some of the most dangerous missions of the October Revolution. It was Russian anarchists who evicted the Whites from the Kremlin, for example. Anarchists dreamt of a new age in Russia, an age in which anarchists and communists could work together for the common good.

That was not what the Bolsheviks had in mind, though, and in 1918 the Cheka, precursor to the KGB, raided more than twenty-five anarchist centers in Moscow. During these raids, forty anarchists were murdered and five hundred taken into custody.

Outside of the USSR, though, Goldman and Berkman still had hope. How could they know what information they were receiving was genuine and what was right-wing propaganda, put about to discredit the revolution that threatened capitalist hegemony?

But that revolution was rotting from the inside. It rejected human rights as bourgeois sentimentality. Lenin personally assured Goldman that freedom of speech was "impossible" during a revolutionary period.

Once in Russia, Goldman learned of fellow anarchists tortured in Bolshevik prisons, of all anarchist activity suppressed. Favoritism and graft made a few schools glorious while most "common schools" were dirty and verminous and unheated, serving children miserable food and punishing them with beatings. Health services, too: doctors and nurses forced to spend their time waiting for a few minutes with the commissar instead of tending to the sick. Goldman visited a special hospital for Communist Party members, with every advanced piece of equipment, every amenity, and she found others without the barest necessities.

There were even plans for a prison especially for "morally defective children."

Only those who have thrown away the last vestige of their humanity put children in cages.

The Party abolished capital punishment, true, with an order that took effect the morning after five hundred "counter-revolutionist" prisoners were executed in Petrograd.

Goldman was horrified. "Five hundred lives snuffed out!" she cried.

"As if a few dead plotters mattered in the scales of a revolution," said John Reed, the radical U.S. journalist, one of only three Americans buried in the Kremlin Necropolis. "Razstrellyat!" The word is Russian; according to Goldman, it means "execute by shooting," but that sounds a little formal to me. I suspect the flavor of what Reed was saying was more akin to a line my mother used to quote from David Peel and the Lower East Side, or perhaps Amiri Baraka, or even Patty Hearst: "Up against the wall, motherfuckers!"

Goldman made excuse after excuse to herself.

Berkman gave the Bolsheviks the benefit of the doubt longer than Goldman did. "You can't measure gigantic upheaval by a few specks of dust," he told her. Doesn't the end justify the means?

Lenin dismissed Goldman's concerns as more bourgeois sentimentality.

But Peter Kropotkin shared her horror, and abhorred the government "that in the name of socialism had abrogated every revolutionary and ethical value."

And then, even Berkman began having trouble justifying the Bolsheviks' actions.

He remarked to a Soviet comrade while walking together in Moscow on the number of children begging in the streets.

"No more than there are in London," the apparatchik replied defensively. (And indeed, when I told this story to my mother, she interrupted to say the same thing.)

Berkman shook his head. "But comrade," he said. "In Moscow, the revolution has already come." (My mother had no answer for that.)

When Berkman tried to implement a plan to renovate the Soviet soup kitchens, to make them pleasant and efficient and their food nourishing, he was told that "It was naïve of Berkman to claim that feeding the masses was the first concern of the Revolution, [and that] the care of the people, their contentment and joy, [was] its main hope and safety, and indeed its only raison d'être and moral meaning. Such sentimentality was the purest bourgeois ideology."

One starts to find bourgeois ideology quite appealing.

The revolution had come and gone, and Goldman, always an endless fountain of ideas, nerve, courage, esprit de corps; a fighter who didn't know when to give in; a perpetual motion machine flying the black flag, her heart beating to the rhythm of a printing press and marching feet, was still. The locomotive lay idle, its black flag hanging straight down, with no breath of wind to stir it.

And then she received another blow. She had been visiting Moscow for a while, and had had no word from America. In fact, a letter for her from her niece had arrived in Petrograd, where it sat for a month awaiting her return. It had never been forwarded because, Goldman was told, "How could anything from America be so important and interesting as what you were seeing in Moscow?"

How, indeed?

Goldman's beloved older sister Helena had died, her death sped by the blow of Emma's deportation.

"Not 'so important,'" Goldman wrote in her memoir, "only news of the death of my beloved Helena. What could personal sorrow mean to people who had become cogs in the wheel that was crushing so many at every turn? I myself seemed to have turned into one of the cogs. I could find no tears for the loss of my darling sister, no tears or regrets. Only paralyzing numbness and a larger void."

The revolution had become a corrupt, hierarchy-bound dictatorship. And her sister had died. And she was far from her home of forty years, never to return for longer than the space of a lecture tour.

Her heart, previously anarchist black and red, was turning gray with grief.

And then she and Berkman were invited to join the Museum of the Revolution. And they said yes.

What a strange thing to do! Goldman could not bring herself to put her nursing skills to use in a corrupt medical system, but she could turn her attention to preserving mementos of the revolution?

What a strange thing to exist! The Party claimed that the only true safety was in worldwide revolution, and it was their only duty to spread that revolution via the Red Army and the Cheka. But it could commit to making a museum in the former Winter Palace?

I approve of preserving history and culture—I am a scholar, am I not?—and I like the symbolism of throwing open palace doors. But it does not seem a natural fit for Goldman and Berkman—collecting historical memorabilia when the suffering and the need were raging around them? On the other hand, the institution was nonpartisan, and Goldman liked the secretary and his staff, who were not Bolsheviks. She would not be constantly under the eye of a commissar. And indeed, she could get the hell out of Petrograd.

For the museum wanted Goldman to join an expedition south to the Ukraine and the Caucasus. She could travel, take an unsupervised breath of fresh air, and speak to people around the country.

So a caravan was found and fitted out, and Goldman and Berkman and several other comrades, only one of whom was a Bolshevik (in the early 1920s, party membership was not open—it required a variety of approvals and an intensive investigation of one's history), set out.

And this is where we join them, between Kiev and Odessa, in the Kiev province, where the wait times to couple their museum car to trains heading south dragged on indefinitely. They spent time visiting little towns and villages, talking with the people there. In late summer 1921, almost twenty years before the Holocaust, most of the people there were Jewish.

The Jewish population of Russia had by 1921 suffered many pogroms as well as assaults by bandits and even the occasional Red Guard. The pogroms during the civil war, 1918–1921, had been as bad as anything under the czars. By 1921, some localities petitioned the revolutionary government for weapons to protect themselves with. They were refused. But to their credit, the Bolsheviks ended the pogroms.

Jews of no particular political persuasion were confused by the revolution. The Bolsheviks had forbidden the trade by which Jewish merchants made their living. Jewish Bundists felt that the corruption, cruelty, and depravity of the Bolsheviks betrayed every revolutionary value they had espoused. Zionists feared the Bolshevik disapproval of specifically Jewish culture, the desire of the Party to assimilate all peoples into one proletariat, to dissolve specific cultures into one.

Goldman did not approve of these criticisms. She thought the critics making them bourgeois. But that does not necessarily mean they were wrong. Sometimes you cannot deny truth, even when it comes in a voice you don't want to hear.

2. THE FANTASY

And so it was that Emma Goldman—stymied, exiled, grieving her beloved older sister and the life she had known, grieving also the hopes she had harbored for the Revolution—walked out of the little Jewish town she had been visiting, and into the Russian forest.

She walked alone, without Sasha, for his heart was not broken by death, though he too was exiled and disillusioned. She walked alone, to listen to her own thoughts, to search the smoldering embers of her heart and find something left to burn.

The day was cold; the woods were beautiful; Emma Goldman walked alone. And she walked, and she walked, and she walked. And eventually she walked right out of Russia, and into the thrice-tenth kingdom.

How long does such a journey take? Kingdom after kingdom after kingdom, until you get to thirty? Well, for us, not long at all, really, for didn't Goldman make it in only a few short paragraphs? This is the nature of time—it dilates during suffering and also during joy, rushes through our fingers into the sea when we seek to hold it tight; when we are depressed, the hours open up indefinitely as we are condemned to endure yet another day of consciousness, and then, and then, we look up and realize that we have lost weeks, months, even years to the sticky-fingered destroyer of joy, never to be regained.

So not long for us, but for Goldman, her walk stretched on and on, and she felt every second it took her to trudge onward, and she was cold in her fingers and in her soul. The color leeched out of the woods, for there was a gray veil separating her from the land of the living. But for us, it takes only a wave of my hand, a scrawl of ink, a metaphorical snap of my fingers, and we are already there, in the land of magic and fairy tale.

Goldman did not know that she had crossed over, of course. There was no billboard proclaiming WELCOME TO THE THRICE-TENTH KINGDOM, WE HOPE YOU SURVIVE YOUR STAY! There was not even a crude wooden signpost, let alone a lamppost in the woods. There was just forest and then more forest, and if there was a warning, a wolf howling at Goldman to turn back, turn back, turn back while you still can, she could not hear it.

And what anarchist cares for borders anyway?

There was no sign of anything strange at all, until Goldman came to the fence. It was weathered and old, and it surrounded a building in shadow. There were twelve fenceposts, and atop each post was a skull, and the twelve skulls were chattering, each louder than the last.

But they were not moaning out warnings. Nor were they groaning ominously in pain or fear, or cackling harshly or anything else appropriate to a skull stuck up ominously on a fencepost. Instead, they were giggling and gossiping.

"Ooooh! She's coming!" squealed one.

"I don't know, that's not how *I* thought she'd look, are you sure that's her? She doesn't *look* terribly dangerous."

"Nobody ever does, I'm not worried about that, but isn't she supposed to be, you know, fast? A bit of a *loose woman*? *I* thought she'd be more alluring. She looks like my old bubbe!"

"She looks like anybody's old bubbe! Ask her for her recipe for blintzes!"

Goldman sighed. As it happened, she made excellent blintzes, but she wasn't going to waste the recipe on a bunch of skulls that couldn't cook, couldn't eat, and had no manners to boot.

That's the thing about depression: it inures you to wonder, even to fear. Skulls are chattering and squealing and all you can do is sigh and accept that they're right, that your best days *are* behind you, to agree that you've gotten too old and fat and aren't good for anything but making blintzes, and blintzes are delicious, but they are no adventure, and you are unable to recognize the adventure going on around you.

Well, perhaps "recognize" is the wrong word, for of course she *recognized* the house. It was a plain peasant home, standing with its back to the bone-gate, ignoring the insulting skulls.

Goldman lingered at the gate for a long time, not out of fear, but in weariness and boredom. She would've drummed her fingers on a femur-fence-slat if it hadn't seemed so infinitely difficult to do so, so overwhelmingly complex to move each muscle, for each muscle to pull the old bones, to maintain even the most basic rhythm: *da-da-dum, da-da-dum, da-da-dum*, the anapest of boredom.

Pull yourself together, she screamed at herself silently, but the thread of being remained slack.

Eventually one of the skulls rotated on its fencepost and

looked at her blankly, which is the only way a skull can look, really.

"Are you going to say it, or are you going to run away? She won't wait forever, you know."

Goldman bridled a bit. "I'm not running away. I don't run away from anything."

"Then you might as well say it," said the skull. "We've all looked at you long enough."

"You're no balm to the eyes, either," Goldman told it, but nonetheless, she squared up and spoke: "Little house, little house, turn and place your back to the woods, your front door to me."

I don't know, perhaps it rhymes in Russian.

The house rose, exposing two scaly, clawed chicken's feet, more like the dinosaur talons we now know them to be, and slowly, deliberately turned. There was a pregnant pause while it looked at Goldman with the knots in its weathered, stained wood. Then the door swung carefully open. A gust of warm air floated out, like an exhalation.

Without looking to either side, ignoring the insulting skulls, Emma Goldman walked into the cottage.

The door swung shut behind her.

The skulls couldn't shrug, of course, or raise their eyebrows, but they allowed a beat of silence before they resumed yakking again.

Once she was inside the house, Goldman couldn't hear them. At first she heard nothing, saw nothing. But her eyes began to adjust to the meager light inside the cottage, and she was able to make out a figure, a figure all harsh angles and stringy muscle, sitting at a table, grinding something with a mortar and pestle. Farther back in the room, a cauldron sat over the hearth. It was very warm in the hut.

All Goldman could hear was the scrape of stone on stone, the fire crackling. A bird sang, somewhere outside the hut.

Finally the figure spoke. "Sit down, Emma." It gestured to a stool on the opposite side of the table.

Goldman sat, her back already hurting from the lack of support.

"Do you know me, Emma?" the figure asked. Its voice was surprisingly pleasant. Instead of the harsh, grating rasp one might expect from a . . . woman, Goldman could now see, a skinny old woman whose tits hung down to her lap, her jaws clamped firmly around a battered pipe, her low alto flowing out like warm honey. Or like pooling blood. "Do you remember me?"

Goldman nodded.

"But do you *really* remember? You were so young the first time we met."

Goldman hesitated. "I was ten. I remember ten."

"That was the second time," said the Baba Yaga, for you must know by now that it was she. "When you came searching for my house after your mother had rebuffed you. You had almost worked up the nerve to step through my door when that older sister of yours came and dragged you back."

"Yes," said Goldman, with some difficulty as she thought of Helena, Helena young and gay, Helena unafraid. "That is what I remember."

"But that was the second time. The first time was when you were a little baby, not even crawling yet, barely sitting. I found you napping outside, ignored by all your family, and I thought, what a pretty child, what a child full of fire and curiosity! I shall take her, and either raise her up as my own or roast her for dinner. These Goldmans don't know what they have and do not deserve her.

"So I did. I took you in my arms and lifted you into my mortar and took you away.

"And I set you down in my garden and left you playing with my hens and their chicks while I went to light the oven, or possibly to prepare a cradle."

"When I was a baby," said Goldman, "we lived in Kovno. It was the capital of the Kovno Governorate. Somebody would have noticed you traveling in a mortar and pestle through the streets."

The Baba Yaga waved a hand irritably. "Disguised, disguised. The mortar was a carriage, the pestle a gray horse."

Goldman shrugged.

"I did not think the Goldmans would notice your absence, but I was wrong. One did, and she was young enough to see that my carriage was no carriage, and my horse no horse. And she came after you, though she was younger than you were ten years later when you sought me out."

"Helena," breathed Goldman.

"Helena," agreed the Baba Yaga. "I saw her though my windows. I pulled back a corner of the curtains and watched as she approached my little house, my garden, my chickens, my new baby or possibly my dinner. I still hadn't decided.

"And as she set her jaw and ignored my chattering skulls and walked steadily into my garden to claim you and bring you home, I thought to myself, *I took the wrong girl. It is this Helena who belongs with me.*"

Goldman's face was impassive, and she remained silent.

"But now that I look back over your life," continued the Baba

Yaga, "I see I was right the first time, and you are the Goldman sister with teeth and a will of iron, and a heart of fire.

"Or a heart that was once of fire. For hasn't her loss left your heart ashes, Emma? Cold and gray with not a spark left with which to kindle the smelting flames that have always before immolated all doubt, all hesitation in your breast?

"Whatever happened to Helena, anyway?"

"She died," said Goldman, and the famed orator hesitated and then added, "some months ago."

"Yes, yes," said the Baba Yaga. "I see that much in your face. But before that."

Goldman shrugged. "She married. A decent man, but no businessman, and there was no passion between them. She had children. She died."

"Ah," said the Baba Yaga, and nodded knowingly. "Such is the lot of women."

There was a pause while the woman and the witch listened to the forest.

"How did you manage to avoid it, dear Emmele?"

Goldman looked at the Baba Yaga. "I have a tipped uterus. I cannot bear children." She tried to summon up her wonted fervor and dedication. "The revolution will be my child."

They listened to the forest again.

"Will it?" asked the Baba Yaga, somewhat delicately. It was a dusty delicacy, long unused.

"I'd hoped so," admitted Goldman.

"Has it not worked out so?" Again, the rare delicacy, and this time Goldman could hear its hinges catch and scrape, protesting such activity after its long sleep.

"No," Goldman said shortly.

"Ah."

The Baba Yaga filled their teacups. Goldman added cherry preserves to hers, and they sipped quietly for a while.

"I suppose it still might," said Goldman at last.

The Baba Yaga tossed delicacy aside. "Here? This revolution? You haven't seen enough? You still believe that?"

"Not here." Goldman shook her head slowly. "But perhaps . . . elsewhere."

"Don't be ridiculous," said the Baba Yaga.

Goldman glared at her. "The working people are a force too potent to be suppressed. All over, we will see uprisings—"

"Do you really believe that?"

Goldman sighed and subsided. "I have believed in this revolution for a long time. Perhaps it is not my belief that matters."

"Certainly not to it," said the Baba Yaga. "In any case," she continued, waving a bony hand, "I have an offer for you."

"A place on your empty post outside?"

"No, of course not. You will keep that space for *me*. You are tired of life, Emmele. Very well, I understand, for I too felt that way, many years ago. And that is when I became the Baba Yaga, when I took my predecessor's place, and she became one with Mother Russia. And now, I feel my old bones longing to dissolve into the earth, and it is time for another to step into the role and occupy this cottage. And Emmele, I think it should be you."

Goldman raised her eyebrows. "But I am not Baba Yaga."

"But you could be," returned the other. "It is a title, not a name, and I can pass it to you, just as the previous Baba Yaga passed it to me."

Goldman considered the prospect with perhaps more equanimity than one might expect from a committed atheist who held that the physical world was all that existed. "What does it involve, being the Baba Yaga?" she asked.

The Baba Yaga was briefly unable to meet Goldman's gaze. "Not as much as once it did," she admitted finally. "The Russian populace is less frightened of my cooking pot than once it was."

"They are less gullible, you mean," said Goldman. "Less inclined to believe in fairy tales."

The Baba Yaga clucked her tongue and shook her head. "Just as gullible as ever, Emmele. They just believe in different fairy tales now. And what a thing to say, as you sit conversing with the Baba Yaga.

"I mostly keep to myself. I cook and eat the odd child who is cruel or thoughtless, or sometimes I give it a charmed life. I consult the skulls for predictions. I keep order among the sun, the moon, the wind, the stars, and the forest. When I am displeased, I add bones to my fence outside. And I am safe, and I am powerful, and I am left alone. It is . . . the best a woman can hope for, in this world."

"Are the skulls always so rude?" asked Goldman absently, while she thought about it.

"Usually," answered the witch. "And I certainly shall be."

Goldman looked at the Baba Yaga questioningly.

"To take over my cottage," the Baba Yaga explained, "you must strike off my head with a cleaver. You must wrench the iron canines from my mouth and affix them in your own. And you must bury my body but put my head on the empty post outside."

"And then what?" asked Goldman. "You sit up there chattering your teeth forever?"

"Not exactly. The part of me that is still mortal dies and melts into the ground of Mother Russia. The part of me that is witch . . . stays on the post and becomes an oracle, and gives light. The part of me that is goddess . . . ascends.

"And you move into my cottage. You practice magic. You aid or eat the Russians, depending on your inclination and whether or not they can find you. You can plot against the Bolsheviks if you like, make them suffer for ruining your beautiful revolution."

Goldman picked up the cleaver that lay on the table between them and fitted the handle to her hand contemplatively. "And Sasha, he can stay with me?"

"No," said the Baba Yaga firmly. "He cannot." After a minute she added, somewhat cruelly, "You know he would never be happy without his girls around him, anyway."

True. Goldman knew it was true. Berkman preferred younger lovers and had ever since emerging from prison. "That old lobster," Goldman muttered, and slashed angrily at the air with the cleaver. It whistled. "Every day one sees decrepit old men of more than fifty-two with girls of twenty. And yet my own longings are met with disapproval, disdain, even disgust among those who claim to be my comrades."

"You see, then," said the Baba Yaga. "There is no true equality. The revolution will never truly come."

"If only I had my old faith," Goldman said, her voice growing stronger with each sentence. "But what is left? I have no faith left in the people. People are venal fools. I have no faith left in the revolution. Look what it has come to! I have no faith left in our own beautiful ideal, even—so much hot air and baseless hopes! What is the *point* of *any* of this?!"

"You might as well strike off my head," murmured the Baba Yaga, who seemed fascinated by Goldman's sudden fury.

"I might as well!" shouted Goldman, gesturing with the cleaver. "I might as well! For what have I *done* with life? Speeches and lovers! One pointless blow against Frick that failed utterly! For all those things avail me now, I might as well strike off your head and take your teeth and live alone in the woods, calling down curses on Lenin's head! I might as well! I will! I *will*! But—" She broke off suddenly.

"Yes?" breathed the Baba Yaga.

"Is it all truly destroyed? Is there nothing left? Is my beautiful ideal really nothing but a mirage? Will I never see it made flesh? You are to become an oracle, so answer me now. If the answer is no, I will strike off your head and take your teeth and live in your cottage and eat the foolish peasants who catch my eye and send poisoned, sorcerous arrows at Lenin's heart! Is there really nothing left?"

"*Nothing*," pronounced the Baba Yaga, perhaps too firmly. "There is nothing. In the shadow of the war to come, the flowering of anarchism shall be crushed beneath the heel of fascism. You may scramble and speechify all you like, but they will be lost. You will lose. Spain will lose."

"The . . . flowering?" asked Goldman quietly.

There was a pregnant pause as the Baba Yaga realized her misstep.

"Spain will lose what?" Goldman continued.

"Spain will be under fascist rule for decades! Perpetrators of atrocities will go unpunished!"

"Spain will lose what?" Goldman repeated.

The Baba Yaga sighed and shrugged. "Agricultural collectives, self-managed factories, schools and hospitals run by and for working people—all crushed. Betrayed! Lost!"

"Lost?" said Goldman. "To be lost, they must first be had."

"For moments only!" cried the Baba Yaga. "And then—into oblivion."

"Moments," said Goldman, "are all any one of us ever has. This moment, and the next, and the next. Perhaps that's all there ever is at all."

The Baba Yaga felt Goldman slipping from her. "But what comes after, eh? Fascism!"

"These moments, they are anarchist moments! And if one moment, why not another?"

"They will be lost!" wailed the Baba Yaga.

"Everything is, eventually," agreed Goldman. "Do you know, once Sasha's cousin told me it was undignified, unbecoming, frivolous, even, for a serious revolutionary, knowing of the misery in the world, to dance with such abandon, even for only a few moments? He couldn't see that those moments are what make it possible to continue the work of revolution. Because the revolution, it must not be heartless and joyless and bloodthirsty, even in pursuit of the highest good, because, Baba Yaga, there *is no highest good*. The means *will always* become the ends. And though I can no longer dance all night, you tell me there are some beautiful moments left to me? Ahead of me, even?"

"You're not going to strike off my head, are you?"

Goldman shook her head briskly. "Not when there is an anarchist flowering waiting for me—oh, Baba Yaga, save your enchantments, for those are the words to conjure with! I have writing I must do. I must warn these Spanish comrades not to be taken in by the Bolsheviks, for one thing."

The Baba Yaga shook her head. "There is loneliness ahead of you," she warned. "And defeat."

"I'm lonely now," said Goldman. "And defeat is not destruction. I will take my leave. Thank you for the tea, Baba Yaga. Good-bye. I hope you do find someone to take your place soon, as you wish it so."

The Baba Yaga snorted. "When you left Petrograd as a girl, you left Russia, and haven't you been unable to return, though you stood on Russian ground? How do you propose to find the forest again?"

Goldman met the Baba Yaga's eyes. "Through the door."

"What door?"

Indeed, when Goldman looked around, there was only a wall with a dusty shelf affixed to it. But she stayed on her feet and regarded the witch stonily. "The door I entered through."

The house began to turn, steadily, slowly, but Goldman stayed on her feet, and her gaze did not waver. The cleaver glinted in the meager light, and the glint was not just reflection. Light arced from the hearth to the cleaver and thence into Goldman's chest as the house continued to spin. She opened her mouth to speak and light crackled through her teeth and tongue. The orator breathed fire. "Little house, *little house*," she called. "Turn and place your back to the woods, and set me free." She slammed the cleaver down into the table.

The house settled with a jolt. A door appeared in the wall. Goldman opened it. As she lifted her foot to cross the threshold, the Baba Yaga called out to her: "Emma!"

Goldman looked back, still holding the door.

"Only a true daughter of the Baba Yaga could command my home against my will. The house knows its mistress."

Goldman shrugged. "I'm not beholden to your chicken-legged house, no matter what it thinks."

"Then take an affectionate warning, daughter. Get out of Russia while you can."

Goldman nodded, and then she stepped through the doorway, and was gone.

3. THE END, JUSTIFYING THE MEANS

I was raised by Marxists, and in the 1980s, that was not so common, not even in New York City. I remember when I proudly told my classmates that my parents were communists (they were never CP, of course; they were 1960s New Left and knew better than that) in fifth or sixth grade—whenever it was that we studied the virtues of capitalism and the unworkable evil of communism. They all seemed shocked and asked what it was like at my house. "You've *been* to my house," I said. "It's just like yours!"

I wasn't sure what kind of answer they were looking for—a big portrait of Papa Karl on the wall, maybe? A dinnertime request to pass the potatoes met with the stern reminder that these potatoes were dug by the workers?

(To be honest, I'm told that my parents did have a big poster of Marx up when I was a baby, but I have no memory of it. Apparently I liked it a lot as a newborn, which my father made much of, but my mother figured it was because it was a stark black-and-white image of a human face.)

My mother repudiated communism when the Soviet government turned the Red Army on the Russian people in August 1991. It's an odd marker, because, as I said, neither of my parents had ever been CP or supported the Soviet Union, but there it is. Life doesn't have to make sense; it just has to happen. That is why art is superior to life. It is why fairy tales can contain as much truth as facts.

When doing the research for this story, I approached my mother with my—as Goldman put it—disillusionment with the revolution. I had always been taught that it had a glorious beginning and that Stalin had betrayed revolutionary principles in order to seize and keep power. But Lenin and his comrades formed a government rotten from the get-go, and Goldman was writing about it from the left in the 1920s, so why were my parents still buying this crap in the 1960s, I asked my mother.

"We all should have known after Kronstadt," she said.

The Kronstadt Rebellion was a rising of sailors, soldiers, and ordinary people on Kotlin Island, in the Gulf of Finland, in March 1921. It made fifteen demands of the Bolshevik government. They included demands for free, fair elections conducted by secret ballot; freedom of speech and the press; freedom of assembly and to form trade unions; the right for peasants to own cattle; the right for workers to engage in handicraft production; the liberation of all political prisoners belonging to socialist, workers', or peasants' organizations.

It was brutally suppressed, with thousands killed, executed, and/or imprisoned.

The Kronstadt Rebellion took place in 1921, thirty years before my mother was born. The Red Army had been turned on the Russian people at the very beginning.

Marx said that capitalism must end in either socialism or barbarism. He did not, I suppose, know about the third option, fascism. Or maybe he included it under barbarism. In any case, it is to fascism that we have tumbled: concentration camps in which children are separated from their parents and brutalized, in which they suffer and die from neglect and worse; a crude, know-nothing leader who sailed to power on cheap racism, backed by elites who believed they could control him; cops who beat and gun down black people more or less at will; our own uteruses being turned into traps as reproductive rights are ripped away across the country.

The administration is empowering a denaturalization task force housed in the United States Citizenship and Immigration Services. This task force is charged with examining "bad naturalizations," revoking the citizenship of the people in question, and deporting them.

I am a Jew and a leftist and, I like to think, a decent human being with more than a shred of conscience, so I fear and abhor fascism, and I am horrified by what the United States is doing and what it has always done. But Marx also said that being determines consciousness, which is to say that my class matters far more than any good intentions or left politics I have. He was probably right, and I am pretty sure that in the event of revolution, I'll end up against the wall as the decadent, white, bourgeois parasite that I am. Razstrellyat.

I know one song, a hopeful song, and I've known it for a long time, that says we can bring to birth a new world from the ashes of the old. But I know another song, too, and I've known it for longer, and that song says ashes, ashes, we all fall down.

The revolution will not be kind. Revolutions rarely are. But the present regime is nothing if not cruel.

Where do those who walk away from Omelas *go*? There's nowhere to go, nowhere moral, nowhere safe, nowhere that does not depend on the suffering of some child. That means you have to stay and fight, and make the revolution as kind as possible.

In the final analysis, I probably am not an anarchist. I think one must have far more faith in people than I possess to be an anarchist. But I believe in this: you do not achieve freedom by abridging people's rights; you do not create joy by enforcing misery. The means do become the ends, because *there is no end*. There are just ongoing moments.

In 1936, some months after Alexander Berkman's suicide,

Emma Goldman visited Barcelona, then controlled by the Confederación Nacional del Trabajo, the anarchist union. The CNT collectivized farms, factories, even hotels and restaurants—all these places run by the people laboring in them. Goldman said that being in Barcelona felt like finally, finally coming home.

Stalin's line was that the abolition of capitalism should be addressed only after the civil war was over, and the more the anarchists resisted that line, the less Soviet aid they got. Barcelona fell to Franco's fascists on January 26, 1939.

Oh, Auntie Em, there's no place like home.

RATS

What I am about to tell you is a fairy tale and so it is constantly repeating. Little Red Riding Hood is always setting off through the forest to visit her granny. Cinderella is always trying on a glass slipper. Just so, this story is constantly reenacting itself. Otherwise, Cinderella becomes just another tired old queen with a palace full of pretty dresses, abusing the servants when the fireplaces haven't been properly cleaned, embroiled in a love-hate relationship with the paparazzi. Beauty and Beast become yet another wealthy, good-looking couple. They are only themselves in the story and so they only exist in the story. We know Little Red Riding Hood only as the girl in the red cloak carrying her basket through the forest. Who is she during the dog days of summer? How can we pick her out of the mob of little girls in bathing suits and jellies running through the sprinkler in Tompkins Square Park? Is she the one who has cut her foot open on the broken beer bottle? Or is she the one with the translucent green water gun?

Just so, you will know these characters by their story. As with all fairy tales, even new ones, you may well recognize the story. The shape of it will feel right. This feeling is a lie. All stories are lies, because stories have beginnings, middles, and endings, narrative arcs in which the end is the fitting and only mate for the beginning—yes, that's right, we think upon closing the book. Yes, that's the way. Yes, it had to happen like that. Yes.

But life is not like that—there is no narrative causality, there is no foreshadowing, no narrative tone or subtly tuned metaphor to warn us about what is coming. And when somebody dies it is not tragic, not inevitably brought on as fitting end, not a fabulous disaster. It is stupid. And it hurts. It's not all right, Mommy! sobbed a little girl in the playground who had skinned her knee, whose mother was patting her and lying to her, telling her that it was all right. It's not all right, it hurts! she said. I was there. I heard her say it. She was right.

But this is a fairy tale and so it is a lie, perhaps one that makes the stupidity hurt a little less, or perhaps a little more. You must not expect it to be realistic. Now read on. . . .

Once upon a time.

Once upon a time, there was a man and a woman, young and very much in love, living in the suburbs of Philadelphia. Now, they very much enjoyed living in the suburbs and unlike me and perhaps you as well they did not at all regret their distance from the graffiti and traffic, the pulsing hot energy, the concrete harmonic wave reaction of the city. But happy as they were with each other and their home, there was one source of pain and emptiness that seemed to grow every time they looked into each other's eyes, and that was because they were childless. The house was quiet and always remained neat as a shot of bourbon. Neither husband nor wife ever had to stay at home nursing a child through a flu—neither of them ever knew what the current bug going around was. They never stayed up having serious discussions about orthodontia or the rising cost of college tuition, and because of this, their hearts ached.

"Oh," said the woman. "If only we had a child to love, who

would kiss us and smile, and burn with youth as we fade into old age."

"Oh," the man would reply. "If only we had a child to love, who would laugh and dance, and remember our stories and family long after we can no longer."

And so they passed their days. Together they knelt as they visited the oracles of doctors' offices; together they left sacrifices and offerings at the altars of fertility clinics. And still from sunup to sundown, they saw only their faces reflected in the mirrors of their quiet house, and those faces were growing older and sadder with each glance.

One day, though, as the woman was driving back from the supermarket in the station wagon, bought when they were first married and filled with dewy hope for a family, the trunk laden with unnaturally bright, unhealthily glossy fruits, vegetables, and even meat, she felt a certain quickening in her womb as she drove over a pothole, and she knew by the bruised strawberries she unpacked from the car that at last their prayers were answered and she was pregnant. When she told her husband he was as delighted as she and they went to great lengths to ensure the health and future happiness of their baby.

But even as the woman visited doctors, she and her husband knew the four shadows were lurking behind, waiting, and would come whether invited or not, so finally they invited the four to visit them. It was a lovely Saturday morning and the woman served homemade rugelach while the four shadows bestowed gifts on the child growing in her mother's womb.

"She will have an ear for music," said the first, putting two raspberry rugelach into its mouth at once.

"She will be brave and adventurous," said the second, stuffing three or four chocolate rugelach into its pockets to eat later.

But the third was not so kindly inclined—if you know this story, you know that there is always one. But contrary to what you may have heard, it was invited just as much as the others were, because while pain and evil cannot be kept out, they cannot come in without consent. In any case, there is always one. This is the way the story goes.

"She shall be beautiful and bold—adventurous and have a passion for music and all that," said the third. "But my gift to your child is pain. This child shall suffer and she will not understand why; she will be in pain and there will be no rest for her; she will suffer and suffer and she will always be alone in her suffering, world without end." The third scowled and threw a piece of raisin rugelach across the room. Some people are like that. Shadows, too. The rugelach fell into a potted plant.

Sometimes cruelty cannot help itself, even when it has been placated with an invitation and excellent homemade pastry, and then what can you do?

You can do this: you can turn for help to the fourth shadow, who is not strong enough to break the evil spell—it never is, you know; if it were, there would be no story—but it can, perhaps, amend it.

So as the man and woman sat in shock, but perhaps not as much shock as they might have been had they never heard the story themselves, the fourth approached the woman, who had crossed her hands protectively over her womb.

"Now, my dear," it began, spraying crumbs from the six apricot rugelach it was eating. "Uncross your hands—it looks ill-bred and it does no good, you know. What's done is done, and I cannot undo it: you must bite the bullet and play the cards you're dealt. My gift is this: your daughter, on her seventeenth birthday, will prick herself on a needle and find a—a respite, you might say—and after she has done that, she will be able to rest, and eventually she will be wakened by a kiss, a lover's kiss, and she will never be lonely again."

And the soon-to-be parents had to be content with that.

After the woman gave birth to her daughter she studied the baby anxiously for signs of suffering, but the baby just lay, small, limp, and sweating in her arms, with a cap of black fuzz like velvet covering her head. She didn't cry, and hadn't, even when the doctor had smacked her, partially out of genuine concern for this quiet, unresponsive, barely baby, and partially out of habit, and partially because he liked to hit babies. She just lay in her mother's arms with her eyes squeezed shut, looking so white and soft that her mother named her Lily.

Lily could not tolerate her mother's milk—she could nurse only a little while before vomiting. She kept her eyes shut all day, as if even a little light burned her painfully. After she was home for a few days, she began to cry, and then she cried continuously and loudly, no matter how recently she had been fed or changed. She could only sleep for an hour at a time and she screamed otherwise, as though she were trying to drown out some other more distressing noise.

One afternoon, when Lily was a toddler, her mother lay her down for a nap and after ten or fifteen minutes dropped the baby-raising book she was reading in a panic. Lily's crying had stopped suddenly, and when her mother looked into her room, there was Lily smashing her own head against the wall, over and over, with a look of relief on her two-year-old face. When her mother rushed to stop her, she started screaming again, and she screamed all the while her mother was washing the blood off the wall.

She had night terrors and terrors in the bright sunshine and very few friends. She continued to hit her head against the wall. She tried to hit herself with a hammer and when she was prevented from doing so she lay about her, smashing her mother's hand. When her mother went to the emergency room to have her hand set and put in a cast the nurses clucked their tongues and told each other what a monster her husband must be.

When she got home she found Lily curled in a ball under the dining room table, gibbering with fear of rats, of which there were none, and she would allow only her mother to speak to her.

Lily did love music. She snuck out of the house late at night and got rides into the city to see bands play, and she loved her father's recordings of Bach and Chopin as well. Back when she was three or four, Chopin had been the only thing that could get her to lie down and sleep. Chopin and phenobarbital. She wrote long reviews of new records for her school paper, which were cut for reasons of space. As she got older, she got better and better at forcing the burning gnawing rats under her skin on the people around her. But she still felt alone because they could just walk away from her, but she could not rip her way out of her skin her brain her breath although she tried so hard, more than once, but her mother caught her, put her back together, sewed her up, every single time, but not once could she clean Lily so well that she didn't feel the corrosion and corruption sliding through her veins, her lymph nodes, her brain, so that she didn't feel the rats burrowing through her body.

Lily ran away to New York City when she was sixteen and a half, and in what her parents loathed, she found a kind of peace, in the neon lights and phantasmagoric graffiti that blotted out what was in her eyes and especially in the loud noises and the hard fast beats coming from CBGB that drowned out the rats clawing through her brain much better than her own screaming ever had, it was like banging her head against the wall from the inside. She knew there was something wrong with her—she talked to other people who loved the bands she saw because the fast and loud young and snotty sound wired them, jolted them full of electricity and sparks, but Lily just sped naturally and all she wanted was to make it stop.

On her seventeenth birthday, Lily went home with a skinny man who played bass and shot heroin. Lily watched him cook the powder in some water over his lighter and stuck her arm out. "Show me how," she told him.

"You have easy veins," he told her, because her veins were large and close to the surface of her skin, fat and filled with rats. They showed with shimmering clarity, veiled only by the fleshy paper of her lily-white skin.

He shot her up and just after the needle came away from her skin—it stopped. It really stopped, not just the rat-pain that she knew about, but the black tarpits of her thinking and feeling—they stopped, too. It stopped, and God, it felt so good and free that she didn't mind the puking, it even felt fine, because everything else had stopped, and she could finally get some sleep, some real sleep.

The next morning she woke up and felt like shit again. And it was worse, because for a while she'd felt fine. Just fine.

We should all get to feel just fine sometimes.

So Lily found some kind of respite on a needle's tip and the marks it left were less obvious than the old dull hard scars on her wrists that she rubbed raw when she needed a fix. She worked as a stripper, using feathers, black gloves, and fetish boots to hide all kinds of scars, and sometimes in a midtown brothel. So she was often flush, and if she was still a holy terror, a mindfuck and a half, now she was flush, and had some calmer periods and a social circle, even if they did sometimes ignore her. She wrote pieces on music for underground papers, and once every two weeks her mother came to visit and bought her groceries and took her out to lunch and apologized when she threw cutlery at waiters and worried and worried over how thin Lily was becoming.

You can't stay high all the time, but you can try.

Lily knew she was getting thin. She would stare in the mirror and not see herself, and when she could put the rats to sleep she wasn't quite sure who she was or how she would know who she was.

Who are you? asked the caterpillar, drawing on his hookah. Keep your temper.

The rats were eating her from the inside out and she was dissolving, she was real only under her mother's eyes—the power of her mother's gaze held her bones together even as her ligaments and skin slowly liquefied, dissipating in a soft-focus movie dissolve.

Dissolve.

Fade in. We are in London with Lily, far enough away from her mother that she could dissolve entirely. Lily had heard that there was something happening in London, something that could shut down the banging slamming violence in her skull even better than the noise at CB's, some kind of annihilation.

There was.

Look at Lily at the Roxy, if you can recognize her. Can you find her? She is in the bathroom, shooting herself up with heroin and water from the toilet. She is out front sitting by the stage, sitting on the stage, sitting at the bar, throwing herself against the wall so violently that she breaks her own nose. The rats are still following her, snapping and snarling at anybody who comes near, and when nobody comes near, they turn on themselves, begin to eat themselves, gnaw on their own soft bellies.

Can you recognize Lily? When her face and form began to dissolve in the mirror, she panicked and knew she had to take some drastic action before she blinked and found only a mass of rats where her reflection should be, a feeding frenzy. In London the colors were bright like the sun when you have a hangover, so bright it hurt to look at them. The clothing was made to be noticed, to cause people to shrink back and flinch away. Lily wanted to look like that. She bleached her hair from chestnut brown to white blond and left dark roots showing. She back-combed it so a frizzy mess stood out around her head like a halo: Saint Lily, Our Lady of the Rats. She drew large black circles around both eyes, coloring them in carefully. She outlined her lips even more carefully, and the shine on them was blinding. Her black clothing was covered in bright chrome like a 1950s car.

She was visible then. She could see herself when she looked in the mirror, bright and blond, outlined in black. Covered in rats.

Her mother thought she looked like a corpse.

Everyone can see her now, everyone who matters, anyway. She is out and about and she is sleeping with the young man playing bass, well, posing with the bass, on stage. He is wearing tight black jeans, no shirt, and a gold lamé jacket. He is a year older than her. Neither of them is out of their teens. They are children. Despite everything, their skin looks new and shiny.

She had been frightened of him the first time they met. Now she was visible, but that came with a certain price as well. Usually the rats kept everyone at arm's length if that close, so that no matter how desperately she threw herself at people they shied away. They knew enough to be frightened by the rats, even if they couldn't see them, even if they didn't know they were there. They told themselves, told each other that they avoided her because she was nasty, the most horrible person in the world, a liar, a selfish bitch, and she was, she knew she was, but really they were afraid of the rats.

But the rats stood aside when Chris came near. They drew back at his approach, casting their eyes down and to the side as if embarrassed by their own abated ferocity. There was something familiar about him, but Lily was too confused by the rats' unusual behavior to think much about what it was. Chris was slight, with skin so pale that Lily longed to bruise him and watch the spreading purple, skin that had sharp lines etched into it by smoke and sleeplessness, and zits all over his face. One of them was infected. When he spoke she could barely understand him, his voice was so deep and the vowels so impenetrable.

When she shot him up he said it was his first time but she knew better from the way he brought his sweet blue veins up so that they almost floated above the surface of his sheer skin. When they fucked later that night she could tell that it was his first time.

Lily didn't have much curiosity left—it hurt too much to be awake, and she tried to dull herself as much as possible. But while they were kissing for the first time she felt a chill that startled her into wakening and she looked over his shoulder and saw what was so familiar about her Chris (she knew he was hers and she his now). Over his shoulder she saw his rats—just a few, younger than hers, but growing and mating and soon the two of them would be locked together, breaking skin with needles and teeth, surrounded by flocks of rats that could no longer be distinguished or separated out, just a sea of lashing tails and sharp teeth and clutching claws. But she wouldn't be alone, he would see them, too, and he wouldn't be alone, she would see them, too, their children, their parents, their rats.

Do you recognize this story yet? Perhaps you've seen the T-shirts on every summer camp kid on St. Mark's Place as they fantasize about desperation and hope that self-destruction holds some kind of romance.

Do you recognize this story yet? Perhaps you've read bits of interviews here and there: she was nauseating, she was the most horrible person in the world, she was a curse, a dark plague sent to London on purpose to destroy us, she turned him into a sex slave, she destroyed him, say the middle-aged men and occasional women who look back twenty-five years at a schizophrenic teenage girl with a personality disorder shooting junk—because here and now we still haven't figured out a way to make that kind of illness bearable, who'd wanted to die since she was ten because she hurt so much, and what they see is a frenzied harpy. She destroyed him.

And her? What about her?

Can we not weep for her?

Look again at those photographs and home movies and look at how young they were. Shiny. Not old enough ever to have worried about lines on her face, or knees that ached with the damp, or white hairs—every ache and twinge is a fucking blessing and don't you forget it.

Do you recognize this story yet?

Don't you already know what happens next?

Kiss kiss kiss fun fun lies. Yes oh yes we're having fun. I'm so happy!

Kiss kiss kiss fight fight fight. He hit her and she wore

sunglasses at night. She trashed his mother's apartment. He left her and turned back at the train station. He was running by the time he got back to the squat they had been sharing—he had a vision of Lily sprawled on the floor dying—not alone, please, anything but alone. He lifted her head up onto his lap; her heart was beating still but her lips were turning blue. His mum had been a nurse and he knew how to make her breathe again.

Kiss.

On tour with the band, away from Lily, he became a spitting wire, destroying rooms, grabbing pretty girls from the audience, shitting all over them, smashing himself against any edge he could find, carving his skin so that he became a pustule of snot and blood and shit and cum where oh where was his Lily Lily I love you.

The band broke up. He could fuck up but he couldn't play. They moved to New York and bopped around Alphabet City. They tried methadone and they need so much they stopped bothering and anyway methadone only stopped the craving for heroin; it didn't give her any respite. When they were flush they spent money like it was going out of style, on smack, on makeup, on clothing, on presents for each other.

She bought him a knife.

If there is a knife in the story, somebody will have to get stabbed by the end.

Lily knows that she can't stand much more of this, much more of herself, much more of her jonesing, much more of the endless days trapped in a gray room in a gray city, and even though it's all gray the city still hurts her eyes it's a kind of neon gray. The effort it takes just to open her eyes in the morning (afternoon), just to get dressed is too much and if she could feel desire anymore, if she could want anything, all she would want would be to stop fighting, stop moving, to sink back and let herself blur and dissolve under warm blankets.

But the smack-sickness shakes her down and she has to move.

Even her rats are weak, she can see. They are staggering and puking. Sometimes they half-heartedly bite one another. She wants to die, but her Chris takes too good care of her, except when he hits her, for that to happen.

When they were curled up together under the covers back in London, which is already acquiring the coloring of a home in her quietly bleeding memory, Lily had asked Chris how much he loved her. More than air, he said. More than smack. Would you douse yourself in gasoline and set yourself on fire if I needed you to? she asked. Yes, he said. Would you set me on fire if I needed you to? she asked. Not that, he said. I love you, I couldn't live without you, don't, don't, don't leave me alone. Not that. Anything but alone.

The regular chant of lovers.

If I needed you to? she pressed. Wouldn't you do it if I needed you to?

He couldn't. He wouldn't.

Then you don't really love me at all, she told him, if you don't love me enough to help me when I need it.

So he had to say yes. And he had to promise.

Now, in piercing gray New York City she puts the knife in his hand and reminds him of his promise. He pushes her away. No. But he doesn't drop the knife. Perhaps he's forgotten to. She reminds him again and somehow she finds energy and drive she hasn't had in months to scream and berate and plead in a voice like fingernails on a blackboard. She hits him with his bass and scratches at his sores. A man keeps his promises, she tells him. A real man isn't scared of blood.

She winds up shaking and crying to herself on the bathroom floor when Chris comes in, takes her head on his lap, and stabs her in the gut, wrenching the knife up toward her breasts. He goes on stabbing and sawing and stroking her forehead until she stops breathing.

The last things she sees are the expression of blank, loving concern on his face and the rats swarming in as her blood spreads across the bathroom tiles.

He watches the rats gnaw on the soft flesh of her stomach and crawl through her body in triumph until finally he watches them lie down and die, exposing their little bellies to the ceiling. The next morning, he remembers nothing.

The police find him sitting bolt upright in bed, staring straight ahead, with the knife next to him. They take Lily away in a body bag. No more kisses.

He is dying now, he thinks. Her absence is slowly draining his blood away. His rats are all dead and their corpses appear everywhere he looks.

You know the rest of the story. He dies a month later of an overdose procured for him by his mother. Why are you still reading? What are you waiting for? The kiss? But he kissed her already, don't you remember? And she woke up, and afterward she was never alone.

They were children, you know. And there still are children in pain and they continue to die and for the people who love them that is not romantic. Their parents and friends don't know what is going to happen ahead of time. They have no narrator. When these children die all that is left is a blank, an absence, and friends and parents lose the ability to see in color. The future takes on a different shape and they go into shock, staring into space for hours. They walk out into traffic and they don't see the trucks, don't hear the horns. A mist lifts and they find that they have pinned the messenger to the wall by his throat. They find themselves calling out names on streets in the dead of night. Walking up the block becomes too hard and they turn back. They can't hear the doctor's voice.

Death is not romantic; it is not exciting; it is no poignant closure and it has no narrative causality. There are even now teenagers—children—slicing themselves and collapsing their veins and refusing to eat because the alternative is worse, and their deaths will not be a story. Instead there will be an empty place in the future where their lives would have been. Death has no narrative arc and no dignity, and now you can silkscreen these two kids' pictures on your fucking T-shirt.

LOST
IN THE
SUPERMARKET

I live in the supermarket now. It's cold, and there's less to eat than you'd think. And I miss the light. I miss sunlight, candlelight, moonlight, starlight, streetlights, headlights, spotlights. All I have now are fluorescent lights, and I think they're the reason that I vanished in the first place. They've turned my skin translucent. By now I'm only held together by surface tension, like the dome of water that rises above the rim of a glass. I worry that if somebody knocks into me, I'll spill. Then the automated moppers will come on their little wheels with their mops and buckets and anti-crime death-rays, and I'll be mopped up in aisle 72 and that will be the end of me right there in front of the three dozen different kinds of cola.

I don't know how long I've been here. I got lost, just like in the song, lost in the supermarket. Joe Strummer and Mick Jones always know what's what and give it to you straight. I miss real music. I miss punk, musicals, reggae, opera, zydeco. All I have in here is Muzak of songs that I didn't even like to begin with. Or Muzak of songs that I did like, and that's even worse. Yesterday, I think it was yesterday, I heard a Muzak version of "Paint It Black."

But then again, my belief matters less and less these days,

just like the rest of me. I can see through my skin, my muscles, my bones. All that's left is my circulatory system, veins and arteries to capillaries so small that they're little red blurs at my fingertips—little rosebuds and carnations floating beneath the surface of my invisible skin. And my heart, beating and fluttering in time to the music in my head.

I think that for everybody else, I've faded away completely. Shoppers walk through me. I blend right into the 853 different kinds of cereal in aisle 206. Or I would, if I could find the cereal again. I found the cereal once, but then I went looking for the milk, and somebody swept away my trail of Rice Krispies, and I never found my way back.

That's when I knew I had well and truly vanished. I found the milk, and my mother came looking for me, and even she couldn't see me. The speakers were Muzaking "Fairytale of New York" and I was contemplating the milk—organic, whole, 1%, 2%, skim, lactose-free, chocolate, Ferberized, 103%—and I heard somebody crying. It was my mother.

She looked terrible. Her clothing was ripped and her makeup was melting off her face. She was calling my name and crying, and I was so happy that she'd come for me at last.

I tried to throw my arms around her, but she couldn't feel me. She kept crying. "Mama," I said. "Mama, look at me! Mama, I'm here." But I knew that I was lying even as I said it. I wasn't there; I was fading under the radioactive lights, fading into the milk with antibiotics and growth hormones and the milk without, the milk in translucent plastic whose calcium has been all burned away by fluorescent light and the milk in waxed cardboard that still built strong bones twelve ways. I tried to grab her again, but the cloth of her coat passed right through my rosebud fingertips.

"Mommy!" I yelled. "It's me. I need you. I'm cold. And I'm hungry. My back hurts and I think I'm fading away. Please help me!"

But she couldn't feel me or see me or hear me and she walked away from me and the milk, still crying, and I know it was my own fault, anyway. I shouldn't have eaten those Fruittles—they're completely artificial, everyone knows that. I think they've turned me plastic, too, and now I belong here. Once I got almost to the registers—I could *hear* the rattling paper bags and the barcode scanners beeping and the credit-card machines spewing printouts, but just before I pushed my cart to the end of the aisle, the Queen of Hearts appeared right in front of me, young and lovely and only just seventeen, or maybe forty-seven, and I had to stop short to avoid running her over.

She was wearing eyeliner in cat's-eyes and black leather boots that laced up to her knees, the kind I always wanted but never fit me, and a red gingham sundress with a white cotton eyelet blouse, the kind I never wanted but always had to wear when I was a kid. She put her hand on my arm. "Don't go," she said. "There's nothing out there. Stay with me. You promised. You promised to be my friend." So I didn't keep going, and she stroked my arm and led me deeper into the labyrinth and then she vanished. I shouldn't have listened to her, but she's the only one who can see me, and that makes it hard to refuse her. I wish my mother could see me. Or maybe Joe Strummer.

I mean, I wish Joe Strummer could see me, not that my mother could see Joe Strummer, which I don't think would be particularly helpful to anybody. I'm certain Joe Strummer could save me. He wouldn't get confused by seventy-six different kinds of yogurt in aisle 3. He wouldn't even notice them. But he was never in this supermarket in his whole life, I bet. I bet he wouldn't have put up with it for one minute, not one damn minute, and I wish I'd never come here, not only this supermarket, but this pathetic excuse for a city. I'm not from here. I'm from the City—the *real* City, the *only* City that matters—and I miss it so much.

I know Joe Strummer could have helped me, but I don't know if he would have helped me. I've read my Lester Bangs and maybe he would've lost patience with me. Sometimes I lose patience with me.

In my neighborhood, there aren't any of these ever-growing supermarkets. There isn't room. When I was growing up we had butchers, bakers, cheese shops, greengrocers, delis—real delis—fishmongers, Indian restaurants, twenty-four-hour Ukrainian diners, the no-pork halal Chinese takeout, cheap sukiyaki for students, hardware stores, baby supply shops, killer bagels, smoked fish, dried fruit, dark chocolate, and real egg creams. Now my neighborhood is rather less humble and it has restaurants that I can't afford and swank bars full of expensive brands of vodka, not bars like Alcatraz, which scared me so much when I was a little girl that I made my mother walk on the other side of the street. Two years ago Alcatraz shut down and was replaced by a very expensive sushi restaurant that only lasted a year.

My mother couldn't feel me.

I thought we had supermarkets. We had a Key Food across the street and a Met food a few blocks away. Each one was about half a block square and they never bothered to play any music at all.

Then I moved here. Not on purpose.

A couple of friends drove me here for a treat. They said that things are cheaper here. There's more room for your shopping cart. It was fun, at first. I ran down aisle 0 and then jumped onto my cart and rode the rest of the way. I thought it was odd when my cart started turning corners without any help from me, but I didn't mind. It was like bumper cars and ice skating and falling all at once, and even vanishing feels good at first, like when you're jumping around to punk rock and the part of your mind that's always obsessively worried about airplanes crashing and being late and being a poser finally shuts up. But then it didn't stop and now my mother can't see me.

The first problem was the bread. I'm picky about bread—if you're gonna eat Wonder bread you might as well make your sandwiches on Styrofoam. At home you could go to the bakery and they'd slice a loaf for you on their juddering shuddering slicing machine. The Queen of Hearts would love that machine. Off with everything, every inch. I could find the Styrofoam bread but I couldn't find the good bread no matter which aisle I whizzed up and down on my magic cart, turns and sticky axles, Muzaking "Walk on the Wild Side" blaring in my ears, turning my brain to oatmeal.

I crashed right into a display of cake mix, which I don't use. I closed my eyes at the last minute when the gingery vanilla-y floury powder was floating all around me and it stopped up my ears, my mouth, my nose, and I couldn't feel anything but the powder. It slid into my eyes and stopped up my tear ducts and even when I opened my eyes I couldn't tell the difference, and by the time my tears had washed away the powder, by the time I could breathe again, by the time those years had passed I was in aisle 30.536992 and going in an ever-tightening spiral until I came to a stop, right in front of the bread.

This supermarket is a nautilus, a big Moebius strip, except that it's all inside and it doesn't connect to itself. I have never found the bread since then. Lucky for me I took a few loaves. It's not bad and I hope I find the butter someday.

But by the time I found the bread my head was spinning, or maybe the building was spinning. But I still needed kidney beans and there were so many different kinds. I need canned tomatoes and I couldn't find them, and then they were all on the very bottom shelves and I had to dig a trench in the smooth faux marble floor of the supermarket, tearing it up with my fingernails and some cheap plastic spoons from aisle 920.

At the very bottom of the trench I found the canned tomatoes, but they didn't have the ones I wanted.

It was the peanut butter that finally stopped me. I was almost done but I went to get peanut butter and I froze like a deer in headlights. It's been so long since I've even seen headlights. Headlights, traffic lights, neon lights, green light, red light, red rover, red rover, let Delia come over. I couldn't move and I felt like I was wrapped up in gauzy ginger powder again, but I was the powder, floating in air in a million pieces. I couldn't remember how to choose peanut butter. There were so many different kinds: chunky and extra chunky and smooth, mixed with jelly and chocolate, made of plastic, natural and organic and unsalted and Valencia, and sometimes a jar looked like it was full of peanut butter but really it had in it something made of olives or almonds or something else. The shelves towered over me and I became afraid that the jar I wanted was the keystone to the whole store; if I took it everything would come crashing down on me, crushing my bones and swallowing up the world, my friends, my mom, Joe Strummer, and my little dog, too.

I don't know how long I stood like that, but eventually one of my friends came back to look for me. I could hear him in the next aisle, calling my name, saying that Cass and Julie had sent him back from the cashiers to get me, where was I? I didn't know and I tried to answer him but I couldn't—I couldn't remember how to start my voice, and my jaw wouldn't move. Finally he gave up and wandered away and then I couldn't hear anything except a Muzak "Heard It Through the Grapevine." I don't know what happened to him, if he ever found his way back to the cashier, and I don't know how long ago that was. Maybe years.

Now I'm sitting in aisle $3\frac{2}{5}$ eating raw spaghetti while trying not to listen to "Thunder Road" when something black and furry clatters down the aisle and cannons into me, ricocheting off and continuing on without stopping, murmuring nervously. I guess I should be more excited, because it's the first thing that could feel me in so long, but honestly, I don't care. I don't care about anything much anymore. But I get up and run after it anyway, because there's this banging, pounding, drilling part of me in my teeth that thinks I should. Maybe it's just a cavity from all the Fruittles I've been eating, but maybe if I do what it wants the banging pounding drilling will stop and I'll be able to curl up and go to sleep, which is all I really want to do, close my eyes and go to sleep forever and ever.

As the furry thing skids around a turn I catch a glimpse of its face. It's a black dog running with its feet caught in disposable aluminum baking dishes that I knocked down by accident yesterday or last year or an hour ago. I follow it, because I know I should apologize and help it get the tins off its feet. They look like steel-toed boots, or maybe silver slippers, and I'm pretty sure that if I can just catch this dog everything will be all right in the end.

It picks up speed and becomes a black blur but I follow it and I'm running and skidding and the carnation blurs in my finger-tips are bubbling. It climbs up the shelves, still clattering like cheap radio thunder, and I'm right behind it, climbing just the way my mother said would pull over the bookcases and crush me flat, back when I was four and she caught me trying it in the living room. I reach out and grab warm squirmy fur before the creature yelps and bounds away and we're off again. I think the black dog is laughing, at least its tin feet are cackling.

We're not looking where we're running anymore and we're running together, weaving across and around each other's paths like maniacs, careening around like drunken teenagers and we don't even notice where we're going and we find ourselves be-hind the meat counter when a hand reaches down and grabs the dog by the scruff of its neck and chops its head off while its mouth is still open and its throat and its feet are still laughing and I stand stock-still staring at the person who has done this.

It is, of course, the Queen of Hearts.

When I first got here I saw her out of the corner of my eye several times, but she just looked like a regular girl somewhere be-tween seven and thirty with dark straight hair in a ponytail. Okay, she was dressed all in red with hearts all over, and I guess that could have been a clue, but I didn't really notice her until I found out she could see me. I was in the fruit aisle. The Muzak was playing "Trouble in Mind." She came toward me and I expected her to walk right through me. But she stopped in front of me and held out a packet of Fruittles, shiny plastic candies like poisoned jewels. She looked into my eyes and I gasped with delight because she could see me. She looked about nineteen, or maybe fifty-nine.

"Have some," she said.

"Um," I said. "No." I'd heard stories.

"Please. I want a friend. I'm so lonely and I do like you."

I said nothing.

"Please. I do so need a friend." And then she looked about six years old.

I said nothing, but I let her put the Fruittles in my mouth.

But immediately after that she vanished, and I didn't see her again until I tried to leave. And Jack couldn't find me and neither could my mother and Joe Strummer would probably write me off as a waste of time.

And now she's here, a cleaver in one hand and the dog's corpse in the other, looking right at me. I try to hide below the counter. She guts and skins the dog, pulling its soft furry hide off with gusto while the Muzak plays "Brown-Eyed Handsome Man." She chops the body up, skewers the pieces, and sets them to roast over an open fire.

At home we don't have a meat counter. We have a Ukrainian butcher, though. Once when I was little he gave me a salami stick to chew on. I haven't had meat in so long, and the smell coming from the cooking dog is reaching right down to my ovaries and twisting them. I feel so guilty, but it's driving me crazy with hunger. The Queen pulls one of the skewers off the fire and advances. I stand up and back away until I'm right up against the counter.

She thrusts the skewer at me and I'm so faint with long-suppressed cravings that I almost pass out.

"Eat."

I shake my head without opening my mouth and try hard to hold on to the feeling of euphoria I had when I was skittering around with the dog. This is your playmate, I tell myself. Don't eat your friends. It's rude.

She doesn't say anything, just stands there looking at me. Her eyebrows are raised and her foot is tapping. I study her wrinkled forehead. She's reasonably patient because etched in every line is the knowledge that I will eventually give in. She can see me and I can't refuse her. The dog could see me, too, and feel me and hear me, but it's dead now and she's alive. She's here. She knows it's only a matter of time. Time has no matter, though, especially here.

I know it, too, and what the hell, if later why not now, and I close my eyes and take a bite. I pretend to myself that this lady is my mother and that the meat is not the cooked body of a friend but instead one of those half-charred, half-fat unidentified shish kabobs she used to get me on the street. It's warm and good. When I was little my mother used to pour the juice from steak, juice made of mixed blood and fat, into a bottle or a cup so I could drink it, so it could give me strength, and that's what the dog meat gives me, strength, but it doesn't taste half so good as my mother's blood.

I open my eyes and notice two things. One is that my bones are visible, and as I watch, my muscles, nerves, and my skin start to come back as well. I wonder whether I'm really becoming visible or if only I can see me.

The meat that is all lovely and warm, cooked and seasoned on the outside, is raw and bloody on the inside. All the blood reminds me that I can't remember the last time I got my period and how much I miss it. There's no blood between my legs now, but there's blood running down my face, over my chin, and dripping onto the sterile shiny floor. The Queen of Hearts takes out a linen handkerchief, spits on it, and cleans off my face. She pats me on the head.

I eat the rest of the dog and go off to hide before the automated moppers come to clean the blood from the floor. I spend several hours admiring my newly visible body in the glass of the frozen vegetables section in aisle 4. Look at the color in my cheeks! My ripped cuticles! My legs, unshaven for who knows how long, my white hairs, my long eyelashes, my bushy eyebrows! Look at the way my skin covers up my heart-lungs-ribs-muscles so completely! I'm perfect, and I even bump into a few people on purpose for the thrill of it. I bark my shins against grocery carts and spend hours admiring the developing and receding bruises, caressing my legs in an ecstasy of wonder at the way my skin obscures the broken blood vessels so that the blue-and-purple mottle gradually fades into green and yellow and is overlaid with the pasty peach pink of my impenetrable, irreproachable skin. I'm in love with the smudges of dirt and dust on my fingers.

I go over to people and I see them taking in the full shopping cart I always lug around and my shattered face (I'm pretty sure I still have dried blood on my mouth) and my ratty clothing. I ask, "Do you know the way out?" and instead I spout nonsense words, I speak in tongues. Panicking, I grab at my mouth, trying to push my tongue into the right shapes, but my jaw moves by itself, it bites my hand so hard that it draws blood that fills my throat—I start to choke because still, still! I'm making these nonsense noises. I've lost my words.

I shut up because it takes all my concentration to keep my thoughts from degenerating, devolving into the gibberish that comes out of my mouth whenever I speak.

I've lost my words and I can't find my way back to them. Sometimes you lose words, you get rid of them when they're useless—they're just sacks for holding meaning, just containers and shapes, and sometimes you can just burn right through them because you don't need them anymore, the meaning is raw and bleeding, electric shockers, fire, a cheese grater shredding your throat, and you don't need words to shape the sounds anymore because that would just be some kind of finesse, something to take the edges off when what you have is pure ripping slashing edge, anger and rage and self-loathing and spitting live-wire third-rail energy and words just blister and shrivel away.

Like the Clash's "Complete Control." Some self-righteous people dismiss it as self-indulgent ranting about the band's troubles with their label, but they're just listening to the lyrics instead of paying attention to the song. That song is the apocalypse. It's the sound of buildings crashing down that summer in New York City when every week another building would collapse at random. It's the sound of water mains exploding, manhole covers shooting into the air, subways derailing, firecrackers blowing off somebody's hand at the Hells Angels' block party, taxi brakes squealing, crowds roaring, the sound of July Fourth when somebody's turned the heat way up by accident, motorcycles flying up First Avenue, dykes on bikes gunning down Broadway, babies howling, cops shooting an African immigrant, mass civil disobedience down at One Police Plaza, riots in the park, teenagers fighting—it's the sound of urban armageddon, of a city exploding with heat and anger and boredom. Strummer holds it together until about halfway through, but there's nobody who can tell me that he's making words after that. There's nobody who can tell me that he's even trying. He's pouring out pure fury and that fury will shred his skin and eat him alive and whoever's listening as well. You don't need words for that. But it didn't shred him or eat him alive. He came back to the words after the song was over, and I can't come back. All I have is frightened, lost, self-doubting gibberish.

I think he could come back because he had the rest of the band keeping him together, winding out a skein of wool tied to his belt as he went into the labyrinth. He had Mick Jones and Paul Simonon and Topper Headon to throw him a lifeline, and the whole time he was using his voice like a five-alarm fire in a bad neighborhood uses gasoline Mick and Paul were chanting "TO-tal . . . C-O-N . . . control" over and over, and Headon was keeping the beat, so Strummer had something to come back to, someone staying steady and holding hard through the pummeling crashing lightning of the song.

I think I could talk to dogs, if there were any in here that I hadn't already eaten. There aren't, of course; no dogs jumping on displays, knocking things over, howling and barking, rolling over and writhing, but what's still here is the Muzak constantly playing, and I wonder what it would be like to buy groceries in silence, what it would be like to curl up in the dark without the glare of fluorescent lights behind my eyelids and a blanket and warmth, and I can almost feel it when a cold damp tendril of Muzak oozes into my ear like a slug. It's got to be something the Queen's doing on purpose.

It's "Career Opportunities." The Clash.

I know why she made me solid again. I'm solid, but I can't talk and I can barely think, and I'm growing hair and soon my ears will grow floppy and a tail will sprout from my ass and I'll shrink right down into a dog and it'll only be a matter of time before I'm skewered and set on fire.

I swing my shopping cart into a new aisle to get some cover while I think, and I push the cart right through Joe Strummer, who's wearing a black T-shirt, black jeans, and motorcycle boots, and is lighting a cigarette. I'm annoyed that I walked right through him like that; I thought I was solid again. I test it out by kicking the only other person in the aisle, who flinches and scurries around the corner. I am solid. Strummer's not.

What he is is annoyed. "Watch it, babe. Don't walk *through* people. Feels weird."

"You're dead." I'm still angry, but also relieved, because he's come to lead me out of this mess, and that means I didn't fuck everything up, not beyond hope, not beyond redemption, not beyond second chances, I didn't screw up anything that can't be fixed, I can be fixed, I'm not hopeless, not if Joe Strummer's come back for me, come back from the dead to help me. He left me, he left me here and I didn't know how to get out of bed and I didn't know why to leave the house anymore but now he's come back and all the grayness will go away again. I feel my ears twitch and start to grow, but I keep them human-shaped through an effort of will.

"So're you," he says. "Almost. Or you wouldn't be here." He takes a drag off his cigarette. "Want one?"

"Nah. I've got asthma," I say, and I try not to cough because I don't want to be an asshole about it.

"Drink?" He holds out a half-empty bottle of tequila, which I grab, even though tequila makes me sick, because I don't want him to think I'm useless.

"You *died*, just when I was getting my shit together, you left me without any directions—"

"Look, I'm not staying here for long. This place gives me the creeps. So pay attention, 'cause I'm only gonna say this once."

My voice cracks. "I can't get out, I can't find the door, but you—"

"You haven't even fucking *tried*," he interrupts, punctuating each word by stabbing the air in front of me with his cigarette. "Screw the door." He pauses, ripples, and refocuses. "You're, uh, you're gonna need to kick it over," he says. "There's no tenderness here. She's got nothing on you, nothing to hold over you. Just kick it over."

He takes another drag off the cigarette. I love smoking. I always have. They can run all the PSAs they want, it doesn't matter, smoking's cool and that's that. He blows smoke out his nose. "But, y'know, dress the part. You'll never do it looking like that."

He hands me a large package wrapped up in brown paper and a beat-up Louisville Slugger and starts to walk past me, up the aisle.

"Hey!" I grab for his hand, but my fingers go straight through.

"Piss off," he growls.

"You can't just walk away and leave me! Aren't you going to get me out of here?"

"I'm not your fucking babysitter," he says. "If you haven't got the balls to get out of this yourself, with everything I've already done to help you, I'm not bloody well gonna take you by the hand."

He goes on for a couple of steps and then stops. Without turning his head he says, "I'll tell you one more thing. When you're done, and you're leaving, don't look back. Don't even turn your head, right? Got that?" Another drag off the cigarette. "Oh, and you can keep the booze, okay?"

I don't say anything, just watch him take another five steps and vanish.

"Son of a bitch," I finally say, after he's gone and can't hear me. I take two more swallows of the tequila. "*Son of a bitch!*" I yell, and hurl the empty bottle down the aisle after him. It smashes into a million pieces, which is very satisfying, and the speakers, which have been Muzaking "White Man in Hammersmith Palais," interrupt themselves in order to squawk "Cleanup in aisle 8002, cleanup in aisle 8002." I hear a squadron of automated moppers massing around the corner, but that's okay, I have a plan. I set my full cart up at the top of the aisle where anyone coming at full speed around the corner is sure to ram into it. I climb up onto the shelves and cling there like a deranged baboon. Those shelves are *tall*, they go up and up and I can't even see the tops, they go all the way up like redwoods, like fire-truck ladders, like train tracks running vertically, the Super Chief to the sky, and I start to wonder, could I climb them? Could I get out that way, just climb up the shelves, up and up until I bust right through the ceiling?

But I don't have any time for that—the automated moppers swing around the corner into my overbalanced cart and they go flying, falling over like empty water bottles. They roll around on their backs, their castors whirling frantically and their death rays firing randomly at the ceiling. I do a maniacal little victory dance, still clutching the shelves.

The death rays are firing randomly but not harmlessly. Chunks of the ceiling are cracking up and falling to the floor and some of them hit the shelves pretty hard, so I have to jump down because the shelves start shaking and cracking and the sky is falling. The Super Chief has derailed and that harmonic wave reaction is tearing up the tracks.

Before the automated moppers can recover themselves, I right my shopping cart and pull out a can of lighter fluid. I punch the can open and fling some of the contents on the moppers, who're still lying on their backs like overgrown water bugs. I rummage some more and find a box of kitchen matches, strike one, and throw *it* on the moppers, too. The fluid catches and burns and the moppers start to melt. The death rays stop.

The aisle's a wreck, and the speakers are blaring out Muzak mixed with more cleanup announcements, and this time, they're gutting "London Calling." Back when I was a kid in the city and then in high school and still in college, I played outfield first in Little League and then on my high school's softball team and then on my college's women's baseball team, and I played right field and left field and center field, any field, because I had a good arm. A *great* arm, and now I guess it's time to see if I still have it. I fish a can of tomato paste out of my cart and hurl it at one pair of speakers. It's been a few years, months, centuries since I last played, but the can crashes straight into the speakers, and they short out in a shower of sparks.

I head for the next aisle, and then the next, smashing speakers as I go. I'm out of practice, and my arm is getting sore, but that's okay.

Finally there's silence. Dead silence, and all I can hear is the fire I set crackling, and maybe the dying burbles of some of the automated moppers. I stop to catch my breath and look around. I'm standing in the middle of a mess, glass and plastic and cans and boxes tumbled all over the floors, a trail leading straight to me, but for the moment, nobody's following it. I'm alone.

It seems like as good a time as any to open the stuff Joe Strummer gave me. The bat is my old bat, back from when I was a teenager playing in Central Park, black and battered. The sticker on it used to say GIRLS' PIRATE ACADEMY, but now you can only read it if you already know what it says. I contemplate it for a little while, trying to figure out where he found it, before I give an experimental swing. It feels good in my hands, and I can't help but admire the movement of the muscles in my shoulders and arms. I rip open the brown paper package and inside is my green skirt, my metal-studded goddess baby-doll T-shirt, a pair of fishnet stockings that I'd lost track of years ago—real fishnet stockings that cut your skin, not that stretchy cotton crap everybody has now, and my oxblood combat boots. Also some huge metal clips for my hair and my snake armlet. My clothing, my

God, I've missed my clothing. It's like gasoline, like a jet pack, like an electric halo helmet, a fire skin, I almost have an asthma attack from the shock. I start to glance around, and then I decide I don't care if anybody's watching, fuck them, and I strip off the boring old clothing I threw on to go shopping lo those many years ago and put on the stuff I love.

Picking up the bat, I face the wall of air fresheners—and I just don't care what they smell like, they all smell like crap anyway. I mark my aim, bring the bat back, and then swing it forward in a steam-powered arc, unstoppable as the end of days, as a supernova, and I just maul the shit out of those shelves, swinging and swinging and swinging until I've smashed out a jagged dark hole to the outside. A chilly breeze comes from it.

I turn back for my cart, and when I face the hole again, the Queen of Hearts is standing between me and the way out. Behind her I can see the night sky and the glitter of the skyline in the distance. She is sixteen, she is sixty, she is every age in between. She wears camouflage, but her shoes have red hearts sewn into them, and she's not fooling me.

"You can't leave," she says. "I made you solid again."

I don't bother to answer.

"You can't take that cart." She's starting to sound anxious. "The cart's supermarket property, it belongs here."

I shove the cart at the Queen, hoping it'll run her over. It doesn't, of course. She catches it with one hand.

"Stay here," she says. "Please." But it's not even a little bit tempting, not now.

I step out the back door, and I don't turn around once, not even to see the Queen standing in her supermarket with the walls crumbling and the shelves crashing and the floor burning and the sky falling all around her. I'm looking straight ahead, at the city lights.

SWIMMING

1. THE HOUSE

Today Adam's parents took us on a tour of their house, which is now larger and more ornate than the gaudiest of Oriental temples dreamed up in the fevered imaginations of barely repressed Victorian fantasists. It is for Adam, and now, for both of us.

They took especial pride in the first-floor dining room modeled on the courtroom of Louis XIV, the Sun King. There is a second dining room that is the whole of the second floor, simpler and rougher-hewn and to my mind all the more cold, majestic, palatial. The tables stretch unto infinity, world without end, and each place is marked with its own silver tankard. Leering, screaming demons are carved into the table legs, the backs of the chairs, the wooden rafters among which ravens soar jeering as if they can see into your very soul and are not at all impressed. And lounging on the table, wearing armor spattered with mud and blood, picking their teeth with sharpened slivers of bone and scratching their privates and flicking the dried or viscous secretions they find there at each other, are an infinite number of women, twice as large as I, toughened, leathery flesh spilling out between sections of armor. They are fat and thin, old and young, raven-haired and redheads. And they were all, every one, glowering at me, glowering and smirking.

Adam has asked me to marry him, and I have said yes, because I love him and I want to spend the rest of my life with him; I want to raise our children together. The only problem is his parents. They are still building this house; they are crazy; they want us to come and live with them.

Adam's mother has the third floor and his father the fourth. Each has a bedroom, a study, a den, a bathroom, a dressing room. On the third floor his mother has a bird room. It is vast, with a brilliant skylight. There are ice floes for the penguins and gum trees for the kookaburras, salt water for the seagulls and peaches for the peacocks. The air is full of whirring brown wings, the smell of feather mites, and falling feces. They shriek and fight and peck each other until the blood comes. And all the time, Adam's mother and father chattered as though their words were what sped the birds through the air.

I love them. I do not mind their madness. After my own family's distance and isolation from one another I find soothing their unnatural chatter and loopy non sequiturs, their inability to allow a pause in the cosmic monologue they are both eternally engaged in delivering. Their fluttering talk floats through my inherited solitude and becomes a blanket covering me, preventing me from levitating indefinitely and steadily away from all that is human and recognizable.

I stared up and farther up, and on this day Adam's parents' words felt no longer like a blanket warming me but instead like white noise, white water, water running into the sink as I stand trying to fumble under the dishes for the sponge and the water level is rising, the water is rising and drowning out the music on the stereo, the water is rising and the waves are rolling in and I can no longer hear words; all I can see as I stare up is a blur as feathers blend into leaves but up and farther up is the ceiling because we are still in the terrible house. It is not a house at all, but a beast, a god, a toad-like Moloch-Baal squatting in the heart of Brooklyn devouring the offerings of labor, love, and material bounty my future in-laws offer up; they offer up their retirement, their sweat and dreams, in an orgy of joy and devotion. And see how it grows, fatter and fatter with each passing year, feeding on human life.

On the fourth floor is Adam's dad's model room, in which they plan each floor. The model is almost the size of the entire room, and leaves us only some inches to stand. Adam tells me what a glorious playhouse this was when he was a child. He thinks he can still fit through it if he crawls. And he does, easy as pie, so to show willing I go in after him. I am little more than halfway when I get stuck in his father's dressing room and no matter how I turn I am wedged in so tightly and painfully with my arm out one window and my foot resting up in the chimney that I can barely breathe, let alone get out.

As I lie uncomfortably, twisted and all out of proportion, I envision layers of the house falling in upon me. There are voices outside—perhaps Adam whispering words of encouragement—but the water is rising and I cannot hear him. I wonder what would happen if I can't get out. Will I just be shut in this box forever while the water rises and the waves roll in?

I could not shed my skin, but I did manage to inch off my skirt, which slimmed me down enough to slither out on my belly like a snake, and then I was out standing in my underwear but there was no shame in it. I put my skirt back on and examined the Ferris wheel on top of the model while Adam steadied me.

Years ago, so many years ago that it is long, long ago, though not far away at all, so many years ago that it is once upon a time, so long ago, and besides, the wench is dead, so many years ago that I have never been sure how old Adam's parents are, whether they grew up in the last century or the one before that, when land in Brooklyn was undeveloped and cheap, they bought some and began building. Perhaps originally their plans were modest, who can say? And who can say when they went mad? They adopted Adam long after they completed the first two stories, and his earliest memories, so he tells me, are of being taught how to hold a hammer, how to use a wrench, how to spread cement for bricks.

I love Adam. But I do not wish to be consumed by that house.

I do not wish to raise my children as little builders, always anchored, dragged down to the seabed by some ever-growing weight in Brooklyn, a mass distorting space and time, energy and light. I do not wish to be sucked into this collapsed star, no, not even if it meant that I could travel in time, not even if it meant I could live forever.

"Of course we're nowhere near ready to finish the roof," his parents tell me. They speak spontaneously in unison, in harmony, one voice rising in pitch as the other falls. "But we plan to cap off the building with a Ferris wheel—an old-fashioned one. We keep making offers to the owners of the Wonder Wheel—we've already worked out how to reinforce the walls and foundation to take the weight because the water *is* rising—they won't sell so far, but you never know. We remember when they built the Wonder Wheel. We were teenagers in love and we were already wizened and gray, even bald. We were little kids playing on the beach as the waves rolled in and we were thirty-year-old construction workers, but we were never lost, not for one moment."

I imagine the Wonder Wheel atop this behemoth of a house, turning steadily in wind and rain and sun. It is not an unpleasant idea, but then out of nowhere, I imagine the wind rising, the sky above Brooklyn darkening, and rain bombs being thrown down onto the borough, and out of the black roaring sea of the sky comes a lightning bolt striking the wheel, crackling around and across the circle, hub and spokes, which turns black and flies into pieces, shooting shrapnel in all directions and the water is rising.

I open my eyes and see that the model Ferris wheel is burnt and smoking and in pieces on the floor.

Adam's mother and father sigh. "Yes," they say. "Yes, well, that does happen, and more often than you'd think. Adam, go downstairs and fetch the broom, please. We can put this back together tonight after you children leave. . . ."

After we clean up the scorched earth of the model room we go upstairs to the carnival floor, the floor that Adam's parents are giving to us. There is a room of bumper cars with flashing strobe lights and a disco ball and loud jarring electronic music as cars speed back and forth slamming into the walls and one another and more than once we have to jump out of the way when a garishly colored car heads for us like a battering ram.

Also on that floor is the room with a huge hand-carved carousel in the center whirling around and around as its internal organ howls out Petula Clark's "Downtown." I wonder whether we could reprogram it to play something else, but doing that would mean going near the clown faces carved on the trunk. I remember my mother taking me to the carousel in Central Park when I was little and part of the thrill was spinning around so close but just out of reach of those scary clowns jeering at you, and I think that was when I began to understand the pleasure, the eroticism, of being just a bit frightened. But I never had to go within reach of those clowns and I will not go near these, not so close that they could reach out with their wooden tongues and painted mouths and get me, drag me into the carved wood, where I would be frozen, trapped in a sharp relief of terror forever and ever. And trapped in wood, I would someday burn.

The next room is not quite finished; it's the one they are currently working on; it's the one they have set aside for me, they tell me, and perhaps someday it will make a good nursery, or perhaps a university, an anniversary, an adversary, a anursereversary. It does not yet have a name.

"We're still working on this," they say. "It's quite tricky, working out how to make these stick together, but well worth the effort, we think you'll agree. . . ."

And I can see that it must be tricky, for instead of bricks and mortar, the walls are built of layer after layer of plastic mannequins, the kind found in shop windows everywhere, from Strawberry's to Macy's. They lie on top of each other, fixed in place by Krazy Glue and their own plastic flesh melted together by a blowtorch. Impossibly smooth and stiff limbs stick out of the walls like swimmers reaching for shore. And this room is not yet finished—a wall and a half remain to be done and cold winds rush in from the open sky outside.

"Plastic repels water," Adam's parents continue to explain, but I have stopped listening. Plastic does indeed repel water, but when I look closely at the wall I can see tiny drops of water in the corners of the mannequins' eyes. They look like the eyes of a baby doll I had when I was very young. She was called Tiny Tears. She was small with a head of short black hair, and she had been my mother's before she was mine. Her eyes opened when you picked her up and closed when you put her down. She came with a little plastic bottle that you could fill with water. Then you would fit the tip of the bottle into her little open mouth and nurse her, and then the water would leak out of the tear ducts in her little eyes, and then you would comfort her. Tiny Tears. These weeping mannequins remind me of her, little Tiny Tears, my mother's doll, and my doll, and perhaps someday my daughter's doll.

Later that night I dream about the house.

In my dream, Adam and I and two tiny weeping babies are living in the Wonder Wheel on top of the house, climbing from one car to another whenever we need to move into or out of a room. The babies love it, swinging from one steel bar to the next with the greatest of ease, like little orangutans, but not I, I slip and lose my grip and then my balance and then I plummet, falling down and down and down until I stick. I try to sit up but I can't move, I'm glued down and I only realize where I am when I see Adam's parents lowering a mannequin smeared with Krazy Glue down to me. I try to yell, but my mouth doesn't open because it's made of plastic, so I can't prevent them from gluing me into the wall of mannequins. My eyes begin to leak tiny warm tears that roll down my face and my feet and gather into a puddle that swells and I wake up with a sound between a gulp and a sigh as the water is rising and the waves are rolling in.

I watch Adam sleeping next to me until the sky turns from black to royal blue. I realize what I have to do.

I will blow up the house.

Then I lie back down and sleep peacefully through the morning.

2. THE PLAN

It is important not to hurt anybody. I would never hurt Adam's parents, not if my life depended upon it. So I must make sure the house is unoccupied when my fuses reach their ends. I do not want to hurt anybody at all, just the terrible house, only the beast of Brooklyn.

I want to kill the house, but I will not. No. To kill the house, to destroy it completely, that would be too terrible for Adam's parents. Their beloved older child, their life project, the house they began back when they were newlyweds, or young teenagers, or perhaps infants—think how it would hurt them to lose their house completely. All their love, all their work, the luxury of their sweat, and sweet Adam's work as well—no. I can't destroy the house entirely.

I will hurt nobody and I will not destroy the house. All I wish to do is to cripple it a little. Scorch it a bit. Nothing that will not heal. Make the upstairs uninhabitable. Not the downstairs. I do not wish to make Adam's parents homeless—then they would move in with us. I just want to make them unable to house us. Adam and I have friends we can impose upon in the event of an emergency.

I can make an emergency.

So. Not to hurt anybody. Not to destroy the house. This will be easy. I have resources. I can get a small bit of explosive and a timer. Oh yes. That is not difficult at all.

And it will have to happen on our wedding day. During the ceremony. How else can I ensure Adam's parents will not be in the house? Adam and I are staying at the hotel the night before and the night after the wedding. The night before in separate rooms, so that the bride does not see the groom before the wedding. No. The other way round.

Yes. Just a bit of explosive on the top floors. On our wedding day. During the ceremony.

Yes.

3. THE WEDDING

It was easy and slightly disorienting, for I had not expected such— what shall I call it? Enthusiasm? Excitement? Cooperation?— from the house. Poor thing, it is as trapped as I am. But no longer. Soon we will both be free.

I'm afraid I got a little carried away, but only because the house was so happy, so helpful. It wants to end. I can feel it. Yes.

It was easy. I slipped out of the hotel at three in the morning. Nobody saw me go. I was too careful for that. I took the subway, slipped my key into the lock, and let myself in. At first I was very careful, anxious lest I wake Adam's parents, but I soon realized I could clatter up and down the stairs as loudly as I liked. We had formed an alliance, the house and I, and it was taking care of me, enveloping me in silence, taking care to muffle my noise.

I started on the top floors, placing bits of explosive in the jeering mouths of the clowns—I knew that the house would protect me, would not let them get me. I put explosive in the reaching, grasping hands of the mannequins and in each careening drunken bumper car, each one nestling lovingly against my shins, waiting its turn. I left a large chunk of explosive in the center of the model, and then I realized that I'd gone farther than I had planned, that I had not wanted to hurt the lower floors, on which the people soon to be my in-laws lived, but there was no going back, the house wanted this, and I could only go on.

On the third floor I held out my cupped hands and the birds flew about me taking bits of explosive in their beaks and brushing me with their wings to say thank you before flying off to place their contributions at the weak places in the walls. On the second floor I approached the dining hall timidly, but the Valkyries bounded over, shaking the house with every step, for they are large as life and twice as natural. They snatched me up on their shoulders and carried me around, cheering "Huzzah, huzzah" and throwing me up in the air again and again until finally *I must go, really, I must go now*, and they took the last of my explosive and each put some into her tankard, and then I really did leave.

I took the train back to the hotel, I was back in bed by five thirty and no living soul the wiser, except, perhaps, the house.

And the rest of the day has been a flurry of kisses and brides-maids and white tulle and now here I am, walking down the aisle, looking at the moist smiles of all my friends and family, thinking of the house in Brooklyn, now only minutes away from freedom, until I see Adam waiting for me, and I feel such a surge of joy and contentment that I think of nothing else.

The justice of the peace first asks Adam to take his vows. We keep catching each other's eyes and trying not to giggle. And then I take my vows, and as I say "I will," the air is filled with a terrible cracking, a joyful shuddering, and we all look up, and the top of the hall has vanished so we are looking up into blue sky.

First come the birds, pinwheeling in reckless gyres, the birds of flight holding up the penguins and ostriches and even a dodo, saying farewell before they rush away in a sudden burst of squawking and crapping. And then the Valkyries ride through the air on their motorcycles, waving swords and screaming full-throated battle cries. They blow me brief, loving kisses before revving their motors and howling off into the distant blue.

And finally, finally, the air is filled with falling mannequin parts, plummeting down soft as snow. I do. They are falling all around us. I do. They become true snow as they land, piling up in haphazard drifts and sliding across the floor of the hall. I do. They're already up to my waist I do and I see Adam leaning over I do and he begins to pat the snow together and make a fort or perhaps a house like my great-grandmother used to build on the Lower East Side when she was growing up I do and I understand. He is not angry, and this will be our life together. I do. He will build up and I will knock down. He will put up buildings and I will blow them apart. He will set the wood and I will strike the match. He will make the fort and I will kick it over. He will make a tower of blocks and I will send a plastic truck smashing, flying, rolling, crashing into it. I do. And one day we will change, and he will tear himself to pieces and I will collect his limbs, his torso, his head, his penis, and put him back together again. And we will live in a Ferris wheel, going up and down forever, together and together and together I do I do.

The snow melts, turns to warm salt water I do which rises just over my head I do I do. Treading water, I turn and see Adam, whom the waves have carried some distance from me. He is bobbing along, looking somewhat confused. I do. I gather my skirts around me and I swim toward him, the warm water carrying me along smoothly. I do. The water is rising, and I am swimming.

LILY GLASS

The girl is gone from the castle and her stepmother wanders the corridors.

Here is another way of saying the same thing: the girl wanders the corridors, but her stepdaughter is nowhere to be found. Neither is her husband; she is alone in this solid, bulky mansion built on endless reels of flickering light.

The marriage was for love as far as anybody knew, and "anybody" included the bride and groom. She was swept off her feet by his worldliness. The lines on his sun-toughened parchment skin exuded an offhand debauchery she could not even pretend to understand. How could she, an ingénue just out of her teens turned leading lady overnight? And the tension she felt in his presence, the sense of familiarity and corrupted need, the fluttering laughter that bubbled up inside her when they spoke— what could this be but love?

The groom was Leo Wredde, Hollywood's most famous rake and ladies' man. He had been struck by the combination of her deceptive beauty, which changed from day to day, and her awkward, gawky movement. She was shy, almost too frightened to speak to him, and her fear made him self-conscious as well. Perhaps this vicarious return to innocence was what caught his heart, for soon the aging roué and widower was enamored with sultry youth.

They met at the screen test for her first film. Casting an unknown to play against such a famous and riveting actor was unusual but not unheard of—it was how stars were made. She had done some modeling, and at her audition Leo watched her for a few minutes and then introduced himself, staring intently into her black eyes, which slanted exotically over high, angular cheekbones. After the screen test, she went back to the small studio flat she shared with her mirror, sat in front of the vanity, and slowly stripped off her makeup. Her eyes, it turned out, were not black and her cheekbones were not particularly high. When she was finished, her face was clean but she barely recognized it. She had a new name now, but she couldn't quite remember what it was. Not Rose anymore, but . . . L-something, she couldn't quite remember . . . Lily, that was it, Lily Glass. It wasn't so different from her old name, after all. One flower became another, and her surname was translated so as not to sound so Jewish—that was important; only producers and comedians were Jewish—but it meant the same thing. It wasn't even the first time she had lost one name and gained another. She could remember being five years old, burning up with fever, and her mother chanting and weeping over her, calling her Rose to fool the angel of death. Rose looked in the mirror but she could not find Lily. She reached for some pencils, just to touch up her eyes.

The movie was a smash, especially after a fan magazine ran a carefully leaked story about the stars' romance. They were cast opposite each other again, and within a year, to the scandalized delight of the moviegoing public, the notorious hell-raiser had proposed marriage to his innocent sweetheart and she had accepted. A love match, as best as they were able, and if the best they were able didn't touch either of them very deeply, well, she didn't know any better and he didn't want any more.

Now she walks through the mansion's halls, searching ever more distractedly for her stepdaughter, who, she knows, is not there.

Nivia was the daughter of Leo's first wife, Bianca, his high-school sweetheart, whose early death had sent him spiraling into brutal decadence as he drank and screwed his way through most of Hollywood, until he met Rose Glaser, now Lily Glass, beautiful, pliant, and only two years older than his daughter. That is one way to tell the story, anyway.

Nivia is almost never mentioned in the tabloids; there is what amounts to a tacit gentleman's agreement between the gossip writers and her father. He will provide them with all the salacious gossip they need, and they will avoid all mention of his daughter. He loves her and wants her to have a normal life. Even when Nivia was forced to leave school for conduct unbecoming a young lady and it had taken all of Wredde's clout and much of his cash to get her into a new one, a boarding school far away in New England, where it snowed during winter, not a whisper of such interesting goings-on made the gossip sheets.

There was no conduct unbecoming a lady at the boarding school. Nivia kept herself cool, alone, untouchable. At first the other girls were excited and curious about her life even though their parents were pleasantly appalled by her trashy, nouveau origins. But every so often, a classmate who had seen one of

Nivia's father's movies or read an interview accompanied by a photograph of him wearing one of his custom-fitted black silk shirts, rolling a cigarette across his lower lip, with his signature half smile—who would have thought he was over forty?—would approach Nivia, half shy, half defiantly hopeful, and ask if it was true that Leo Wredde was her father. And could she, perhaps, be persuaded to invite him to the school? Or invite *her* home for the holidays?

The answer was always no.

And then, perhaps out of spite, perhaps out of snobbery, the questions got worse. Was it true that her father had requested, or perhaps rented, the attentions of a dozen young women to help celebrate his best friend's forty-second birthday? Was it true that her father had screwed the waitress at his favorite after-hours club on the bar in full view of the other drinkers? Was it true, what his last mistress had said when she Told All to the lowest scandal sheet in Hollywood, about the handcuffs and the leather and the riding crop?

In case you are curious: all of these tales of Leo Wredde, aging libertine, are true, though he himself is fictional. He is a good enough father to deny them in Nivia's hearing, though she has her suspicions—after all, she must have inherited her unbecoming conduct from *somebody,* and surely it was not from her sainted mother—but he is also a good enough movie star to wink at the press and answer evasively. You can hear his fans gasp at the thought of his rapacious appetites and the barely plumbed depths of his perversities.

He *is* a good father, though, and in Nivia's mind their time together is limned in sunlight. She adores him for what he is, though she also hoards a secret, cramped hatred of him for what he is not.

Is it true he pulls young men into his bed as eagerly as young women?

Is it true that he is engaged to Lily Glass, a starlet only two years older than his daughter?

Is it true that he is larger than life, more brilliant than truth, the horned man, the fertility idol, the god of fucking and desire, a creature of blood and muscle maintained only by our urgent outpourings of aching, pathetic, low-rent, unimaginative fantasies, rehearsals of the same tired taboos over and over and over again, a sex god for this age of mass reproduction?

And your stepmother? What is she?

Not even Lily knows the answer to that; she strips off her makeup every night in front of the mirror and she does not know what she has become. She sees posters of a perfect face outside of cinemas and in press kits, and then patterns of light and shadow resolve into that same luminescent face on screen and she cannot tell what kind of creature she has become. She hears a constant hissing around her ears and she looks into her mirror and turns herself to stone.

The movie was a smash and Lily was a star—she was made for the pictures, everybody said, with her slim body and slightly too-large head. On screen, her face glowed as though it was the source of a cool, constant light, rather than the projection of a burning bulb. She had a kind of face perfect for film acting—mobile, expressive, and malleable. It took on any shape the makeup artist chose. Her hair could be arranged in any style demanded. Her features composed and recomposed themselves on a director's or producer's demand. She could be anything, any woman at all. She was a find.

She had worked at it. Growing up in tenements with a single mother, even at a very young age, even when she couldn't get the money to go to the pictures, which was most of the time, she sat outside the cinema and stared at the posters, imagining a world free of the sounds of fighting in the next room at home and the sounds of sweatshop machinery she associated with her mother, a world free of men and women begging on the street, a world silent but for the appropriate piano accompaniment. The young Rose had papered part of the wall of the room she shared with her mother with photographs from old fan magazines she'd scrounged from trash cans.

After a few years, the movies were no longer silent, but they were still quieter than any place Rose had ever known.

She is a star now, and in the year leading up to her marriage, the studio puts her to work in five pictures—the bosses are worried that she will fall pregnant after her marriage, and they want to get as much out of her as possible beforehand. She plays tough-talking sexy broads (twice), a treacherous femme fatale, a tragically fallen woman, and a touchingly pathetic waif. She often dies at the end. While she is working on the last picture, playing the touchingly pathetic and consumptive waif, Leo comes to visit her on the set.

She is glad to see him—despite all the work, she has very few friends and no family in this city. She thinks of herself as a mascot, whatever the equivalent of a Shabbos goy would be among the goyim themselves, a girl playing dress-up with clothing much too big for her. Shylock's daughter in the perfect garden during an evening made for ill-fated romance, she who pawned her mother's ring and broke her father's heart.

She thinks she looks very beautiful as this girl, a young thing with long black hair and very pale skin who is driven out onto the streets by a cruel, jealous mother. She runs over to Leo and kisses him on the mouth, but he pulls back, holding her at arm's length, and stares at her in silence. Finally he opens his wallet and shows her a photograph. It is of his daughter. She has seen it before, but now she realizes that in the makeup and wig she is uncannily like the girl in the photograph. Leo stares at her accusingly, as though she'd had some hand in this.

"I'm sorry," she says.

The director smirks.

The wedding was simple and brief and it took place on the same day as Nivia's commencement. Leo had wanted to watch his only daughter graduate, but she had asked him not to come; she could not stomach the thought of her classmates' quickened breath at the sight of her father. In his turn, Leo asked Nivia not to come to his wedding, in order to keep her as far as possible from the limelight.

As Nivia received her diploma, Leo slid a gold ring onto Lily's finger; as the headmistress shook Nivia's hand, Leo kissed his bride.

When Lily meets Nivia for the first time, she cannot look away; Nivia is the most beautiful thing she has ever seen. She almost reaches to touch Nivia's sharp, square jawline, her dark lips, the indent at the base of her strong pale throat. But she doesn't. She doesn't touch her stepdaughter at all.

Lily and Nivia, much to Leo's pleasure, get along like a house on fire. Lily feels braver, less lonely, and together they go to zoos, shows, movies. Nivia loses her glacial pallor as well as the sobriety she had always thought defined her character. She feels almost giddy.

When Lily makes love to Leo it hurts her, and this is the secret of her love for him. He makes her feel pain and she craves it, he makes her beg for it, and it feels right, but not only right, she feels her blood bursting in ecstasy, the velocity of her fall rushing through her skin, she feels herself ripped open and in burning convulsions. Leo ties her so tightly that livid red lines burn on her wrists for hours afterward and beats her until she cries and still it isn't enough. Still something eats away at her from the inside out, something that she fears will eventually crack and destroy the masterpiece that she constructs in the mirror every day.

Nivia eschews makeup, but Lily finds her more beautiful every day and every night.

One afternoon Lily finds Nivia asleep in the sun in the backyard, her black hair pulled sharply away from her white face, her lips deep red in the sunlight. Her strong-featured face reminds Lily of a woman she had met years ago, when she was first starting out as a model and was still Rose, who had taken her to a bar in Greenwich Village where she had drunk wine and danced, whom her mother had forbidden her to see again. "Darling," her mother had said. "There is no future in this. It's as easy to fall in love with a rich man as anybody else. Catch a rich husband, be settled, be happy." Rose did not argue. She knew that when her mother said that she had eaten dinner at work and so was cooking only for Rose, it really meant that her mother was not eating dinner at all to save money, and she also knew that it would break her mother's heart if Rose revealed she knew. So Rose could not argue with her mother, not about anything.

But here, now, having caught a rich husband, Lily is almost overwhelmed with the desire to curl up next to Nivia. Instead, she takes Nivia's face in her hands and kisses her slowly on her red lips.

Nivia opens her eyes and smiles.

Lily could watch Nivia smile, could kiss her again, the story could end here, end happily with stepmother and stepdaughter stepping out of those roles and into each other's arms.

And it almost does. Lily kisses Nivia again, but this time when they part it is to see that Leo has come into the backyard and is watching them with not a muscle moving in his face.

Lily leaps up and runs into the house, away from Nivia, past Leo, up to her private room, the small studio with her vanity and makeup and mirror. She tries to repaint her face, repair her lipstick, but her hands are shaking and she loathes the sight of her own face, so finally she hangs a towel over the mirror and curls up on the chaise longue under a blanket. She thinks incoherently about killing Nivia so she could be at peace again, a cold porcelain peace behind her makeup, and then she thinks no, that's wrong, Nivia is not the problem, Lily herself is the problem, she is the one who cannot be content even when she has everything. She thinks of her mother telling her to be grateful for the food on her plate, but her mother is speaking a different language, a harsher language than the one Lily speaks now, and calling her a different name as well, not even the name she had when first she came to this golden town, but her first, earliest name, the name she had before the fever.

She cannot remember that language; she can barely remember

that name. The problem is in herself, she should kill herself, but she is too tired to do anything more than hold her arms up, hold them out to the malekh hamoves.

In the backyard, Nivia slowly and deliberately empties a watering can onto some flowers. She does not meet her father's eyes. She cannot bear to look at him. For the first time, he looks old. Leo does not demand that she go, but he does not ask her to stay, either. She goes inside to pack and Leo puts her on the Super Chief that evening. It is worse than when she left her first school. She leaves no message for Lily, and Lily does not come down from her private room.

Leo and Lily have never spoken of what he saw in the garden. Perhaps his heart is broken. He and Lily are civil to each other, but days and then weeks go by without either one seeing the other. He never hurts her anymore, he never makes love to her at all. One day he leaves for Ireland to film a swashbuckling historical romance in glorious Technicolor, and Lily knows that he will start to sleep around again, with his costar or perhaps a local boy or both. She doesn't care. She hasn't heard anything from Nivia, not even a postcard. Not even good-bye.

Leo has exchanged a few letters with Nivia. He is her father, after all. She is fine, and far away in New York City, where she lives the bohemian life, writing poetry and spending her evenings in Greenwich Village's bars and cafés. She has bobbed her hair and has a different woman for every night of the week—her father's daughter—but her heart is ice. For money, she writes novels whose lurid covers show cruel brunettes staring possessively at soft, melting blondes. Both brunettes and blondes are in brassieres. Many of them have wicked, unloving stepmothers.

Lily continues to work. She is not pregnant. She is starring in a romantic comedy set in New York's demimonde, and her scenes are the only social interaction she has all day. She has no one to talk to—even the skeleton staff at Leo's mansion look past her, or through her. One evening she stays late on the set and falls asleep alone on a fake stoop in front of a building front in a faux Greenwich Village on a back lot soundstage.

She wakes up on the genuine, cold stone stoop outside the building that contains Nivia's flat. Nivia is standing in front of her, holding a bag of groceries. When she recognizes her stepmother, her face becomes even whiter than usual and the paper bag slips from her grasp. Lily helps her pick up the groceries and follows her into her apartment with her hands full of apples.

Nivia locks the door and waves her hands vaguely at Lily. "I thought I shouldn't see you," she said. "Dad said you weren't well. I've been so cold without you."

Lily strokes Nivia's short black hair. "Your hair is a mess, my love." So Lily combs her hair.

Lily touches the ribbons crisscrossing the back of Nivia's dress. "Your ribbons are tangled, my love." So Lily untangles and reties Nivia's ribbons.

Lily pauses, afraid to speak or move, not wanting to take her hands from Nivia's waist. Nivia is afraid to breathe, afraid that if she inhales too deeply, Lily's hands will slip away. Finally, she turns around.

"This is for you," she says, holding a rough red winesap apple in the palm of her hand. Lily closes her eyes and bites into the apple. It is painfully tart, moist, and earthy. She can taste the roots of the tree in the juice of the apple. She kisses Nivia's temples, her forehead, her mouth, and the taste of Nivia's mouth is the taste of one hundred apples. Nivia kisses the cobwebs that Lily can no longer remember painting on her own face. There are ribbons and zippers and buttons and clumsiness and then just the two women murmuring with the pleasure of each other's skin. Lily feels her blood humming a deep chord and the motion of Nivia's hands and mouth is so beautiful, so beautiful that she feels herself shaking apart, falling from the inside out, and she knows Nivia can put her together again, more beautiful, stronger than ever she has been before.

"You're so beautiful," she gasps. "More beautiful than anyone else in all the world."

Nivia cries with happiness, and laughs, and says, "No, you are so beautiful, and I have always loved you, ever since I saw you."

Lily wakes up and she is still in the real Greenwich Village, still in Nivia's bed. She kisses Nivia's spine and the soft skin of her belly but Nivia is sleeping soundly and doesn't wake. She wraps herself in Nivia's clothing and inhales the scent.

Then she sees herself in the mirror.

The colors in Lily's mind become ash. She dresses herself haphazardly and walks slowly into the mirror. The glass opens up to receive her, pulling her in like swampland, like quicksand. She cannot breathe inside it. Then she finds her way out from the mirror and she is once again in her own room in Leo's mansion.

She sweeps all the bottles off her vanity, hurling them to the floor, at the walls, into the windows. She wrenches off one shoe and smashes the mirror.

She sits down amid the shards of glass and dripping stains and finds a broken jar of cold cream and some tissues. She begins, finally, to remove her makeup.

All mirrors, everywhere, are connected.

Safe in her small flat, Nivia slept on.

The mirror in Nivia's studio reflects a needle of sunlight directly onto her closed eyes. After a few minutes she wakes up and looks around for Lily.

Not here, she thinks, but the door is locked and her keys are still where she dropped them, near the pile of apples. She checks the shower in the small bathroom and finds nobody. She sits down and stares directly into the mirror.

"Where are you?" she asks.

And she gets an answer.

Nivia dresses herself and walks into the mirror.

She feels herself shattered into a hundred pieces, feels herself become needle-sharp shards driving into her own heart. The pain is almost unbearable and her thoughts scatter until all she remembers is that she is determined to go on.

Nivia finds herself in Lily's room, standing on shards of broken mirror-glass. She steps forward and vials and bottles crunch under her boots. The walls, papered with reviews and posters of Lily's own movies, are streaked with red and black. Lily herself sits disheveled at what remains of her vanity, a round frame with only a few bits of jagged glass still stuck around the edges, like a set of gaping jaws. She is wiping her face with cold cream.

"Lily," Nivia calls softly. Her lover doesn't seem to hear her, but goes on savagely stripping her skin. "Lily?" Nivia is frightened.

"That is not my name!" Lily spins around and—a blank, a space, a clear oval where her face should be. Her knotted hair curls wildly around empty air. "I—I don't know my name!"

"Rose," says Nivia. She steps forward and, closing her eyes, she finds Rose's mouth with her fingers. Keeping her eyes closed, Nivia kisses Rose and colors flow from her mouth. When she opens her eyes, Rose's face, her true face shimmers like a pool of water in a rainstorm, and then settles. Her face is plain. She looks tired.

"I can't do this," says Rose.

"You can," says Nivia. "Dad won't mind. He'll get over it. He's done worse. He's done worse to me." Each sentence is a lie.

"Not that, not just that." Rose shakes her head. "I—I—"

Nivia starts to panic. "It doesn't matter. It doesn't matter, we don't have to be together, you could just leave, come back to New York, we'll just be friends again, all this makeup, you could paint, I'll help you, you'll be fine, you—"

"I—I—I—" Rose is whispering, looking wildly around her, staring at the gaping maw where the mirror used to be. Finally she stops, shakes her head, and looks at Nivia again. "No." Her face smooths over and Nivia is too frightened to scream as Lily's face becomes, for an instant, a mirror, and Nivia sees her own horrified eyes, her own mouth straining to scream, before Lily shudders and dies, and her face in death is nothing familiar.

"Rose," Nivia whispers, and lifts her eyes to the mirror on the vanity, which is once again whole, unmarked, flawless.

Leo comes home to Hollywood to bury his young wife. He is showing his age at last. Within a few years he is being cast in fatherly and then grandfatherly roles. He doesn't mind. He still has the odd fling here and there, but he is content to be a father, in the end, and he is proud of Nivia and how she has turned out. He knows that she has not had an easy time of it, being his daughter.

Nivia takes Lily's mirror back to New York and sets it up in the corner of her small flat, where it changes with every person who gazes at it. Eventually she falls in love again, because that is what the living do, and each time, each time it is a miracle.

THE
REVENANT

The revenant is the one who comes back. The revenant comes back from the dead, but home is gone, so all that is left is haunting. And the revenant is a fantasy that our emotions and will are powerful enough to overcome even death. The revenant tells us that all is not dust and ashes, our pain persists, our pain *matters*. That we can leave a mark on the spaces and people we knew, we can force them to witness our suffering. Our rage. The revenant comes back, because even death cannot blunt the edge of our thirst for revenge, cannot salve our wounds. Because there is no solace for what has been lost, even in death.

We all die in the end, and sometimes we die in pieces, not all at once. Like phantom limbs—phantoms, revenants, only come into being once something has died. The arm, the eye, the breast, once vivid and pulsing with blood—for the blood is the life—is no longer part of you, it has died, but its pain remains. Often the phantom limb feels like it is in a distorted, painful position. The sensations are not only pain; sometimes someone with a phantom limb will feel as if they are gesturing with the missing part, or try to pick something up with a hand no longer attached. The literature tells us that phantom pain usually decreases in frequency and intensity as time goes by, as the death of the body part recedes further and further into the past.

There is something missing from me. Sometimes I forget it's gone, and try to use it, like I see other people doing. But you can't hold a teacup with a phantom hand, and soon enough I am reminded of what is missing.

Here is a girl. She is sixteen years old, but not the sexy sixteen of television and movies. She still wears the clothing her mother picks out for her. She is skinny and gangly. She doesn't wear makeup. Her hair is a mess. She likes science fiction and watches a lot of BBC shows like *Doctor Who* and *Blake's 7*. She has a group of friends, geeky, just like her, although she is beginning to fall in love with punk rock and they are not. She is reasonably happy.

This will not last long.

If you are a married forty-five-year-old man who notices that a teenage girl has a crush on you, there is a variety of things you might think and do.

You might think, *This girl is young enough to be my daughter,* and stay away from her. You know this is nothing but trouble waiting to happen.

You might talk to her, hear about her father's recent desertion, and see the desperation in her eyes. You could then be straight with her, tell her that what she wants isn't what she thinks it is, and you won't do it.

You might just enjoy flirting with her. There's nothing wrong with that, after all, and everybody deserves a bit of fun.

Or you might have her give you a blow job in the urine-soaked hallway of the apartment building where she is living, and if you do that, it really doesn't matter what you were thinking.

You're an asshole.

In the 1970s, a folk practice never before seen sprung up across the United States. Teenage girls assured each other that if you turned off all the lights in the bathroom, and brought in a lit candle, and chanted "Bloody Mary" three times while staring into the mirror, Bloody Mary would come out and wreak horrible violence, drinking their blood, scratching their eyes out, or sometimes, taking revenge on those who had wronged them. Sometimes.

Alan Dundes, the venerable folklore scholar, theorized that this practice has something to do with anxieties about menstruation and all it symbolizes. And maybe he was correct. But maybe not. Maybe the blood drawn by Bloody Mary isn't a metaphor for sexual maturity, or womanhood, or anything like that. Maybe it's exactly what it seems, the blood of undirected rage, of violence. After all, adolescent girls have a lot to be angry about.

Of course, there is no Bloody Mary in the mirror. Everybody knows that. All you ever get in a mirror is a reflection yourself, captured pieces of your own soul.

Phantom limb pain can be treated by watching yourself in the mirror moving the missing limb into a more comfortable position (remember, in the mirror, left is right and right is left). It seems genuinely to work.

I have looked into many mirrors in my time. Bathroom mirrors, subway windows, plate glass shop windows, dressing-room mirrors, but I have never chanted "Bloody Mary." Not yet.

* * *

The same girl, a year later, under a mask of liquid eyeliner and bright red lipstick. She spends two hours every morning blow-drying her hair straight. She wears Lycra miniskirts and torn fishnet stockings. She looks absurdly young and almost feral. She has thrown all her geeky science-fiction books away and the group of friends has long since expelled her from their ranks. She comes home at five in the morning with beer and whiskey on her breath. Her schoolwork lies untouched.

I've never had a romantic relationship that's lasted longer than a handful of months. Well, twenty years ago, I had a long-distance relationship that lasted a year and a half. It ended with my partner saying, "I think of you more as a best friend than a lover," and breaking up with me, and I thought it was pretty rich given that we'd been having sex for quite some time with every evidence that he had enjoyed it, but he's not the only one to have said that. They can't quite articulate what's missing, these partners. They think I'm an awesome person, and I am so important to them, and they love me. They're just not *in love* with me. They don't feel *romantic* about me. The sex is awesome, they assure me, that's not it. It's something else. They can't quite put their finger on it. They don't know why.

I know why. Don't bother trying to find her; she's not there.

If you are a forty-five-year-old married man and a teenage girl has a crush on you, here is an easy way to captivate her: take her seriously. Almost nobody takes teenage girls seriously. If you do—if you sit and listen to her and respond to her interests, her likes and dislikes, as though she were a real person with real, legitimate thoughts and opinions, she will be yours.

It helps, of course, if you have had interesting experiences to tell her about. If she likes punk rock, for instance, and you were in a band that played CBGB and Max's Kansas City back in the day, you can be sure that she will want to hear all about it. While you are telling her, she will gaze at you with wide, impressed, admiring eyes.

If you are the sort of man who is doing this, you should try not to pay attention to the fact that they bear a striking resemblance to the eyes of a child.

Here is what happened: one morning over the summer she was sixteen, she woke up late and staggered into the bathroom to brush her teeth, and overheard her parents talking. Her mother happily told her father that she was off to buy him a present for their twentieth wedding anniversary. Her father responded by announcing that he had met someone else and was leaving her. The girl sat on the edge of the bathtub in her pajamas and listened to the conversation. Her father was very calm and collected, which was unusual. Usually he stormed and raged during fights. Her mother was neither calm nor collected. She sobbed hysterically, and her daughter hated her for it. It was embarrassing, was what it was, and frightening also.

During a lull in the conversation, the girl crept back into her bedroom and got dressed in the clothing her mother had picked out for her: a white T-shirt, pink shorts, and white sandals. She looked clunky, with too-long limbs. When she finally went out into the living room, her mother was immobile on the couch and weeping. Her father gave her twenty dollars and told her to go away. She took the money, bought some women's magazines, and went to a local café.

There's more to the story, of course. Her father does not stay this calm. Eventually her mother stops crying and gets up off the couch. And that café isn't there anymore.

The neighborhood I grew up in is almost unrecognizable now. I used to have friends who weren't allowed to come visit; it was that kind of neighborhood when I was young. But it was a mix of working-class families and bohemian artists and musicians and there were baby supply shops and there were dive bars. Now it's very chichi and only stockbrokers and rock stars can afford to live there. And my mother, whose apartment is rent-stabilized.

But I can still see echoes as I walk down the street. I still know where everything used to be, so I wait until late one night, after dark, and I leave my four-year-old son with a sitter and head down to Avenue A, which is of course alive with light and noise at that hour, even on a Tuesday. So I go into one of the side streets, where a certain café used to be, an Irish café where I ate brown bread with butter and drank tea while my mother sobbed on the couch, and I lean in close to the plate glass of the jewelry shop occupying the space now.

And I whisper, "Bloody Mary. Bloody Mary. Bloody Mary."

There is a pause, pregnant with the possibility of my dead self reborn. And into it, I whisper, "Wait."

And then I go home, and pay the babysitter, and check on my

sleeping son, and slip back into my own bed, and wait for him to wake me up in the morning.

The thing you want to remember about teenagers is that while they like to act cynical and like they've seen it all, they're really very naïve. As you can imagine, this is quite an advantage if you are a married forty-five-year-old man and trying to seduce one. All sorts of lines that would send a grown woman into gales of laughter or cause her to roll her eyes at you will have their full *romantic* effect on a teenage girl. You can tell her, for instance, that she resembles the girlfriend you had when you were eighteen, and she won't snort scornfully at you, even if she is a New York City Jewess and you grew up in southeast Ireland, and the likelihood of you having known anyone who looked like her in your youth is close to nil. You can even stare deeply into her eyes and tell her that age doesn't matter, the only thing that really matters is how two people feel about each other, and she won't shake her head in disgust and immediately dismiss it as a pathetically transparent attempt at emotional manipulation, to say nothing of nonsense. Instead, it will work.

Years later, she will come to regret this, and feel deeply ashamed of her own naïveté.

But you needn't worry about that. If you are the sort of middle-aged married man who is doing this sort of thing, no doubt you won't.

Who doesn't love the first few weeks or months of a romantic relationship, those giddy, heady times when you're drunk on love and sex and the new partner seems perfect, and all you want is to stay in their arms all day and all of the night, and then maybe wander hand in hand, presenting each other with flowers and staring deeply into each other's eyes over glasses of champagne at brunch and maybe take long walks on beaches?

I don't. You can't trust all that. People say things they turn out not to mean. The first few weeks for me are full of painful disbelief. "I love you," they say. "You don't have to say that." "I love you, though." "It's okay if you don't, if you want to go on dating other people, we haven't agreed to be exclusive." "I love *you*." But they don't mean it. Because a few months later, *I* really fall in love. When I feel secure, when I feel like I can trust them, really truly trust them, and then it's like relaxing into a deep warm bath, and I finally allow myself to believe every word they said. By that time, they're no longer so enamored, and it's unfair, because they *said*, and I believed them, and now they're saying they didn't mean "I love you" like *that*, they didn't mean *romantic* love, they meant camaraderie or some such nonsense, and all the water turns to ice and I'm trapped, I can't move.

There's something missing from me, some piece of my soul that just isn't there anymore and I can't believe in the champagne and the long walks on the beach while they are happening, I can't trust the—what's the word?—oh yes, the *limerence*. The missing piece, she died a long time ago. I was so young. She was so young.

She loses most of her friends after her parents' split—after all, they're only kids, too, and don't know how to deal with her constant simmering tension and anger. She spends school lunchtimes huddled by herself at the top of the elementary school jungle gym listening to punk rock on her Walkman. So she finds refuge in a downtown bar that doesn't take the drinking age too seriously.

The bar hosts a local band on Saturday nights. It's made up of men who've been on the scene for years, men in their forties. The music is good and the bar is packed and she's heard that Joe Strummer used to hang out there when he lived in the city. Eventually she develops a crush on the singer, who has a certain amount of seedy, dissipated charisma.

At first he doesn't pay her any mind. Not only is he much older than her, and married, but he also has a mistress. She is only four years older than the girl in question, with long black hair, perfectly arched eyebrows, and Celtic knotwork tattoos around her upper arms. She is an artist. So the singer doesn't have the time or the inclination to notice the girl. But you shouldn't mistake this for an ethical or moral choice on his part. Right now she is still gawky, awkward, and gangly. Eventually she will stop straightening her hair and wear slightly longer skirts. Eventually she will become lithe, even somewhat appealing. Eventually his mistress will move to another country.

I am the belle, they say, of Avenue A,
And if you're strolling down that way,
You're pretty sure to see me on the street.
'Cos I'm something of a walker,
And the fact that I'm a "corker"
Is the talk of every copper on the street.
Billy McNeill, he is my steady,
And you'll always find him ready
For a scrapping match or any sort of fight.
He's the bouncer down at Clary's
And he says of all the fairies,

I'm the only one he thinks is out of sight!
Get off the earth, and don't attempt to stay!
'Cos I'm a queen, the belle of Avenue A.

—Safford Waters, "The Belle of Avenoo A" (1895)

One thing you should prepare yourself for, if you are a middle-aged married man bedding a teenage girl, is the difference between porn-movie virgins and an actual real live teenage girl who has never had sex before, or even been kissed before you met her. In porn, or perhaps in your fantasies, a virgin is dewy, pliable, and wide-eyed, given to making unsolicited gasps at the size of your cock, amenable to your every guidance and suggestion.

A real teenage girl, however, one who hasn't had sex before, is considerably different. For one thing, she will be painfully self-conscious and extraordinarily anxious about what you think of her. She will not know what she is supposed to be doing at any given moment or how she is supposed to be feeling. She will very likely freeze up.

Of course, you can make this sort of thing work to your advantage. You, after all, will know what you are doing, what you like, and what you want, and she will not be in a position to question you or object. After all, she won't want you to think she's not cool. She doesn't want to be a disappointment to you. But be aware that she's probably not enjoying herself, she's quite likely numb with terror and embarrassment, she's dissociating like mad. Of course, that may be precisely what you want.

She does know one thing, however. She does not like it when

you push her head down. I have never met a woman who does. But you don't have to care about that.

When the revenant emerges from the plate glass shop window onto the East Village, she is in the form of a young woman, of course, the Belle of Avenue A, as the song goes. Poor girl! She must be so confused. The city has changed around her so drastically. Well, that is what cities do, of course, but without even Trash and Vaudeville as a reliable landmark, how will she find her away around?

Where is she going? Well, I imagine she has an appointment, don't you?

For so long I felt only guilt and shame and humiliation about that part of my life, for so long. But revenants come back thirsting for vengeance. And blood as well, of course. And they have already died, so there is nothing left to lose.

Still, Manhattan is mostly a grid, and the street signs are the same, so I think the revenant corner of my soul will get her bearings soon enough. I think. And when she does, she'll head for SoHo.

The girl becomes friends with the mistress, which complicates her feelings to no end. Does she have a crush on the man, his mistress, or both? She certainly thinks she is beautiful, with her long black hair and her complicated tattoos, and she admires her hard-bitten attitude and her self-reliance. The mistress thinks of her as a kid sister.

She always knew that the girl was still—in all the ways that mattered—a child.

But eventually she moves away, across the ocean, leaving the girl to her own devices.

The girl doesn't have many devices to speak of, not now. Later, she will. She will have friends, plans, projects, a career she loves. She's good at all that, and she's lucky. But not now. Now all there is is the loneliness, the black tar pits of self-loathing, the bar, the band, the man. If only we could go to her and reassure her that there will be more, much more for her. Perhaps we can. But then this would be a very different story, wouldn't it? Best, then, to leave her to her own devices.

Soon, very soon, after the mistress moves away, the band's singer approaches the girl. Perhaps "approach" is the wrong word.

Sooner or later, the question will arise of how you can get rid of this smitten teenage girl. If you have not sufficiently prepared yourself for the experiences described in our last tutorial, it may well arise the first time you take her to bed. It may arise the first time you take her to bed in any case, if you are that sort of man. You will want to be prepared.

One option is, of course, to talk to her. Play the guilt-ridden husband. Tell her that you adore your wife and you simply can't go on in this way. Of course, it is hard to actually pull this off if you have been fucking a woman only four years older than this girl for several years without displaying a single pang of conscience.

Another option is to simply ignore her. It is easier to do this if you have been growing tired of her and dialing down the level of your attentions for some time. Be this as it may, simply ignoring her the next time you see her may not be quite enough. She may first react by going to ever greater lengths to coax a smile from you, and you will have to remain steadfast in your disdain. You must behave in such a way as to make her wonder if she was hallucinating your earlier pursuit of her. If you persevere in this, she will come to be completely off-balance; if you play your cards right, she will even blame herself for having been so foolish as to expect you to care about her. Remember, she has never done this before and she has no standard against which to measure your behavior. You are her reality check. This gives you an immense advantage.

There is one danger to this approach that you should be aware of. Teenage girls are, by definition, immature. If you flirt with other young women while standing directly in front of her, she may haul off and kick you on the ankle, causing you to fall over in front of the other young woman.

If she does, it will be the only part of this experience that she does not later regret.

The Belle finds SoHo more familiar than she did the East Village; it is the same, only more so. More gentrified, louder, more crowded. But the grid hasn't changed, the street names are still the same, and nobody pays attention to a twenty-year-old girl wearing bright red lipstick, combat boots, and a miniskirt making her way down Mercer Street. She seems a little dazed, a little disoriented, a little out of place, but she is not what has changed. She has not changed at all. She looks vulnerable. And she used to be vulnerable. But now she's dead, and she's come back, so what is there left to hurt her?

She drifts into Fanelli's, a bar on Prince and Mercer that's been there forever. Well, since 1922, and that's close enough. They used to serve good mussels, she remembers vaguely, and then remembers that she doesn't eat anymore, not food.

And then she sees him sitting at the bar. He's drinking a pint of Bass, as always. He looks . . . older, but in the bar's dim light it's not as obvious as it would be in sunlight. Strawberry blond hair is now mostly white. The lines in his face are deeper than they used to be. Even so, he looks exactly the same.

He hates this bar, has hated it for years, but it's so close to home, it's hard to eschew it completely. And the mussels are good, though he's not eating them tonight. He's just in for a pint before he goes home, before he spends the evening with his wife, doing . . . whatever it is they do together. I actually have no idea, so neither does the Belle. He's almost finished, almost ready to put on his motorcycle jacket and leave, when he sees her.

What is she doing here? he thinks, flashing back twenty-five years, before realizing that's ridiculous, that can't be her. She'd have to be . . . middle-aged by now, in her mid-forties, probably, just about the age he was when they first met, and hadn't he heard through the grapevine that she had a kid now? Something like that. Even if she still dressed the same, her hair should be threaded with white, her own face should now be lined, and surely she wouldn't still be so slim, her limbs wouldn't still be so coltish. That girl can't be her.

But he looks again, and they make eye contact, and it is her. She looks a little wan and forlorn, and he almost feels—not sorry, what's the word? *Responsible*—for her. Perhaps he should approach her, make sure she's all right? But then he remembers the hours and hours of couples therapy that was the price of keeping his marriage intact, and he remembers how he never even brought her up, because why bother? She was a mild fling, some fooling around in taxis, one or two trips upstairs to the room she rented on Ludlow Street, not worth mentioning, not when he and his wife had years and years of his infidelity with his mistress to unpack. Nothing serious. No bones broken. So there's no need to acknowledge her now, not so close to home, not when he's on his way home to his wife, and he finishes putting on his jacket and he picks up his guitar case and heads for the door. But to get there he has to walk past her, and as he does, she puts out her hand and grabs his shoulder in a far more decisive gesture than she'd ever allowed herself all those years ago. She spins him around with more strength than he ever thought she possessed.

Revenants are strong, for they have overcome death, and draw on their will alone for power. She could throw him into the wall if she wanted to. But that's not what she wants right now.

So they are face-to-face.

"Hey," he says. "How've you been?" It's a ridiculous question because she clearly hasn't aged at all, time hasn't passed for her, she's exactly the same as she was, but he's freaking out a little and is playing for time.

She nods. "Come with me." She transfers her grip to his arm above his elbow and stands up.

"What are you doing here?" he asks. She doesn't answer. "I can't go with you," he says, but she's strong-arming him out the door into the dim evening, down the block and around the corner, into a niche sheltered by some scaffolding, and he can barely keep up.

What do I want the Belle to do to him there? He wants . . . what he has always wanted, until he didn't want her anymore. I would like her to lean in and suck all the love that has been given him out of his soul. I would like her to breathe in and strip him of his decades-long marriage, of his memories of first love in Ireland, of his time with his mistress, of every significant romantic relationship he's ever had, and then to release him, let him go home to an empty house and a life without the kind of love he took so much for granted. I want her to take from him what he took from me.

But don't be ridiculous, that's not possible, not even for a revenant. What do you think this is, Azkaban? And revenants don't come back to rip away your memories and love.

Revenants come back for vengeance.

Revenants come back for blood.

Why now? you may be wondering. Why now? Why, after so many years, did I call her out for vengeance now, when he's an old man already? Why not earlier?

Trauma is suffering that will not stay in its temporal position. It comes for us long after it happens, intrudes on us when we're least expecting it. Memories flash before my eyes and my body physically recoils, I turn my head away and shiver from shame. Sex is so fraught with anxiety that it chokes me and I cannot speak. Trauma recurs, time and time again, pushes you into repeating patterns you thought you had long since put to bed.

Why now? Why not just let it go?

I will not let it go because it will not let me go. Twenty-five years later blow jobs are still fraught with shame and anxiety. Twenty-five years later I still occasionally have a memory that causes me to physically pull away in an effort to shake it. Suffering shared is suffering halved, they say, and what is vengeance but suffering shared?

Let me tell you a story. Recently, I had dinner with some old friends, friends whose daughter I used to babysit. She's eighteen now, and giddy in love with her first girlfriend. Her eyes glowed and she blushed as she told me all about her new love. Her skin shone with happiness and youth and innocence. And I remembered the child I had taken care of fourteen years ago, so little, so vulnerable. How I held her hand to protect her when we crossed the street. How I gave her piggyback rides. How she cuddled on my lap while I read to her. And she is still that little girl, glowing with happiness.

What kind of monster would have pushed that child in front of the oncoming cars instead of holding her hand and guiding her to safety?

What kind of monster would see that glow, that potential for happiness, that trust, and instead of treating it tenderly, transmute it into humiliation and shame? Smear it with shit? Just to get his rocks off?

Monsters walk among us.

And I thought, looking at the teenager who used to be the child I protected and played with and put to bed, I thought, once, I must have been like that. Once, I must at least have had the potential to be like that. To trust like that.

Monsters walk among us.

And in that moment, I felt rage.

When the Belle emerges from under the scaffolding, leaving a crumpled, distorted heap behind her, there is blood on her hands, blood under her fingernails, and blood smeared around her mouth, but that kind of thing doesn't arouse much notice in New York City, not even now. What people do notice is her weaving walk, her air of confusion, and they steer clear, because an unpredictable person is a dangerous person, even if she is only a young woman.

The Belle is confused. Why is she still animate? Why is she still alive? A revenant that has achieved its goal is allowed to pass on, according to all the stories. That is the point. Is there more to her goal than she thought? What is she doing still here?

But she feels a familiar tug, the same tug that brought her to SoHo, and this time it's pulling her to Brooklyn.

That's the secret, of course. That piece of my soul, of my self, he's not the one who killed her. He never had that kind of power. Only one person had that kind of power.

I killed her. I killed the Belle of Avenue A.

I had tried first to kill my sexuality, my desire, on the grounds that if I never felt desire again, I would never fall for that kind of manipulation, and indeed, it went dormant for years at a time, only to reemerge at unpredictable intervals. But I met with only mediocre success; I tend to dissociate during sex, to find myself somehow *not there*, unable to feel anything at all. My libido vanishes for years at a time, without any indication of its reasons. I have never quite shaken the sense that sex is something I am obliged to do under certain circumstances, whether or not I feel like it. But my desire had the wiry strength of a weed, and I could never uproot it completely.

So I killed the Belle instead, so I wouldn't believe in the first flush of love again, so I couldn't be taken in by *romantic* notions, and that worked. She was already injured, and suffering, and she was willing to die. When I smothered her, she barely even put up a fight. And I thought I was protecting myself.

As she walks slowly over the Brooklyn Bridge (revenants do not take taxis and they certainly don't crowd onto the subway),

I wonder what will happen when she reaches me. Will I have to kill her again? Will her teeth meet in my throat?

Or instead, will I hold out my arms to her and bid her come near and let me comfort her, let me smooth her hair and wash the blood off her face, let her cry in my embrace? Will I give her what every revenant wants—affection, apologies, a loving welcome home?

BURNING
GIRLS

In America, they don't let you burn. My mother told me that.

When we came to America, we brought anger and socialism and hunger. We also brought our demons. They stowed
away on the ships with us, curled up in the small sacks
we slung over our shoulders, crept under our skirts. When
we passed the medical examinations and stepped for the first
time out onto the streets of granite we would call home, they
were waiting for us, as though they'd been there the whole
time.

The streets were full of girls like us at every hour of day
and night. We worked, took classes, organized for the unions,
talked revolution at the top of our voices in the streets and
in the shops. When we went out on strike, they called us the
fabrente maydlakh, the burning girls, for our bravery and dedication and ardor, and the whole city ground to a halt as the so-
ciety ladies who wore the clothing we stitched came downtown
and walked our lines with us. I remember little Clara Lemlich,
leaping to her feet at a general meeting and yelling, "What are
we waiting for? Strike! Strike! Strike!" Her curly hair strained

at its pins as if it might burst out in flames, the fire that burns without consuming.

I was raised in Bialystok. I was no stranger to city life, not like those girls from the shtetls who grew up surrounded by cows and chickens and dirt. Though I had my fair share of that as well, spending months at a time with my bubbe, who lived in a village too small to bother with a real name, three days' journey from the city.

My sister, Shayna, she stayed in the city with our dressmaker mother and shoemaker father and learned to stitch so fine it was as though spiders themselves danced and spun at her command. Not me, though. I learned how to run up a seam, of course, so that I could be a help to Mama when I was home, but my apprenticeship was not in dressmaking. Mama could see from the beginning that I was no seamstress.

Mama didn't have the power herself, but she could find it in others. Eyes like awls, my mama had. Sharp black eyes that went right through you. When I was born she took one look at me and pronounced, "Deborah—the judge."

When Mama saw what I was going to be, she knew that I would have to spend as much time with my grandmother as I did with her, and so when I was four years old, my father rented a horse and cart and drove me out to my bubbe's village. That first time, I sobbed all the way there as if my heart would break. Why would my mama and papa send me away? Why could I not stay with them as I always did? I imagined it had something to do with my mama's rounding belly, but I did not know what.

My bubbe was a zugerin in her village, one who leads the women in prayer at shul, and after only a few hours by her side

I was so happy to be with her that I barely noticed when Papa left. Over that summer and the ones that followed, she kept me by her side and taught me not only the proper rites but how to conduct myself toward other women, how to listen to what's not being said as well as what is. She was a witch, looking after the women of her village, because the kinds of troubles women have are not always the kinds you want to talk to the rabbi about, no matter how wise he is.

If her village made Bialystok look like a metropolis and we had to be afraid of the Cossacks, it was as close as a girl like myself could get to cheder, the Jewish schools where little boys began their education in Hebrew and reading Torah. Every day my grandma set me to learning Torah and the Talmud and even some Kabbalah. None of these are for girls, say the wise rabbis, but for the working of pious magic, what else can one do? I studied the sacred words and memorized the names of God and his angels, and I liked that best. Within a few years, I was able to help my bubbe as she wrote out amulets to preserve infants from the lilim and prayers for women whose men were wandering out in the world, peddling in each little town in order to keep their families in bread. I couldn't get away from the sewing, though. Still I had to sew simple shirts of protection to preserve those same peddlers from harm, and every time I pricked my finger and bled on the fabric, I had to start over again.

When I returned home after that first summer, Bubbe came with me, the first and last time she ever did so. She did not like the city, though she admitted it was safer for us than a town exposed to the wild like hers. And so the first birth I ever witnessed was that of my little sister, who from the very beginning was wreathed in dimples and golden hair. She blinked her green eyes up at Mama and smiled so bewitchingly that Mama smiled back and whispered, "Shayna meydle." So Shayna was her name.

I did not get the golden hair or green eyes, but then, Shayna did not get any of our bubbe's powers. When I examined myself that evening in my mama's hand mirror I saw sharp angles, even at four, coarse black hair, and eyes like Mama's. Eyes like ice picks. I was not an attractive child, not like Shayna.

But I had the power. I knew already that I could be useful.

The following summer, when Papa drove me to Bubbe's, I bounced up and down in my seat as though I were one of the horses and could speed the cart on its way. I did not like to think of pretty Shayna at home with our mama and not me, but my bubbe's house was where I was the favorite. My fondest memories are of sitting at her kitchen table writing out the names of angels and symbols of power while she praised my memory and confided that there was no shame in making up names and symbols when one ran out of traditional ones—for is it not true that all things are held in the mind of God, and so anything we create has been created already?

Less to my taste, but even more practical, were the lessons I learned from watching Bubbe's visitors. Women from the village came to see her, both the shayna yidn and the proste yidn. They came in and my grandmother would offer them coffee and talk to them as if they were old friends just come over to pass the afternoon. Then, usually, just as they were leaving, they would turn and say, as though they had almost forgotten, "Oh, Hannah, a puzzle for you," and my grandma would usher them back to the kitchen and listen intently as they poured out stories about sick children, women's illnesses, being with child when one more would be more than a woman could ever want. Most problems my grandma could solve with a jar of her broth, seasoned this way or that, but this last was always trickier, and was when Bubbe welcomed another pair of hands most. I could not manipulate her instruments as well as I liked with my smaller hands, but I could boil them and watch and learn. And when it was time for a baby to come, my smaller hands were a great help.

What was hardest for me to learn was tact.

Once when I was eight and I was studying the holy symbols and how best to combine them with the various names of God, a local woman, a nobody to my mind, a maidservant home for a visit, for heaven's sake, rushed into my grandma's cottage and stood there looking around her. I did not like her at all. Her stupid stuttering interrupted my thoughts and she looked like a lost cow as she stood there blinking, unable even to articulate her need. I scorned her, knowing in my child's way that I would never be at a loss for words like this, no matter my trouble.

"Well?" I asked her.

Nothing. She said nothing for a long minute and then she stuttered out my grandmother's name.

"Fine," I said. But instead of running to fetch my bubbe from the other room, I just stuck my head in and hollered, "Bubbe, another pregnant maid for you!"

Two things happened. One was that the girl burst into tears, and the other was that my grandma appeared in the kitchen and slapped my face so hard that it felt as if one of God's angels had smitten me. I landed on my tuchus.

"Dry your eyes, my darling," said my grandma to the girl, while I stood rubbing my jaw like an idiot. "And please forgive my granddaughter. She is sharp enough, but there is no heart in her chest, only a steel gear."

I ran out of the house and into the garden, where I climbed into my favorite spot in an old birch tree that my bubbe used for tea leaves and tar. Not pretty and no heart, only a steel gear. There was not much future for a girl like that, I thought. No marriage, certainly, and thus no children. No wonder my mama did not delight in me as she did in my sister. Papa loved me best, in his quiet way, but he did not have my mama's sharp eyes; most likely he just could not see my emptiness. I wept, feeling sorry for myself, but only a little. Well, I thought, if I cannot be pretty and I cannot be kind, I can be powerful. I *would* be powerful, and make everybody see it. More powerful than Bubbe, even.

Despite my renewed vow to study, I was not to learn anything for a week. Instead, I had to keep house as well as I could while my grandmother stood over me and harangued me.

"You think you are somebody special, a queen, maybe, to be so cruel to someone coming for help? Smart you are, and a witch you may be in time, but a zugerin, never, never so long as you keep like this! You will never command respect, and you will never be able to practice your skills, for nobody will come to you! People must come to us with trust, and if you must speak sharply to a girl you do it in private, so that she understands that you do it for her own good! Not hollering contempt like a Cossack!"

"I was not like a Cossack!" I said. "I hurt nobody!"

"So that girl was crying because she stubbed her toe? She's not the first to be taken in by the master of the house and she won't be the last, and anybody who comes for help should get a hearing and not be scorned by a child too young to lace her own boots!"

I cannot say that, after this incident, I felt kinder toward those visitors of my grandmother's whose problems were, I felt, of their own making, but I learned to school my face and my tongue and even to feel some compassion for their suffering. When I was at home, though, I would pull Shayna aside to tell her the gossip of

Bubbe's village. She would have been about four or five then, the age I was when first I went to my bubbe's, and she always wanted to know what it was I was doing.

"What am I doing?" I would toss my head. "What am I doing indeed but cleaning up the mistakes of dullards who should know better!"

Shayna's eyes grew wide. "What kind of mistakes?" She was at the age when she was always spilling her milk or tripping over nothing, and she had great sympathy with those who made mistakes, but I did not. After all, my grandmother rarely had to correct me more than once on the same matter.

"Foolish girls!" I told her. "Foolish girls who watch the horses and cows but don't know enough to keep their own legs closed if they don't want to foal or calve."

Shayna chewed on her lip. "Well," she said, "you can't keep your legs together while you're walking, or you'd fall. Do they fall a lot, like me?"

I tossed my hair again, annoyed to be talking to such a baby. "You don't know anything," I said. "Just like them."

But it was only to Shayna I would whisper such scornful things. To everybody else, and especially to my bubbe, I listened patiently and even kindly.

And so almost eight years passed, with Shayna learning to sew dresses from our mother and me learning how to use my powers from our bubbe. And then one evening, in the middle of winter, my best friend, Yetta, banged on the front door of our house, and when I answered, she pulled me out onto the street.

"It's Rifka," she said. "She's in trouble."

Rifka was Yetta's older sister, and I did not wonder what kind of trouble she was in. She had been almost engaged to a butcher's son, but they had fallen out over his attentions to another girl.

"Poor thing," I said, unthinking, and then Yetta smacked me, just lightly, but enough so that I paid attention.

"Don't give me 'poor thing'!" she said. "Everyone knows how you spend your summers, and I will not go to anyone who might tell Mama or Papa. If you are a friend to me, you will come help Rifka now!"

Of course, I was only too pleased to be asked. I collected my bag of tools and herbs that I had put together under my grandma's green eyes and set out, telling Mama that Yetta and I were going for a walk. Rifka was not far along—anxiety had made her careful, and I could have mixed up the powders she needed blindfolded, but she clasped me to her and wrung her hands as though I had moved heaven and earth. When she miscarried the following day, tears of joy ran down her face as I held her hand.

She did not tell her mama or papa, but she did tell her friends, and soon enough I was called upon for various illnesses and childbirths and other women's matters. It got so I could no longer go to my bubbe's for more than a month every year, for the women of Bialystok's Jewish Quarter could not do without me. I missed the idyllic months with my bubbe, but I was proud of my learning and new status. And I do not regret this! Learning and skill are things to be proud of; they are the stars that light the sky of one's lifetime.

By sixteen, I was bringing in as much money as my mother and sister combined. For not every family can afford dresses, but every family will have a sick child, or a distressed daughter.

When I did go to my bubbe's, I took over more and more of her work in order to give her some rest.

"I *do* manage without you," she'd say, as I'd come home late from sitting up with a child with whooping cough.

"Yes," I'd say, "but you shouldn't. I can hear your bones creaking from here."

I don't think she minded such comments as much as she pretended to. I think she was proud of me. She called me her good right hand. I was there with her when she fought the lilit at the bedside of Pearl, the butcher's wife. It was a strong demon with wild long hair and claws that stuck out from her fingers like nails from a plank of wood. She raged and raged outside our circle of protection. I knelt at Pearl's hips, supporting the coming baby with my hands while my grandmother chalked stronger and stronger charms of protection on the wall.

The lilit howled like a livid wind.

"Don't look!" I shouted to Pearl. "It's unclean! Think of your little one!"

Pearl shut her eyes tight and clutched the silver knife we had placed in her hands when labor started. She added her own voice to the whirlwind in the room while I slipped my hands inside to loosen the cord around the baby's neck. I felt it straining tight against my fingers.

"May the foolish woman who brought clothing for the new babe into her house before the birth be left with nothing but an armful of cloth!" shouted the lilit. "May she claw at the dirt like a dog, searching for her baby's bones! May she—"

"In the name of Eloe, Sabbaoth, Adonai, let your mouth fill with mud and your voice be stopped!" said my grandmother firmly, putting herself between Pearl and the demon. As she cut off the lilit's words, the cord loosened, and my grandmother went on to bind the lilit with the names of the heavenly host. Finally all was quiet and Pearl's baby spilled, healthy and ruddy, into my arms.

I held him up in triumph to the new mother, but Pearl's face was a mask of terror.

"What ails you?" I asked her. "All is well." Then I turned to follow her look and saw that although my grandmother had bound the lilit, she was deep in conversation with the creature when she should have been doing the work necessary to banish it. I handed the baby to his mother and turned to my grandmother.

"Look to your own children, Hannah," said the lilit, cutting her eyes at me. "You think she will thrive here? Trouble is coming to your daughter and her family in Bialystok."

"Bubbe, what are you doing? Banish the unclean thing and be done with it!"

My grandmother pursed her lips. "Deborah, tend to Pearl and her son. This creature and I are speaking."

"Then speak outside!" I told her. "Speak outside if you must speak to it!"

"Very rude," said the lilit, clacking her claws at me.

My grandmother held the door open pointedly, always keeping her body between the demon and the new baby. I waited for half an hour before she came back.

On the way home, I exploded in a way I only ever did with Shayna and with Bubbe. "What were you thinking, listening to a child-killer?! What filth did she pour into your ears?"

"All creatures have some knowledge," my bubbe said patiently, "and it's as well to find it out."

"Very wise," I said sharply, "but perhaps now I should find it out, too? What were you talking about?"

"The future," said my bubbe, and she refused to say any more.

I returned from that trip and found that my mother and Shayna had not been having an easy time of it. Business was slow. One day I found them together pinning up a dress onto a pattern. They didn't know I was there, and they were talking in low voices, intimately, in a way I'd shared with my bubbe but never with our mother. I became green with jealousy, and lingered in the doorway to listen.

"Pass me that pin, darling—ugh," said my mother, sitting back on her heels to look at her handiwork. "You know, when I was a girl, with a needle in your hand your life was golden. Always you would have work, always you could support your family."

"And so I shall!" said Shayna sunnily. She had long ago grown out of her clumsy phase and now everything she did was graceful and delicate. "Already you see the embroidery I do, Mama! The stitches so tiny, only an ant could see each one."

Mama pressed her hands to the small of her back. She was starting to show, and I was not the only one who'd noticed. "Well . . . no. Not anymore. Already you see us scraping and scrimping for business. The new factories open up and machines can do more work for less pay, and the factories do not hire us. I begin to think that my mother is right . . . perhaps we should send you and your sister over to America. They say there that Jews can work in factories as well as gentiles—indeed, that without us there would be no factories."

Shayna's face turned pale, and I was sure mine had, too. It was rare not to know a family that had sent a daughter or husband over to America, di goldene medine. Yetta's family owned a sweetshop, and even they had sent over Rifka. I had always thought it was because they had found out about her disgrace, but perhaps it was not. Money came every week, and letters, too. In America, Rifka wrote, children went to school together, Jews and gentiles, with no fees to pay and no limits on the number of Jews. There was not gold on the streets, and she lived with a family that had her sleep on a board placed on two chairs and made her do most of the housework, but still she sent home more money in a week than her parents could make in a month.

"Bubbe would not want that!" I cried. "How could you say so? How can you talk about sending away your own daughters?"

Mama was so surprised to see me that she nearly swallowed a pin. She coughed and said, "But she wrote to me about the idea. She didn't say anything to you?"

"Not last I saw her, and that was only a month ago."

"Well." Mama sighed. "My mother keeps secrets. She keeps secrets and she makes plans and catches us all in her net. Her own feet, too, sometimes, she tangles." She looked at me tenderly. "I have wanted to warn you sometimes, darling. You need to be careful of my mother's plans. Once when I was young she decided—"

I did not wait to hear what my bubbe had decided. "Bubbe would not send me away! She needs me!"

Mama frowned. "Well, I would never force either of my girls to go. But you should think hard about it, both of you. Bubbe has sent me a letter and she is unhappy with what she sees in store for our city. I shudder to think of any danger, and between that and the money. . . . Now, you go away, Deborah, go chatter with Yetta or brew up some broth. Your sister and I have work to do."

I wandered out into the street. It was true what Mama said, that business was not good for her and Shayna, but to go across the sea! It was not as if we lived in one of those places where, as Bubbe said, they killed you after every bad harvest. Bialystok was modern and the chief of police was a man of decency, who did not hold with the killing of Jews. Besides, our young activists had formed a self-defense league, and I would not have wanted to be on the wrong side of those knives and guns. I thought we were safe; at least, we did not fear every moment of every day.

I kicked sullenly at rocks until I wandered over to see Yetta, and then we played at singing games, which we could only do when Shayna was busy, because her voice sounded like a sick cat.

Later that year, Cossacks killed my grandmother.

My grandmother's village was too small for word to reach us before we visited. Papa and I found most of the village's houses destroyed. Just cottages, built of mud and straw. Easy to kick apart. Easier to burn.

Papa had grown up in a village like this one, and his face twisted as he surveyed the wreckage.

"Back into the cart, young one," he said. "We leave now." He didn't raise his voice, just spoke as if what he said was fact.

"Without burying Bubbe?" I said, trying to match his calm.

"Where is there to bury her? The shul and graveyard are destroyed. We will take her back with us. This is not a good place to be."

"Papa," I said. "Let us at least say Kaddish—surely we have enough time for that?" The wind blew my hair in my face.

We went inside and I laid my bubbe on a ragged old blanket, too worthless to bother taking. I cleaned her body with water from the well and closed her eyes, arranged her arms and legs decorously alongside her body, not all splayed out at odd angles like we found her. I do not think she had died from violence; I think the terror was too much for her heart. When I was finished, she looked almost as if she had been sleeping when the Angel of Death took her, not cowering and hiding as men no better than beasts destroyed her village. But I could not wash away every sign of decay, and one look at the remains of her home showed the peaceful arrangement I had made for the lie that it was. Papa said Kaddish over my grandmother. He let me have another fifteen minutes to go through the house and take what was left to bring home to Mama. I found Bubbe's box of needful things behind the loose stone in the hearth where she usually kept it, and a small pouch of old jewelry with it. That was all.

In the cart I cried all the way home.

Mama and Papa had grown up in small villages, and they feared the pogroms every time the wind changed. But I had not been touched by such fear before. Hadn't our own chief of police said, "As long as I live, there will be no pogrom in Bialystok"?

Soon after Papa and I had returned with the news of my bubbe's death, Shayna and I were sitting together in the main room when Mama came in with sadness in her eyes and the box and pouch in her hands.

"You should have these to remember and think on my mother by," she said.

She took out a locket, an ivory cameo carved with the profile of a fancy lady, and stroked it with one finger. "Shayna, darling, you look like my mama did when she was young, when I was little—hair so gold it puts the sun to shame. You should have this locket. Mama wore it when I was a little girl, and she said it was fine protection." My mother looked near tears. "I hope the new one coming is another girl. A girl I can name for my mama."

Then she turned to me and tilted her head, thinking. Our sharp-eyed mother was back.

Mama took the ivory box from her lap and shook it

suspiciously. "I can't open it, and believe me, I've tried. But the symbols carved into it—I suppose they mean that Mama would want you to have it."

I took it and traced out the carvings with my fingers, the same way Mama had touched Bubbe's cameo.

Mama stroked my coarse black hair. "Be careful, baby girl. Use your judgment."

Deborah was a judge in the land of Israel, and Mama never let me forget it.

That box was where Bubbe kept prayers for women whose husbands traveled, special inks, blessed talismans, and one photograph of Mama, Papa, Shayna, and me that we'd paid a traveling salesman for. I'd never had any trouble opening it. I was different from Mama.

I waited until I had some time to myself and went to a place I knew, secluded by bushes, not too far from our home. There I opened the box, expecting Bubbe's familiar collection of blessed things to tumble out onto my lap. What I found inside was a length of deerskin wrapped around a silver-plated knife, the photograph, and a piece of paper. It wasn't a blessing. It was long and complicated and seemed to be some kind of contract.

I tried to puzzle through the contract, but the words swam in front of my eyes and made me dizzy.

As I refolded the paper and put it back in the box, I heard a rustling in the bushes.

"Who's there?" I called out, a little frightened.

No one answered, so I picked up a stick and walked briskly over to the bushes.

"Come on out!"

There was another rustling and then the patter of a large rat scampering away. I parted the bushes with the stick and saw some long gray hairs stuck to the tree branches, and a trail like something made by a long, ropey tail dragging in the dirt.

Our baby brother, Yeshua, was born three months later.

After the baby came, we began working the clock around in order to get to America, where, Mama said, they didn't let you burn. Papa began working seven days a week; he wouldn't handle money on the Sabbath, but he would go to his workshop instead of to shul, and Mama prayed the whole day for God's forgiveness. I already was working as hard as I could—I had never turned down anyone who called for me, and I didn't start now. But I worked harder at home, casting spells of protection around each of us. Mama wouldn't let me or Shayna talk to boys—she said that we had enough trouble saving for five tickets without one of us girls dragging a husband or baby into things. This was fine with me; I never had much use for boys. When I could sneak away, I went to Yetta's family's sweetshop. Sometimes Mama and Papa talked about sending Papa over to America first, so he could send money back, but everyone knew women who'd done that and then never heard from their husbands again, and I was not sure my protection could keep him safe far across the sea, so we just stayed the way we were: Mama, Papa, two sisters, and baby Yeshkele. And every week, we put what money we could spare in a jar that Mama kept buried in the back garden.

Mama was always telling me, "Look after the little ones," as though I was not already wearing my tongue thin speaking spells of protection over Shayna and Yeshua. It did not come without cost, the work I did, and I grew tired of Mama's constant worries, especially because in my heart I did not believe that anything could happen to us. Not in Bialystok.

Every so often I would take out the contract and pore over it. But trying to read it hurt. The ink seemed to be made of blood and vomit. A stench like cow shit rose off the page. My stomach churned every time I unfolded the paper. The writing itself snaked obscenely in my brain, displacing any meaning the words themselves might have. I would spend hours and come away with a headache strong enough to make gravel of boulders and only enough words to know that my bubbe had signed a contract of some kind.

What this meant, I had no idea.

"Take care of the baby," Mama said.

Yeshua was always wandering off. He would get bored watching Mama work, and of course it was always I who had to fetch him back. He crawled through and smudged the circles of protection I drew around him and it was almost impossible to get to the end of an invocation without Yeshua trying to eat the herbs I placed around him. I cannot count the times I had to break off in the middle, redraw the circles, and start over. I cannot count the number of amulets I drew up for him, as he chewed each paper with its magic symbols and prayers to bits. It got so I could not tell if any of my work was worthwhile—he seemed so set on undoing it all.

It became simpler just to take him everywhere I went. That way I could protect him in the moment and keep him out from under Mama's and Shayna's feet. The only places I did not take him were to women's childbeds. Otherwise he was a constant presence on my hip.

One day, coming home from Yetta's sweetshop, an old woman with long, straggly gray hair, who looked like a heap of clothing with a cord tied around the middle, stopped us.

"Lovely baby," she said. "Lovely baby boy."

I waited for her to make a sign warding off the evil spirits she'd attracted with her compliments, and when she did not, I knew she meant us no good and tried to push past her. As I did, she grabbed Yeshua out of my arms. He began to wail and reach for me.

"Get your pigkeeping hands off my brother!" I yelled, grabbing for him, but she swung him away from me.

The old woman looked me full in the face and I fell back— her eye sockets were empty holes, and fires burned in them. The creature was a lilit, the lilit my grandmother had spoken with.

"Pigkeeper, is it, granddaughter of Hannah? Your brother, is it? The boy is mine, and none of thine."

I pulled out the silver-plated knife that had been in my grandma's box. I'd kept it in my apron pocket ever since that day I'd found it. "He's mine and I'll send you to the fires of Gehenna if you don't give him back."

Instead of answering, the old woman sprang away from me. I stabbed at her with my small knife, but my aim was no good and all I managed to do was slice into her arm.

The creature fell to her knees, screaming in pain. Some kind of mucus poured from her cut arm. I grabbed Yeshua back while she pressed on the wound, vainly trying to stanch the flow while she raged at me, spitting and cursing. The mucus ate away at the blade of my knife. I clutched Yeshkele to my breast as though he were made of gold and bolted for home.

By the time I got there, frightened and out of my breath and my wits, Shayna was the only one at home. I flung myself into her arms and cried while Yeshkele squirmed impatiently to be put down. But I couldn't force myself to relax my grip.

"Deborah!" Shayna exclaimed. "What's happening?"

"He's our baby, ours!" I rocked back and forth on my heels.

Shayna unbent my fingers, took the baby from me, and set him down gently.

"Our baby, ours," I kept saying while Shayna patted my hair and wiped my face. Yeshua crawled off to play with some toy horses our papa had carved for him.

Finally I ran out of sobs and told her what had happened, that a demon had tried to take our baby brother, who was chewing thoughtfully on one of the horses.

"How could it?" Shayna asked me. "After your work?"

I wiped my face. "I must have forgotten something," I said. "Something that makes him vulnerable. Or I'm just not strong enough yet. Or—" Suddenly I thought of the mysterious contract in Bubbe's box and of her long talk with the lilit that had been trying to take Pearl's baby.

I ran and got the paper from the box. "Shayna," I told her, "these words are sick—can you smell them?"

"I can't smell anything," she said. "It's just a blank piece of paper."

"It's not," I said. "If I keep these words in my head my eyes burn and my thoughts curdle. So I'm going to read out each word I can to you, not keeping it in my head at all. And you write them down."

Shayna looked a little frightened, but she did what I said.

"Baby," I finished, and Shayna gasped.

"Oh, Bubbe," I whispered. "Oh, Bubbe, how could you?" For our bubbe had killed our brother with ink as surely as if she'd taken that silver knife to his throat.

The long and the short of it was that our bubbe had struck a bargain with the lilit, whose name resisted my reading, for the power to get us safely to America. In return, she gave the demon the right to take the next baby of the family.

I'd never realized how much Bubbe wanted to get us out, and I wondered what the lilit had told her about Bialystok.

Well, she'd been cheated—the mob had taken her and we were still in Bialystok. But our baby brother wasn't safe yet, and the demon was trying to collect. I tried to put a brave face on for Shayna's sake.

"The contract can't be good still," I told her. "Bubbe can't see us safely to America now."

But in my heart, I knew the demon didn't see it that way, and so did Shayna.

"Don't be an ass, Deborah! If that were true, you wouldn't have had to fight it off this morning."

I didn't know how to keep Yeshua safe. But I did know that it was no use telling Mama and Papa, and Shayna agreed. After all, they were working as hard as they knew how to get us across the sea, away from the old demons, and what more could they do if they *did* know? It was down to me to take care of this kind of business.

For two weeks, Shayna and I hovered over Yeshkele like two cats over a mousehole. When one of us slept, the other one watched. We took him everywhere with us, and Mama appreciated the help, even if she didn't know its reason.

After two weeks of my eyes falling out of my head with exhaustion from useless charms and wardings and my brain boiling with effort, I reasoned like this: Everyone knows the power of a contract. The contract was what put Yeshkele in danger. So, if we destroyed the contract, we would release the power and dispel the danger.

I tried throwing the thing on the fire, but it wouldn't burn. I stuck it right in the heart of the blaze, but when the embers had burned themselves out, I stirred the ashes, and there the contract would be, with not even a smudge.

Sometimes you need more than herbs and spells of protection. Sometimes it is not enough merely to defend. So Bubbe had taught me the evil eye. The evil eye, everybody knows, works by concentrating the element of fire, infusing it with the power of God's curse, and directing that cursed fire with one's vision. Under Bubbe's supervision, I had practiced by glaring my heart out at dust, at flowers, at old rags. Lines formed in my face ahead of their time and eventually I got good enough to set regular bits of paper alight with my gaze. Now I needed to direct my anger at something more powerful than rags. I could feel the anger at my grandmother for making this cursed bargain massing behind my eyes like lightning in a black cloud. And I could hear the crackling in the air around me. Shooting pains ran through my head and I could feel my hair start to snake out from its braid. When the pressure was like a blacksmith's vise, I'd open my eyes and send my pain at the rag or the paper and it would burst into flames.

When I felt that I was ready, Shayna and I took Papa's cart outside of the city and made a pile of oil-soaked rags and dry leaves. We put the contract in the center. Then she held Yeshua and drove the cart well clear of me and the kindling. I had told her to go half a mile; she went barely a quarter mile, which was just as well for me, in the end. When she and the baby were safely away, I focused on my rage at Bubbe, at the demon trying to take Yeshua, on the mob that had killed my grandma. I heard the crackling and felt my head pulse with pain, and when I turned my gaze on the mound we had built, there was a sound like a hundred gasps, and a tower of flame shot from the small pyre up into the cloudy sky.

My joints felt like they were made of moss and I fell down hard, hitting my head on a rock. My muscles like cobwebs, too weak to move or even to call for help from Shayna, I watched the fire burn itself out in clouds of oily, acrid smoke so thick you could have cut it into slices and spread butter on it. It took close to an hour to clear, and I could hear Shayna stumbling around with Yeshua in her arms, calling for me. Even when she found me, I wouldn't let her start for home until she'd sifted through the ashes and found nothing left of the contract.

I had succeeded.

Shayna had to almost drag me back to the cart. I was sick, she said, so sick that it looked like I might not wake up. Mama and Shayna told me that my fever burned so hot that when they dunked me in ice water to bring it down, the water turned warm as blood. Mama longed for her mother to come and put together one of her brews, but Bubbe was gone and all Mama knew how to do was boil up a chicken and try to make me eat. They said that I fought her, that I said she was trying to drown me. And then, as suddenly as I got sick, I got better. I woke up one morning and asked Mama for something to eat. By the next day, I'd had enough of lying in bed. But Mama didn't want to let us out. Something had happened while I was sick. The skin around her eyes was taut and she had chewed her lips so hard that they bled.

"The chief of police is dead," she told me. "Dead and gone. And there's bad feeling in the air."

"I don't feel anything," I said. I suppose I was still sick, to have said something so stupid.

She clipped me around the ear. "Not your kind of feeling,

child! The chief didn't up and die of a chill, idiot! Someone killed him. And the army says it was the Jews."

Shayna broke in. "Everybody knows that the chief was a friend to us! Didn't he say—"

"Yes. Yes, he did," said our mama. "And now he's dead and the chief prosecutor is no friend of ours. The self-defense league has been patrolling every hour of the day and weapons are appearing on the streets outside of the quarter, and for all it's a bright June day, there's a dark fog lying over the city. I don't want you two going out."

"Mama," I said. "You can't keep us in forever. How long must we wait until this fog lifts? I haven't been outside for so long. This is the gentile Holy Week and things will only get worse. Better now than Easter Sunday."

Mama looked like she might slap me again. "Headstrong girl! I should have sent you both to America already, for here you have the survival skills of an infant!"

To hear such a thing after what I had done! That she wished me far from her side, that she did not trust me to take care of myself even after she had depended on me for charms and amulets. An infant, she called me! Me, who had fought off a demon and destroyed its hold over our family! Still, I kept my temper in check, as I had learned.

"Mama, if times are so bad, it's all the more reason for me to go out. With the protections I put on the family, my supplies are low. Let me get what I need to protect us, and when I come back, you'll have no more worries."

And Mama relented, I think as much out of a desire to see roses in my cheeks again as anything else. I took Shayna with me to help carry my supplies, and as we stepped over the threshold, I looked back at Yeshua. But I shook myself. He was safe now; if Mama was to be believed, taking him with me would only be putting him in more danger. So Shayna and I left together, and Yeshkele stayed with Mama while Papa worked in his shop next door.

After I got the herbs I needed, Shayna and I walked over to Yetta's sweetshop, so I could make sure she was all right. It was a long walk for me; I was weak, and the colors didn't look quite real—everything was thin and watery. The sun hurt my eyes.

At the sweetshop I fell into conversation with Yetta, who was minding the shop while her parents were out. Shayna eyed the candies. We could hear the sounds of some kind of parade from far off, but Yetta was catching me up on the gossip I had missed during my weeks of illness, and I was enthralled in the story of her other sister's betrothed's time at *gymnasium*. I didn't even notice the sound of a gunshot, which I later learned had been the signal for the processions to turn on the Jewish Quarter. We didn't hear the shouts; it wasn't until Yetta smelled smoke and looked out the door to see a mob yelling and throwing stones that she grabbed me and Shayna and pulled us into the stone cellar. I helped pull the rug over the trapdoor in the back room as we went down and wrestled the bar into place.

We heard glass shattering, and then sounds of violence were right overhead. We could hear barrels being smashed, the counter splitting. My mind was still weak from the fever, or I think I would remember more clearly. But I do remember knowing as strongly as I had ever known anything that Yeshkele needed me, only me, and he needed me to come quickly, to run to him. I remember the sound of flames crackling, my hands on the barred trapdoor, Yetta grabbing my arms from behind and yanking me back down the stairs. We stayed there a long time. We ate the sweets and dried fruits that were being stored and used an old barrel to relieve ourselves. We slept and woke and still the sounds of the mob carried down to the cellar.

Finally there was quiet.

Shayna crept upstairs and put her head out the trapdoor while Yetta made sure I stayed still.

"Everything's burnt," Shayna said. Her whisper cracked.

Yetta and I followed her upstairs.

The shop looked like—nothing. Everything burnt or smashed or both. We picked our way across the floor, silent and reverent as Adam and Eve on the first day of the world, but it felt like the last.

The streets were empty, but fires were still burning down the block.

We didn't speak. Other people were just as silent. I remember one man watching a building burn. Tears dripped steadily from his eyes but he didn't make a sound. Some wandered aimlessly; nowhere left to go, I guess. I saw two women meet each other in the middle of a block, saw their eyes widen in shock and relief, and then they threw their arms around each other. Without a word. I never heard a silence like that before.

I don't remember saying good-bye to Yetta. She went to look for her family, I think, and Shayna and I needed to find ours. I didn't see Yetta again. I don't know what happened to her. My best friend, and I never saw her again.

I don't remember walking home, either, but I must have. Not all the streets were destroyed. We found out later that in some places the self-defense league had managed to fight off the attackers: civilians, police, an army with bombs and guns. And some streets that held places like butchers' shops, places where men and women brought out the long knives, they made it through all right, too. I do remember that Shayna insisted that we would find Mama and Papa safe at home, Mama with her dressmaker's shears and Papa with his awl, but I knew different.

Our street was always quiet, mostly private homes.

Shayna said she had to lead me home every step, because if she let go of my arm I'd just stand in the middle of the street like a lamppost. I allowed her to pull me along, but I paid no attention to my path, stumbling once into a pile of broken glass. I did not feel the fall, though the cuts hurt sharp enough as they healed. Shayna spent almost an hour picking glass out of my flesh that night. When we reached home, my arms were coated red with my own blood.

Mama and Papa and Yeshua, they were dead. Shayna closed Mama's eyes before I went to see her. I couldn't bear to stand before those eyes. I remember holding Yeshua's little body against my breast and crying, trying to wake him up. But I could not wake him, and all my embraces did was stain him with my blood.

The day after we buried Mama, Papa, and our brother, I went into the back garden and dug up our savings. It was enough for two of us.

That is how Shayna and I came to America. In America, Mama had said, they don't let you burn, and I repeated it to Shayna every night on the boat.

We had enough when we got here to rent a room and buy some new clothing so we didn't give ourselves away as a couple of greenhorns before we even opened our mouths, but not enough to last for long. A business like mine needs word of mouth, needs local knowledge, so it's not like I could just set up shop. Our landsleit group got us work at one of the tiny sweatshops in the neighborhood, no more than six people crowded into the boss's front room, his wife cooking dinner on the same stove he used to heat the irons. But it was such a little shop—you couldn't live on what they paid. The boss sweated every penny out of you and the shop was no good for rebuilding my own trade, because there were so few of us working there. I had no intention of living out my life like that, and I would not allow Shayna to do so either. I saw what had happened to women who had been sewing their whole lives—hacking coughs from the cotton dust, eyes bleary and half-blind from peering at seams and threads all day, fingertips like leather from stabbing themselves with needles.

Those small sweatshops were the past, they were the old country, like we'd never left. America, everybody knew, was in the modern factories, where dozens of girls sat together and earned a respectable wage, not subcontracted out to tiny shops that took their profit out of your skin.

Not that the factories were any picnic—women there could still end up blind, coughing, and sick, but it was more congenial, friendlier, and most important for me, had lots of girls together in one place. We needed to get out of the small shops, and Shayna was the one with the skills to get us hired. Lots of these factories broke down the work so that you didn't need much skill, but nonetheless, it was useful to sew more beautifully than a machine.

When we walked into Shlomo Cohen's, they barely gave us a second glance.

"Mister," I said to the foreman, "we're looking for jobs."

"And you can keep looking," he said to me, but when Shayna pulled out a blouse she had stitched and embroidered on the ship coming to America he sang a different tune.

"This is something special," he said, addressing Shayna this time. "We can use someone like you, and you could go far here, maybe be stitching samples in a little time."

"And my sister," said Shayna firmly.

He shrugged. "And your sister." We were put to work on the spot.

So, we worked twelve hours a day, six days a week, at Cohen's shop, one of the smaller factories, only about fifty girls, and we got by. There was always work. You could hear sewing machines on the Lower East Side every hour of the day and night, every day of the week, Sabbath or no Sabbath. The Italian girls worked Saturdays and the Jewish girls worked Sundays and most of us didn't observe so much and we worked any day we could. That was the way of the New World—even the most pious would eat ham sandwiches in the New World. And be glad to get them, too.

Shayna's talent shone through. She was made a tucker on the ladies' skirts, a high-paying job, with the possibility of becoming a sample maker, where she could follow a garment from fabric to its final form, doing almost the same kind of detailed craftwork she had done with our mother.

On one side of me was Ruthie, another girl like me who could run up a seam but not much else. Ruthie had bright blue eyes and she laughed like the shop was a party. Something about her black brows and brown braid reminded me of Yetta, and I started spending less time with Shayna. Shayna would stay late, so eager she was to become a sample maker, and I would walk home with Ruthie instead. We would eat dinner together, talk. She was like me, no interest in the young men, but she was friendly enough to me. She said my eyes were like awls. And she said this like it was a good thing.

Ruthie was a firebrand, had been at *gymnasium* back in Riga and had become a Bundist, a revolutionary. Like many of her comrades, she was also a freethinker.

"No gods, no masters!" she would tell me passionately, before stabbing her finger with the machine's needle. "These others," she'd say, swinging her arm around to take in every girl in the shop, "these others are only interested in catching a rich man, but I have bigger dreams! Look here, here is opportunity for a world not bounded by fears of superstitious whispers! Here we can cast off such foolishness, do away with rich men and cruel gods together! We can throw away fears of demons and see evil's true face, the faces of depraved men!"

I was so captivated by her speech that despite what I knew she had me half-ready to forswear any belief in God or devils as well. I had never been very political, but in the company of someone like Ruthie, I found myself stirred by visions of justice, by a world aflame with possibility, the blossoming of a new era in the New World.

Ruthie always told me that she became a Bundist after learning of the misery suffered by the poorer members of her father's shul. Back in the old country, her father was a rabbi and a Zionist, a man who believed that safety and justice for Jews would be found only in our return to our ancient land. I half think Ruthie became a Bundist in part to anger him. Ruthie had Shayna's sense of excitement along with some real order to her thoughts. She'd had to leave Riga when the police found out that she'd been the author of certain pamphlets.

After work Ruthie would let me practice my English on her, or we'd go to the movies or wander the streets, arm in arm. Never was the Lower East Side so wondrously beautiful as on those nights, especially after it had rained and washed away some of the smell.

On my other side in the factory was Rose, who had been abandoned by her no-goodnik husband and left with four children. One day she came in with more lines in her face than usual. Her youngest, Fanny, had been up all night with what Rose claimed was the croup.

"The croup is bad," I said, "but not terrible. You can paint her throat with iodine."

Rose nodded, but she didn't look less worried. I almost put it down to a mother's heart, but still I kept pushing. "I can come over after work and help you."

"No!" she cried fearfully, and then subsided. "No, I can do it myself."

"Rose," I said. "It's not the croup, is it?"

"How can you know?" she asked.

I was pleased—close observation can take the place of any more mysterious power when necessary. "I know," I said.

She looked around furtively and edged closer to me. "You mustn't tell anyone," she whispered. "I can't afford to stay home in quarantine."

I knew then what the next words out of her mouth would be.

"Scarlet fever," she whispered.

"Rose," I said. "I can help with that."

"How?" she asked, a little suspicious. "I can't pay."

"So who said anything about payment? I'm offering to help."

I put all I could of myself into the broth I made that night, and I had faith in it, even though the ingredients I got here were not quite the same as those I would have used back home; vinegar and red pepper were easy enough to find, but I searched hours in the markets for myrrh gum. For double measure I made up an amulet for the baby as well, and added into it something new that I found in the markets: powdered foxglove. When Rose saw the amulet her face lit up.

"Now," I said, handing over the amulet and the medicine, "you must be sure to give Fanny hot baths—she needs to sweat out the illness."

I prayed every night that the child would recover. I had done everything I could, but there is no knowing with scarlet fever. It can recede only to come back worse than ever. But Fanny did recover, and Rose believed it was my doing.

She came back to me when her sister was in trouble. Her younger sister, she told me, had started walking out with a worthless boy, and wouldn't take anybody's words of warning, even their father's. Rose was worried the girl would fall pregnant, and then what would become of her?

"I can help with that," I said.

"I will pay you," she said.

So I made up pessaries for Rose's sister. "It's good you had the brains to come to me early on," I told her. "It's easier now than later."

Little by little I built up a group of women who knew me— Rose's sister had a friend with female troubles, that friend had an aunt with a sick child, the aunt had a friend with a child coming after two miscarriages who wanted every amulet and charm I could provide for her. After a few months I was able to stop working at the shop, and that week, Ruthie came to live with Shayna and me. The family she boarded with had decided to move to Boston, and it seemed only natural for her to come stay with us. In fact, it was no trouble at all, because Shayna was home less and less. When I asked her where she was going, she would just tell me that she was spending time with some of the better seamstresses from the shop, that they were giving her tips on becoming a sample maker. As I was so busy lately, I was just grateful that Shayna had made some friends. Between my work and Ruthie, I barely got to see Shayna some weeks. Ruthie and I often had the room to ourselves. I was grateful that Shayna understood.

About a month after moving in with us, Ruthie left the shop as well, putting her troublesome writing to good use. On the Lower East Side, there were so many newspapers! She was hired as a writer by *Der Schturkez,* a socialist paper put out by immigrants who had come to America after the failed 1905 rebellion. They made even Ruthie look mild.

I'd hoped the three of us could celebrate together, but when I went to Shlomo Cohen's to pick up Ruthie and Shayna, only my friend was there. I couldn't find my sister with any of the other girls, but I wouldn't let it ruin the evening. Ruthie and I went uptown and waited for standing room tickets at the opera, even treating ourselves to a glass of wine each at the intermission. At the bar, I leaned over and saw my sister on the arm of Johnny Fein.

Johnny Fein had a handsome face and he dressed well, but he was a dangerous man to know. He ran numbers, drugs, women. His girls came to me for help all the time. But he never had any trouble getting a pretty girl on his arm. He wouldn't have had much trouble even if he'd been a tailor, I think, because of his sharp features and lantern jawline, but it didn't hurt that he always had a lot of money to flash around, and he was flashing it that night, treating Shayna to a bottle of champagne. I hadn't seen them in the standing room section, that was for sure. And Shayna didn't see me now, as I turned away and went to find Ruthie.

We missed the final act of the opera, as I was staging my own melodrama outside with Ruthie as audience.

"How long—how *long* do you think she has been walking out with him? With a *criminal*?"

"Calm down," said Ruthie. "You're doing nobody any good tearing your hair out like this, least of all me. This is supposed to be a happy occasion, remember?"

"*Happy?* I should be happy with my sister, my baby sister whom I'm supposed to protect even now, sipping from the cup of iniquity? Willingly chaining herself with fine gold and silver filigree to a man of evil? How could I not know?"

"I can't imagine," Ruthie said dryly, "why she wouldn't have mentioned it to you."

"Such a man! A man to make small children scream and run away in the streets!"

"He gives the children candy," said Ruthie. "They like him."

"Yes, well, I imagine he gives Shayna candy as well." I subsided. "But she will have some talking to do when she gets home tonight."

She did not come home until very late indeed, that night. She and Johnny Fein must have gone to a dance hall after the opera. I waited up, and when Shayna came in, I launched into her. Ruthie tried to make herself not be there by curling up in a chair in the corner.

"Girl! We did not come all the way to the New World so that you could get yourself killed by hanging on the arm of a shtarker like Johnny Fein! What do you think you're doing?"

Shayna gasped. "Witch!"

I snorted. "You think I needed witchcraft? I saw you all right—I saw you at the opera house! You know, I looked for you to celebrate with us after work, but you were already gone. I thought you were out with the girls—some girls!"

"What do you care where I am?" she asked plaintively. "You've been happy without me, I could tell! I'll do what I like!"

"I guess I know now why you were really staying out so late!"

"You know nothing about it!" Shayna yelled back, her shock and quailing gone. "Nothing! My Johnny is a hero! You should have seen how he was with that Cohen!"

"So tell me. How was he? A brutal thug? Because that's what he is at other times."

"Not a thug! You don't know! You were over on the other side of the shop with that dirty atheist you call a friend—"

"Ruth is sitting *right here*!" I shouted. "Don't you dare call her names! If not for her advice I would have dragged you home the minute I saw you, and this is the thanks she gets!"

"You be quiet and listen to me for once, Deborah!" Shayna dismissed my interruption. "There was that Matthew Cohen putting his hands all over me and calling me filthy names and nobody near who could help. But one day Johnny came in and told Cohen that was no way to treat a lady and offered me his arm to walk home. He's been a perfect gentleman. You never noticed any of it from the first day to this, and now you want to tell me what to do?"

I felt terrible. I had seen the way Matthew Cohen eyed Shayna, and I knew he thought he was such a big man—son of the owner and all, palling around with a brutal goniff like Johnny Fein. They both thought they were big men, real Americans, calling themselves "Johnny" and "Matthew" when everybody knew they had been born "Yakov" and "Moishe." But I had not been paying enough attention to the danger Shayna was in. Even so, I was not going to let my guilt get in the way of a fight. "So Johnny Fein claims you and that turns him into a righteous man?" I said. "If you're really this stupid you *deserve* to end up like the rest of his girls!"

"What do you know about what I deserve? You'd rather see to every other woman in town than to me," Shayna blasted back. "I've always come last for you! Your customers, Yeshua, Yetta, and now Ruth! You're not Mama, and if you weren't so unnatural, you would see yourself how Johnny really is!" She gestured over at Ruthie, who was trying to make herself unseen. "And you have your friend," Shayna said. "You leave me to mine."

"Unnatural?" I yelled back. "Fine! You won't have the bother of my unnatural help ever again!"

Shayna stormed out, slamming the door, and didn't come home again until early the next morning. In general she stayed out later and later, and soon she didn't come home nights at all. I barely saw her—just a glimpse in a crowd, really, at a dance hall, maybe. But she was still a tucker at Shlomo Cohen's shop and that, I thought, should tell her something. If Johnny Fein really meant right by her, wouldn't he have pulled her out of factory work by now and made an honest woman of her?

"Your Johnny, the hero," I said sharply to her one morning when she was still sleeping at home. "Why are you slaving over a sewing machine in that factory if he's so righteous?"

Shayna pressed her lips together and glared at me. "I like it there well enough," she said. "I like the girls, the talking. And it's good to make my own money. I suppose you'd miss it if I stopped paying my share of the rent!"

"It's not your own money that bought you that ring," I told her, pointing at her finger wearing a golden ring with a real sapphire.

She twisted the ring around and said, "Johnny says I shouldn't talk to you so much, anyway. You don't understand." She walked out.

Oh, but I understood. I understood, and I'd seen this sort of thing before. It started with opera and new hats and dance halls and sparklers on your wrists and fingers, but that wasn't how it ended.

Weeks later Shayna came home wearing a scarf around her head, shadowing her face. A scarf of the highest quality, no question, but a scarf nonetheless, like she was a greenhorn.

I have sharp eyes, though. I can see through shadows and scarves, and I could see the bruises she was covering.

"What's happened to you?" I asked, as if it wasn't obvious.

"Nothing," she muttered, drawing the scarf tighter around her head.

"That's not nothing," I said, jabbing a finger at the shiner over her right eye.

"So I slipped," she said. "You know how clumsy I am."

I snorted. "I know how clumsy you were when we were girls, but even then you never wound up with bruises on your face. Let me help you."

"I don't want your help!" she said harshly, and turned away from me.

"You must wait, my love," said Ruthie, which was pretty rich talk coming from the girl who counseled violent revolution. "She'll come back to you eventually."

She did.

I had a nice piece of meat made for dinner, and I had enough for three or even four, when Shayna came in, her eyes red from crying.

"Shayna meydle," I said. "Baby girl, what has happened to you?"

She waved her hands vaguely and sat down at the table, her head bent.

"I've done a terrible thing, big sister."

"Nothing so terrible that I cannot solve it," I said. I didn't have the heart to give her the tongue-lashing she deserved. Ruthie ran to the kitchen we shared with the other tenants to make some coffee, leaving us alone.

"I am through with Johnny Fein! Through!"

"Good," I said. "But tell me what has happened to you."

"What has happened to me? Better you should ask what I have done!"

"I'm asking," I said, coming to the end of my patience. "I can help, but I must know the ill."

"You think I am crying tears?" Shayna said. "These are not tears streaming from my eyes! This my heart's blood for what I have done!"

"Stop squawking and tell me what is happening," I said sharply, but Shayna only drew breath to wail again.

Ruthie came in with the coffee and intervened in what was clearly going to become hysterics. "Tell us," she said quietly.

Shayna told us.

"I have meant to talk to you for a long time," she said, "for weeks, but I haven't had the nerve. Johnny is a man with a temper like a demon, and he does not like to be crossed. Better that I should wait for him to tire of me than bring down his wrath on us."

"I can take care of us," I interjected.

Shayna smiled wanly. "I'm sure you believe so, but even you cannot turn aside a bullet. A few days ago, I was working in the shop, waiting for Johnny to come pick me up. But he came in late, and he came in with Matthew Cohen.

"They'd been out drinking and gambling that afternoon—I could tell—and Johnny told me that as I was a sporting girl I'd want to know about a bet they made. But I didn't! I didn't!" she sobbed.

"But we want to know," Ruthie said gently. "You can tell us."

I was not half so calm inside as Ruthie appeared to be.

"Johnny had been bragging, how pretty I was and how nimble with my fingers, and he'd bet one of his friends that I could turn out a hundred shirtwaists a day for three days. Me, by myself! No piecework—just me!"

"Nonsense," I snorted. "Nobody can do that!" Ruthie put her hand on my arm. I think it was meant to calm me, but I felt it as a warning as well.

"I know!" wailed Shayna. "I told him I could not, but he told me I'd better, for he and Cohen had wagered more money on it than my life was worth."

Shayna's fingers were twisting her fine shawl like a dusting rag.

"I worked my fingers raw all day, but the pile of pieces got no lower. I knew I could never get everything done by midnight. Oh, Deborah, how my foot ached from the treadle and how my hands shook. It was worse than our first days in that little sweat-shop on Delancey. My eyes stung and my fingers were dead at the tips. I never even stopped to eat, and then I stuck my finger with the needle twice and started bleeding on the cloth. I put my head down to cry."

"Poor child," murmured Ruthie.

Silly goose, I thought, but did not say. She should have come to me long ago.

Shayna looked at Ruthie, not at me, as if she could read my mind, and went on. "After a few minutes, I picked myself up, ready to try again, when—such a sight, oh, God! Out of the pile of cloth next to me a terrible old woman came. She had long gray hair that hung in rattails and her nails curved out in claws. She was hunched over, covered in warts, and reeked like rotten meat in the sun. Her skirt was held up with a frayed rope, and coming out from under it I could see the tip of a tail. Her eyes glittered like broken glass. Oh, I was terrified—my blood froze and I gasped for air!

"But I remembered what you said, Deborah, about sometimes God's host taking ugly forms to test us, so I did not show my horror."

"What I said?" I interrupted her tale. "That was no angel of God's, that was a demon!"

"I didn't know!" wailed Shayna.

"Be quiet," said Ruthie to me.

So Shayna resumed. Her breathing had become less ragged as she fell into the rhythm of the story. "'Tut, tut, Shayna meydle,' said the woman. 'Why do you cry?'

"So I told her my sorrows, and how soon the clock would reach midnight and how Johnny's face would darken when he saw how little I was able to make, nowhere near a hundred, and how I didn't know what he would do.

"'Dry up your tears,' said the old woman. 'I can sew up those pieces no problem, and all I need from you is your pretty ring.'

"It was the ring Johnny bought for me, with the sapphire," explained Shayna. "I love that ring; it made me feel like a movie star to walk down the street on Johnny's arm with that ring on my hand, but I figured that a ring does no good to a corpse, so I took it off and gave it to the old woman."

Taking her out from under Johnny's protection, such as it was, I thought to myself.

Shayna was lost in memory. "Oh, you should have seen that old woman sew! Her hands and feet and tail were a blur. When she stopped, there was the pile of shirtwaists done and dusted, and she vanished into thin air just as Johnny and Matthew came in. They were thrilled to find that I'd won their stupid bet, and I thought that once they had sobered up the next morning, they would see what a foolish bet they'd made and that everything would go back to normal. But the next morning I came in to find a pile of cloth higher than my head. I worked my fingers raw and until my eyes were burning and bloodshot, but by eleven o'clock I had more than half the pile to go. I stood up to stretch out the cricks in my neck and back, and when I sat back down, I was face to face with the ugly little woman. Again, she asked what my trouble was, and again, I told her.

"'Don't you worry about a thing, Shayna meydle! I can sew these pieces for you, no problem, and all I ask from you is that pretty locket around your neck.'"

Again, "Shayna meydle," I thought to myself. A familiar address, like the demon knew her—and then I realized it did.

"But it was Bubbe's locket!" continued Shayna. "I didn't want to give it up, especially since Mama had given it to me, but what could I do? I figured that Bubbe wouldn't begrudge me a finished task, and I took off the locket and gave it to the gray-haired woman."

Taking her out from under Bubbe's protection, I thought. If this was the same lilit as the one that had plagued us in the old country, it didn't want rings or lockets, not really. I went cold and ran my eyes over Shayna's figure. She looked as trim as ever.

"Again the old woman set to work, and when she was done, the entire stack of shirtwaists was sewn up perfectly. On the stroke of midnight, she vanished, and Johnny and Matthew stumbled in and I really thought that this time it would be enough for them, that surely they wouldn't go through with a third night!

"But the third night," Shayna said, her hysterics rising again, "the third night, the old woman didn't ask for my hat or my locket, but for my firstborn baby! And what could I do but say yes, and now I've lost my firstborn before I've even borne him!"

How did it find us? I thought frantically. I knew it had been spying on us in Bialystok, or how could it have known to tell Bubbe that we were in danger, but how could it have followed us to this New World? Ruthie said America was free of those old fears, but she was wrong. "Are you carrying?" I asked.

"I don't know!" Shayna cried. "I want free of Johnny and his wagers." She buried her head in her hands and wailed.

Oh, I felt that wail in the pit of my soul. To have failed not only Yeshua but Shayna as well! The one with my inattention and the other with my arrogance. "But a mistake is a mistake," I said. "Maybe I'm not above making them as well. And I can help with yours." After a minute I added, "I can take care of Johnny." Ruthie put Shayna to bed, but I sat up a long time, planning how.

The next day I went out and dug up some clay from the street. I came home, molded it into the shape of a man, and named it. I took the silver knife and slashed open the sides of the doll where Johnny Fein's pockets would be.

With his money no longer flowing, Johnny Fein's body turned up in the river, a week later, broken and twisted.

Matthew Cohen, I hardly had to do anything about. Without Johnny to cheat and threaten for him, he started losing his bets, and no one else would cover him. He lost his money, all his family's money, inside of a month. A broken man, too, he was. He ended up in the back room of a saloon with a bullet in his head, so I guess he finally tried to stiff the wrong bettor.

Shayna, well—she wasn't the same, but after Johnny had been dead for a while she picked up her head again and smiled a little at the world around her. She had not been with child after all, so that was one less worry for us. Ruthie and I made enough money between us that she didn't have to go back to work for a while. Shayna started seeing a kind young man, Solomon, a quiet fellow, so steadfast and calm. He worked behind the counter at his family's appetizing shop, which was how they met. They were a good match, and before their first trip to the movies, Shayna brought him home to meet me and Ruthie. He was very respectful. Shayna began spending more and more time with him, but just as often as they went out, she would bring him over, and the four of us would have dinner. Sol even came to me when his younger sister came down with the croup. After some months, Sol and Shayna were married in a very small ceremony, just Ruthie and me and Sol's family. After a month or so, the four of us moved into a small apartment over his family's shop, next door to his parents and aunt and uncle. Shayna had long since left Cohen's shop, and now she worked with Sol's family at his store.

One day, she came to me with her face drawn and tight, just like when we were little and she was in trouble.

"Sister, sister," she said. "I've got news—a little one coming." She made the sign to ward off the evil eye.

"Mazel tov, Shayna," I told her.

"For another, maybe," she answered. "But what will happen to my baby? That lilit will come take it away. Or will it end up like our baby brother?"

"I haven't forgotten," I told her. "This is America. I won't let

that creature take your baby away. Don't worry yourself anymore. I burned that contract once and I can take care of things
again."

I knew the demon wouldn't take Shayna's baby while it was
in the womb, but I took every care anyway. Not a stick of furni-
ture or a scrap of clothing for the baby would I let Sol bring into
the house before it was born. He had to keep everything in the
store. I made up amulets and cast charms of protection over her
just like I had done for Yeshua back in the old country. When
Shayna started to feel pain I put the silver knife in her hands and
chalked a circle, wide enough for her to walk around in, around
her bed. I chalked every charm of protection that I knew on the
door. Sol, I sent him to shul to pray for her and recite psalms.
He went. A good man, Sol. Good enough to know when to do
as he was told.

While Shayna labored and suffered, I did what our bubbe
had taught me. First I recited the prescribed benedictions. Then
I picked up a new pen, an unopened bottle of ink, and the ko-
shered deerskin parchment from Bubbe's box. I wrote out the
finest amulet ever made for a newborn—no rabbi could do better. I used every symbol of protection I'd ever seen and some I
made up. Shayna whispered to me the name she was going to
give her baby girl—by now we both knew it was going to be a
girl—and I wrote it into the most elaborate, complex, and powerful prayer of protection I could, invoking every angel and every
name of God I knew or imagined.

"Beauty isn't enough," Shayna said hoarsely, between contrac-
tions.

"No," I agreed. "It's not."

"My daughter will be a fighter."

So in the amulet, I wrote for the protection of Yael, daughter of Shayna.

When Shayna, sobbing as though her heart would break, had pushed Yael out, I rolled up the deerskin, slipped it into a deerskin bag, and hung the bag around the baby's neck. I peered into little Yael's eyes and already saw the fighter she was, anybody could see that, and a true Hebrew name is true power, everybody knows that. So when Shayna sat nursing her for the first time, gazing happily at her daughter, I sat on the edge of the bed and said to her, "We must call her by her true name only if nobody else is near. Otherwise call her Alte, the old one."

I hoped we could fool the lilit. Even if we slipped up, though, I had confidence in my magnificent amulet.

Shayna insisted on singing to the baby, and Yael seemed soothed by her songs, but the rest of us! Such a caterwauling would scare off my customers, I was sure. Still, it's not good to argue with a new mother—it might sour her milk—so I held my peace and tried to get used to the horrible sentimental songs. She liked one in particular, "Ev'ry Little Movement," and would rock the baby while humming, "Every little movement has a meaning all its own. Every thought and feeling by some posture can be shown. . . ." A more insipid song I've never heard.

Seven months passed before our old troubles from the Cohens' shop came back to haunt us.

It was a Sunday; Sol and Shayna were at the store and Ruthie and I were home. Yael started screaming, angry and frightened in one sound. We ran to her and found a bent old woman with a naked rat's tail leaning over her crib and tickling her under her fat chin. She was as ugly and shriveled as Shayna had said, and covered in bristly fur, but I knew her at once. Her eyes were the fiery pits I remembered. I knew we had no time to lose. I darted in front of Yael and spat out all the names of God I could think of:

"By El, Eloe, Sabbaoth, Ramathel, Eyel, Adonai, Tetragrammaton, Eloyim, I command you to be gone and let this child be!"

But the lilit just picked up Yael, who screamed and kicked out at the old woman's warty skin with all her strength. I steeled myself and again commanded the demon to be gone, this time calling out the forty-two-letter name of God, as dangerous to those who speak it as to those it is spoken against. But the demon only grinned more broadly.

"Your prattling means nothing to me, witch," she said. "Not even God will break a signed contract." She shoved what I recognized as a deerskin parchment filled with writing in my face. It was a duplicate of the one I had burned a few years ago in Bialystok. But there was one difference—below our bubbe's signature I saw my sister's. I grabbed Ruthie's arm and pulled her close.

The demon shot claws out of her gnarled fingers and shredded my perfect amulet. "I claim what is mine, the child Yael, daughter of Shayna, and depart, for not all the names of the heavenly host will break this contract."

Yael was screaming her lungs out and flailing at the demon with her tiny hands balled up into fists. I realized how useless it had been to try fighting this creature by hiding the baby's name and calling her "Alte," by chanting the names of God.

And then I realized how to defeat the monster.

"Ruthie," I whispered. "I need time. I can save her, but I need time. A week."

Ruthie was no dummy. She fell on her knees and burst into

stage tears. "By the mercy in heaven and earth, by Adonai and all his angels, Uriel and Zadkiel, and I don't know the others, not like Deborah does, but I beg for the mercy shown in the past. As the Lord God spared the Jewish babies over the eight days of Pesach from his righteous wrath, I beg you to grant us eight days to say good-bye to our baby, to prepare her for a motherless life."

I would never have tried such a stunt—for one thing, Ruthie was mangling the story of Pesach—but how could a demon resist comparing itself to God? That is the very root of a demon's evil. It fluffed up its hideous fur, looking like a large, horrible spider. "In the name of Adonai, Uriel, Zadkiel, and all the heavenly host, I *am* no less merciful than your God. Take your eight days. Say your good-byes and make the child ready."

And then she was gone.

I paced back and forth all day, wearing a hole in the carpet until Shayna came home from work. I went downstairs to talk to Sol twice, but each time I stopped outside the door to the store and went back up without even putting my head in. It wasn't my place to tell Sol about Shayna's previous troubles—that was between husband and wife. But when Shayna did get home, I let her know in no uncertain terms that we had big trouble, and keeping it from Yael's father would not be right. I told her what had happened. She blanched and turned on me.

"You said the amulet would keep Alte safe!"

"Well, you never said you made a covenant with this creature! You never said you signed a contract!"

"How should I have said such a thing?" she cried. "Bad enough, a shonde, to have done it. But to say it? I grow tired of your scorn, Deborah." She pushed herself away from the table, and in the same tired voice said, "We'd better start packing. A week's head start is a good one; we should be able to get pretty far."

I gaped at her. "Goyishe kopf—what have you got for brains, girl, kasha? Maybe you think you're dealing with a little dyb-buk? No such luck—you've got hold of the Devil's own right hand here. There's no running away from that thing. You are just going to have to be brave."

"Me?" she asked.

"I can help you, tell you how to hold on to Yael, but do it for you? No. That I cannot do. She's not mine to hold on to, and I signed no contract. You will have to face this demon yourself."

"Face a demon? *I'm* supposed to face a demon?"

I fought the urge to shake her and demand she be the woman our mama would be proud to own as her daughter. "Maybe you'd rather give up Yael?"

Now Shayna looked as if *she* wanted to hit *me*. But she swallowed her temper, as I had swallowed mine. "Of course I wouldn't." She sounded stronger by the minute. "But how do I fight a demon?"

A person can get tired of looking after her little sister. So guilty I'd felt, ever since Johnny Fein had hurt Shayna, that I hadn't asked her for anything since, like she was a baby herself. But she wasn't, she was a grown woman. And a person can get tired of being looked after, as well, of being the little sister. I suppose that's why Shayna went with Johnny—to get away from me and out from under my gaze. I am bossy, or so they tell me. I looked at Yael again and she looked at me. I remembered Yeshua peering up at me from the cradle of my arms.

"Let's find out," I said.

Together Shayna and I spoke to Solomon. I told him that the best thing he could do would be to stand ready when the time came, holding the baby, and if Shayna failed or if I was wrong, run as fast as he could for shul with his daughter. It would never work, of course. The demon would catch him before he made it out the door, but what could I tell him? That he was about as useful as a groom at a wedding? Ruthie we told the truth, and to her credit, she believed. She determined quietly that if Shayna and I failed—and if we failed, we would die for our treachery—she would grab the creature's tail and follow her wherever she took the baby. Never would she give up.

I did what I had to do. For six days I fasted, and on the seventh I went to the mikvah, bathed, and returned home. I ate matzoh with honey, prepared by Shayna, and plain fish. I lit a candle and set it on the table next to a clay bowl full of good wine. I kept a pen, ink, and paper nearby. I swallowed a mouthful of sweet wine and then I began to chant:

"I conjure you by the Lord who created heaven and earth to reveal to me what is true and to conceal from my eyes what is false; I conjure you by the staff with which Moses divided the sea to reveal to me what is true and to conceal from my eyes that which is false; I conjure you by the heavenly host, the hands of God, Akriel, Gabriel, Hatach, Duma, Raphael, Zafniel, Nahabiel, Inias, Kaziel . . ."

While I chanted I watched the wine intently. If I had stopped chanting even for one moment, the spell would cease, so I listed every magical name I knew, every name I could imagine, every feat of every great Jewish hero and heroine as the wine bubbled, frothed, churned, and finally smoothed out as still as glass. Then letters began to appear, as though they were being slowly etched into the surface of the wine. Without breaking my chant, I groped for paper and pen and copied the letters exactly. When no more letters appeared and the wine was still again, I finally brought the chant to an end, and the wine became plain wine once more.

I took a couple of deep shuddering breaths, feeling sick to my stomach. I had never properly been trained for this and I didn't know the safeguards that I should have had in place, that my bubbe would have had in place if she had been casting this spell. I felt very ill, weaker than I ever had before.

I called Shayna in and showed her the letters written on the pad.

"Not the Lord nor all the heavenly host will break a signed contract," I told her. "You will have to do it yourself."

"And how am I to do that, big sister?"

"You must *force* the demon to tear up the contract. Then she will have no power to take your little one. The demon does not have to listen to the names of the Lord and his angels, but she must answer to her own." I tapped the paper. "This is her name. You must bind her with it and force her to make you free of the contract. It is the only way."

Shayna took the paper and started to sound out the name. Quickly, I put my hand over her mouth. We didn't want to attract the creature's attention before we were ready.

At sunset the next evening, we waited in one room: Shayna, me, Ruthie, and Sol with Yael in his arms.

And then the lilit strolled into the room. She looked like me, this time. Just like me.

Shayna started to shake. I took her hand. "Don't be frightened," I told her.

Then Shayna turned to look at me and I saw that she was not frightened. She was angry. I gave her hand a squeeze and hoped that she wouldn't let anger overwhelm our planning.

The demon chuckled and spat. Her spittle sizzled and burned through our rug, my wedding present for Shayna and Sol. "Your bubbe is suffering a thousand torments as she reviews the ways in which your troubles are her own doing. You, Deborah, I will deal with later, for we have so much in common, after all."

I shook my head—*no, we have* nothing *in common*—and heard the demon say, "Now, Shayna meydle, give me Yael. Give me the baby girl." She cracked her knuckles and grinned my grin, our bubbe's grin.

Sol tightened his arms around the baby while Shayna stared at the demon.

The demon smirked and displayed the contract that had been signed twice, once by my bubbe and once by Shayna. "I fulfilled my end of the contract twice, giving your grandmother powers and doing your sewing. It's not my fault she was killed before she could use them or that the mob took your brother before I could. I'll just have to do what I can with this one instead." She snapped her fingers. Yael disappeared from Sol's arms and reappeared in the demon's. Yael began to scream and claw at the demon's hands with her tiny nails.

"*Abomination!*" Shayna screamed, extending an arm and shaking her finger at the creature. "*Abomination!* Cursed in the sight of Adonai, Tetragammaton, and all his host! Abomination! I, Shayna, daughter of Rokhel, conjure you to forfeit the child Yael, daughter of Shayna! I conjure you to release me from our contract, a contract shameful in the eyes of God and man, a contract conceived and gotten by you, the lowest of the low, the slime of worms and shit of pigs! I conjure you to destroy this contract and leave this city, leave this earth, and spend eternity in the realm of unspeakable things! I conjure and bind you by your own soul, your own self, your own name—" Shayna pointed her finger at the creature's heart and yelled, "RUMFEILSTILIZKAHAN!"

The demon turned gray and began to spin in place. "The devil told you that!" she howled. "The devil told you that!"

"Not the devil, unclean thing," Shayna said, triumphant. "My *sister.*" And she seemed proud to have me by her side.

The demon spun and howled wordlessly until the very air burst into flames and she and the contract she was holding imploded into burning embers that vanished in midair. Sol leapt to catch Yael before she fell to the ground. The only sign that a stranger had been in the room was the hole in the rug.

We had Yael, ours to keep forever, but not without cost. Finding the name of the demon had been powerful magic, and the exhaustion that followed, the weakness that comes when you do a great feat for which you have never been properly trained, made me sick, sicker than I had been for many, many years. Sicker than I had been since the old country.

I tossed and turned with fever for days and a livid rash spread across my face and limbs. I burned so fiercely that Shayna brought in a doctor, who looked me over and pronounced, "Scarlet fever."

Scarlet fever! A child's disease, after all—insult to injury, that was. But then again, conjuring the demon's name had left me as weak as a child. My skin burnt so fiercely that it turned bright white. Shayna held cold compresses against my skin, but within minutes the heat from my body made them feel like they'd been warming in the stove for an hour. My fever climbed every day, burning what little sense I had left. Ruthie stayed home from work for days trying to spoon broth into my mouth so I wouldn't dry out entirely, or so I am told—for again, I don't remember much of those days. But with Ruthie home and me too sick to do any business, we were short of money, and Shayna went back to factory work.

Sol's mother found it a shame, a married woman in a factory, but Shayna told Ruthie that, actually, she did not mind. "With Sol and his brothers and his parents in the store," she told her, "all I am is underfoot. In the factory, I'm somebody. I'm good at what I do there. I'm good enough that I think that someday I'll get to be a sample maker, maybe even a designer."

And she was so happy, said Ruthie, with the work she found—a modern factory, large, airy, three floors, imagine that, she said, and so high up the girls needed elevators to come and go. And so easy it was for her to get the job there, she didn't have to pay off anybody, she said—it was like magic, like an angel was watching over her.

Too easy, in retrospect.

I don't remember any of that. All I really remember are the dreams—every hour I managed to sleep I was plagued with nightmares, dreams in which my eyes were worms of fire burrowing through my head, or my head and hands became so swollen that I was sure they would burst, or I was falling, falling so far that I would never stop, never come to earth again. The pink rash had become raised crimson blisters. For weeks this lasted, and then . . . one night, late in March, the fever broke, and I sweated through three blankets. Ruthie washed linens all night, and that morning I woke up hungry. Ruthie fed me some breakfast: a little soup, a little milk, a soft-boiled egg. For two or three days she tended me while I regained my strength, and then she went out to work.

I was weak, and for most of the day, I sipped tea and tried to rest, but as morning shaded into afternoon the watery sunlight finally pulled me to my feet. Taking slow, tiny steps, I dressed myself and made my way down to Sol's store, where I found him behind the counter and his mother minding Yael. His mother agreed with me that fresh air would do me all the good in the world, so slowly, painfully, I stepped out into the street.

The sunlight, weak as it was, was painfully bright to my eyes. It bounced harshly off cold streets, all sharp angles and hostile edges. I pulled my jacket closer around my body; when Shayna had first stitched it for me, it had hugged me close, displaying my figure, but the weeks of illness had wasted me. A chill wind cut through a near alley and I trembled.

What struck me most about the street was how quiet it was, unnaturally quiet. There were no children playing skip rope or taunting each other, no peddlers trying to sell their wares, no friends arguing good-naturedly or couples screaming at each other. Just my soft, frightened footsteps and the wind. For a minute I was convinced that the illness had taken my hearing as well as my figure.

I walked carefully, keeping one hand on the buildings for support. When I finally got to the end of the block, the sounds of street life flooded back and I became dizzy with relief. I caught a bit of life from the remaining sunshine and went where my feet took me. I didn't know where I was going, only that I wasn't strong enough to get there as quickly as I needed to. But still, behind the street sounds, beneath the bustle, I heard that sinking silence.

I was three blocks away from the park when I heard the fire engines coming up behind me. They passed me easily, and by the time I arrived at the Asch Building I barely had breath enough to push through the crowd.

The silence was gone. Screaming and roaring filled my ears and poisonous black smoke filled the sky. I didn't understand what was happening—bundles of clothing trailing flames seemed to be falling from the sky while the few doors of the Asch Building were choked with people clawing and crawling over one another in order to get out. Once they did get out, though, they just joined the yelling throngs across the street, watching the falling bundles hitting the street with solid, damp thuds, one right after another. It wasn't until I saw one of the bundles trying and failing to push itself to its feet that I realized what they were.

This was Shayna's modern factory, I knew it, and I knew it had been no angel that had gotten her the job there.

I found myself out in the street, where firemen were frantic with their own futility. Their rescue ladders went up seven stories—the factory was on the eighth, ninth, and tenth floors. One woman staggered out of the building and immediately turned and tried to run back in. The firemen had to knock her out; she kept yelling about her daughter.

I looked up. One girl stood on the window's ledge. Already her skirt was beginning to smolder and even though she was so far above me, I swear I could see her face, unnaturally calm as she opened her purse and threw the money inside down to the street—and I remembered Shayna saying that today would be payday.

She took off her hat and sent it sailing in the direction of the park and the wind whipped her hair around her face. I could see flames as well as smoke coming out of the windows now.

Her dress was on fire.

She smoothed her hair back and stepped off the ledge as if she were stepping off the curb and crossing the street. She plummeted and her skirts rose up around her, a flower of flame.

She landed only six feet from me. A cinder hit my cheek and bounced away before I could move.

Three women stood on another window ledge together. They linked arms, closed their eyes, and jumped, and their aim was good, but they tore right through the bottom of the safety net, and the firemen holding it were splattered with blood.

"I didn't know, I didn't know they would come down three, four at a time, arms wrapped around each other's waists," the fire chief wept when Ruthie interviewed him later.

I searched the faces of the women pouring out of the building, running to avoid being hit by the falling girls, their friends, but I didn't find Shayna there. I ran through the street, pulling away from the men who tried to stop me, looking at the fallen, but I could not find my sister among them either.

I looked up at the flame-filled windows. There was no more jumping now.

"I'm sorry, Mama," I whispered.

I wept while the building flamed with girls burning, burning here in America.

ACKNOWLEDGMENTS

I am grateful to my agent, Jennifer Udden, for her care and work with this collection, and I have been so fortunate to work with the amazing people at Tordotcom Publishing. Thank you to Ellen Datlow, an incisive, perceptive editor, and to Ruoxi Chen, infinitely patient, professional, and enthusiastic. Publisher Irene Gallo, whose faith in my work has bolstered me on many an occasion; and Emily Goldman in editorial, Mordicai Knode in marketing, Lauren Anesta in publicity, Amanda Melfi in social media, Christine Foltzer in art, and Lauren Hougen in production, sterling professionals all.

My greatest source of support is also my longest-standing: my mother, April Schanoes, brought me to fairy tales and to Oz when I was a little girl, and has always had infinite reservoirs of faith in my work and love for me. I could not have written any of these without her.

I would be remiss if I did not thank my fairy-tale crew: Cristina Bacchilega, Sara Cleto, Jeana Jorgensen, Linda J. Lee, Jennifer Orme, Psyche Ready, Claudia Schwabe, Kay Turner, Brittany Warman, and Christy Williams.

All of us working in fairy tales owe a debt of gratitude to Terri Windling, and I particularly do. Terri brought into the world so much of the fairy-tale literature that has inspired me, and she has always encouraged me in my work. I am honored to know her.

My friends have been a source of unstinting support and kindness: K. Tempest Bradford, Gina Costagliola, Rose Fox, Gavin Grant, Miles Grier, Sara Eileen Hames, Corey Hindersinn, Josh Jasper, N. K. Jemisin, Ellen Kushner, Amy Kwalwasser, Rowan Larson, Erika Lin, Marissa Lingen, Kelly Link, Kathleen Luce, Farah Mendlesohn, Stacey Merel, Miriam Newman, Chelle Parker, Ri Pierce-Grove, Xtina Schelin, Delia Sherman, Barbara Simerka, and Emily Wagner. Thank you all so much, from the bottom of my heart.

I'm grateful to all my family, past and present, for their kindness and support, especially Suzanne Berch, Vanessa Felice, Barbara and Steve Goldstein, Paula Gorlitz, Gene Heyman, Georgia Hodes, Bonnie Johnson, Jonas Oxgaard, Helen Pilinovsky, David Schanoes, John Semivan, and Steven Zuckerman.

Let me thank also the former and current children who have inspired me: Sophia and Asher Decherney, Emma and Cora Hodes-Wood, Sofia Rabaté, Kit Schelin, and Poli and Dasha Sotnik-Platt. I am grateful in particular to my marvelous godchildren, Bear and Aradia Oxgaard, and my miraculous, amazing son, Solomon Schanoes. Bear, Aradia, and Solly, you are my great loves, and I cannot imagine what life would be without you.